THE GAME IS UP

"We've been found out," Margaret said.

"How many others did you agree to meet tonight?" Jess asked.

Margaret drew herself up to her full height. "I don't like how you're talkin' to me."

"You liked it when you were spinnin' a yarn about me bein' the kind of man you had been lookin' for all your life."

"She told you that, too?" Heck despondently asked.

Ethel took Margaret's hand. "We'd better be on our way."

"You're not going anywhere," Jess Donner informed her.

"No, you're surely not." Out of the darkness came Grat Vanes. Rusty was at his right side. The brothers had their hands close to their revolvers.

"Who are these two?" Margaret asked.

"We didn't agree to meet them," Ethel said.

"We're acquainted with these cowpokes," Grat said. "We couldn't help but overhear, and we think it's a downright shame what you did to these boys. But I guess it's fittin'."

"What is?" asked Margaret.

"That all of you are goin' to die together."

Rusty Vanes slid his hand to his Colt. "Who wants to be first?"

Ralph Compton

Bucked Out in Dodge

A Ralph Compton Novel
by David Robbins

A SIGNET BOOK

SIGNET
Published by New American Library, a division of
Penguin Group (USA) Inc., 375 Hudson Street,
New York, New York 10014, USA
Penguin Group (Canada), 10 Alcorn Avenue, Toronto,
Ontario M4V 3B2, Canada (a division of Pearson Penguin Canada Inc.)
Penguin Books Ltd., 80 Strand, London WC2R 0RL, England
Penguin Ireland, 25 St. Stephen's Green, Dublin 2,
Ireland (a division of Penguin Books Ltd.)
Penguin Group (Australia), 250 Camberwell Road, Camberwell, Victoria 3124,
Australia (a division of Pearson Australia Group Pty Ltd.)
Penguin Books India Pvt. Ltd., 11 Community Centre, Panchsheel Park,
New Delhi - 110 017, India
Penguin Group (NZ), Cnr Airborne and Rosedale Roads, Albany,
Auckland 1310, New Zealand (a division of Pearson New Zealand Ltd.)
Penguin Books (South Africa) (Pty.) Ltd., 24 Sturdee Avenue,
Rosebank, Johannesburg 2196, South Africa

Penguin Books Ltd., Registered Offices:
80 Strand, London WC2R 0RL, England

First published by Signet, an imprint of New American Library,
a division of Penguin Group (USA) Inc.

First Printing, October 2004
10 9 8 7 6 5 4 3 2 1

THE IMMORTAL COWBOY

This is respectfully dedicated to the "American Cowboy." His was the saga sparked by the turmoil that followed the Civil War, and the passing of more than a century has by no means diminished the flame.

True, the old days and the old ways are but treasured memories, and the old trails have grown dim with the ravages of time, but the spirit of the cowboy lives on.

In my travels—to Texas, Oklahoma, Kansas, Nebraska, Colorado, Wyoming, New Mexico, and Arizona—I always find something that reminds me of the Old West. While I am walking these plains and mountains for the first time, there is this feeling that a part of me is eternal, that I have known these old trails before. I believe it is the undying spirit of the frontier calling, allowing me, through the mind's eye, to step back into time. What is the appeal of the Old West of the American frontier?

It has been epitomized by some as the dark and bloody period in American history. Its heroes—Crockett, Bowie, Hickok, Earp—have been reviled and criticized. Yet the Old West lives on, larger than life.

It has become a symbol of freedom, where there was always another mountain to climb and another river to cross; when a dispute between two men was settled not with expensive lawyers, but with fists, knives or guns. Barbaric? Maybe. But some things never change. When the cowboy rode into the pages of American history, he left behind a legacy that lives within the hearts of us all.

—*Ralph Compton*

Chapter One

The sun baked the prairie and the three thousand head of cattle strung out from north to south. The cloud of dust they raised hung thick in the air. Thick, too, were the flies, and the smell of sweat and other odors.

Jess Donner was on drag when Tom Cambry trotted wide of the herd and came up alongside him, grinning fit to burst. But then, Tom Cambry nearly always smiled. He had the sunniest disposition in the outfit.

"Have you heard the news, sprout?"

"How could I with my ears plugged full of dust?" Jess responded. "And I'll thank you to quit pokin' fun at my age, you sachet kitten. I'll be sixteen next week, as you keep forgettin'." He was touchy about his age, as he was about a lot of things. His family had moved to Texas from Alabama six years ago, and he had a distinct Southern drawl. He was caked whitish-gray from head to toe, and his saddle and horse, besides.

Tom Cambry, who cut a fine figure of a man with his wide-brimmed hat, red bandanna, and blue shirt, was strictly Texas born and bred, as were most of the hands on the drive. "I'm glad my drag days are over." He swiped at the choking cloud. "I'd almost forgotten how bad it gets back here. A cowpoke can hardly breathe."

"Then spout your news and go breathe somewhere else," Jess suggested. He was of middling build and close to six feet when not slumped in the saddle. At the start of the drive Stu Wilkins proposed nicknaming him Bucktooth because two of his front teeth stuck out from the rest, and Jess had said that was fine so long as Stu didn't mind if everyone took to calling him "Manure Mouth."

"Sheathe your horns, consarn it," Tom scolded. A shock of black hair framed his uncommonly handsome face. He wore a belt made of solid silver with the biggest buckle anyone ever saw. "I just reckoned you'd like to know we strike Dodge in two days."

Jess eyed the *segundo* from under his hat brim. "Did the Almighty appear to you like he done to Moses?"

"No, you lump of coal," Tom said. "I've got it straight from Rafe. He says we'll reach Mulberry Creek, about ten miles south of Dodge, by the day after tomorrow."

Jess Donner couldn't help but smile, too. But his smile faded and he worriedly asked, "He'll let us go on in, won't he? I mean, it wouldn't be right to have us nursemaidin' these critters with all that prime entertainment so close we could practically reach out and touch it."

"What would you know of entertainment?" Tom scoffed. "You've never been up the Western Trail before—or any trail, for that matter. Why, you're a regular green pea."

"Another thing I hate," Jess said, "is havin' my flaws pointed out. My ma and pa made that a habit and it got so I couldn't walk right, to hear them squawk. It's why I lit out on my own."

Tom sighed. "You're techy as a teased snake, and that's not healthy. I should know. I was the same at your age."

"Yet you managed to become ancient," Jess said; the *segundo* was all of twenty-four. "So I don't see where it's anything to harp on."

"Suit yourself, you darned grump." Tom gigged his sorrel on up the line.

Jess opened his mouth to say something but closed it again. Adjusting his bandanna over his mouth, he reined toward a few stragglers. "Get along, you turtles. I move faster in my sleep."

Another flurry of hooves preceded Steve Ellsworth, who reined up sharply and exclaimed, "Have you heard the news, pard?"

"I'm danged popular today," Jess said. "Yes, I've heard it. And you'd best get back on swing or Rafe is liable to get his bristles up. You sure as blazes don't want that."

Steve was too excited to care. "Dodge City! Can you imagine? They say it has more saloons and dance halls than a man can count." His freckled cheeks split in anticipation. "Dance halls!" he repeated. "Do you know what that means?"

"You aim to show the world what a sorry excuse for a stomper you are?"

"Aren't you hilarious?" Steve said. "Don't you have any romance in your blood? Think of all those *females*." He said the last word as if it were God and gold all rolled into one.

Jess shook his head in mild disgust. "I've never met anyone so fond of calico in all my born days. To hear you talk, the only reason you joined this drive was to get roped by some sage hen."

"A man is never too old to find himself a good woman and settle down," Steve said a trifle resentfully.

"Old, hell. You're not but a year older than me," Jess said. "You've had women on the brain since you sprouted fuzz on your chin, and that's no lie. Why, one whiff of perfume and you're like a buck in rut."

"You're lucky you're my bunkie," Steve said, and headed back to take up his position as swing rider.

"With friends like these, who need hostiles?" Jess muttered, and used his rope on another cow. "Lazy critters," he snapped. There were always three or four knotheads that refused to keep up. Some outfits would eat the sluggards but Rafe Adams refused to lose a single cow.

Suddenly, from out of the dust, came the trail boss himself. Rafe was a big man with strapping shoulders and a broad chest. What he did not know about cattle was not worth knowing. He got his start working for Shanghai Pierce, about as famous a cowman as ever lived, and the past several years he had been leading herds up the trails for various buyers. Reining his big gray in next to Jess's bay, he casually asked, "What are you sellin', whiskey or tobacco?"

"How's that again?" Jess asked, thoroughly confused.

"You've had so many visitors, I figured you must be sellin' something," Rafe said, and grinned.

"Oh. That." Jess relaxed. "Everyone is excited about us hittin' Dodge." He paused. "We are going to get to go in, aren't we? I haven't seen the inside of a barbershop in months. And I could stand a bath."

"We're all a mite whiffy," Rafe conceded. "Those dance hall doves will take one sniff and run." He pulled his hat brim low against the burning sun. "I just hope Mr. Carruthers will be there to meet us." Rafe then stared so hard and so long at Jess that Jess shifted uncomfortably in his saddle.

"Have I broke out in hives?"

"I have this little speech I always give the new ones," Rafe said. "Words to the not-yet-wise, you might say."

"I ain't no greener," Jess said, standing up for himself.

"You're not no ranny yet, neither, although you've got the makin's of one. Two or three more drives should sweat away the fat between your ears."

"Thanks heaps."

"Don't take it personal. It's just that I would hate to have to send word to your folks that you were bucked out in gore."

Jess shook his head. "You needn't worry on my account. I'm not hankerin' to swap lead. All I want is a haircut, a bath, a new set of clothes, and to take in the sights."

"It's those sights that can kill you," Rafe said. "Gamblers out to fleece you of your hard-earned money, doves out to fleece you of however much you're willin' to pay for their attentions, however much they can pick from your pockets. And don't forget the lawmen." He said the last with distinct scorn.

"What's wrong with them? Aren't they supposed to uphold the law and such?" Jess asked.

"That's the general idea, but you can count the number of honest tin stars on one hand and still have fingers left over. Bat Masterson is one, but I'm not sure he's still there. The thing to remember is that a good portion of the money they earn comes from the fines they hand out, and they're not shy about finin' someone. Then there are the killers like Mather."

"Who?" Jess asked. The name was slightly familiar but he could not place it.

"Dave Mather. Mysterious Dave, they call him. Anyone who so much as looks at him crosswise eats lead."

"Aw, he can't be that bad. All that talk of killers and such is more hot air than anything else."

Rafe gazed into the distance. "Some years ago I

came up the trail with another herd. I wasn't foreman, just one of the hands. We went into Dodge to take in the sights. I drank some, played cards some, but nothin' that would get me in trouble."

"I'll do the same," Jess promised, but the foreman did not seem to hear.

"One of the other fellas let a little whiskey go to his head. He sat in on a crooked game, then raised a fuss when he lost. We tried to calm him down but he always was pigheaded. He marched to the livery, armed himself, and came back to the saloon to put the fear of God into the gambler."

"What happened?" Like all the hands, Jess loved a good story. Each evening after the herd was bedded down, the men spent hours around the campfire swapping yarns. The best storytellers were always called on to relate new tales, or repeat favorites. Rafe rarely told any, which made this a special treat.

"Floyd, that was his name. Floyd Higgins. He walked up to the tinhorn, pointed his six-shooter, and demanded to see the deck so he could prove the cards were marked. The gambler refused. I tried to convince Floyd to hightail it out of there before it was too late, but Floyd always was a stubborn cuss. The next we knew, in walked Bat Masterson."

Jess listened with rap interest. Masterson was a famous cowtown lawmen. Whenever the subject of killers came up, his name was sure to be mentioned. He was widely regarded as one of the most fearless men alive. He also had a reputation for honesty and fairness, which was rare.

"Masterson tried to reason with Floyd," Rafe had gone on. "He asked Floyd, real polite, to put down the revolver and come along quietly. He even promised to have a word with the judge about goin' easy on Floyd since Floyd had never been in wrong with the law before."

"That sure was decent," Jess commented.

Rafe's rugged countenance clouded. "Floyd should have listened. But he was young and headstrong and he told Masterson he couldn't turn himself in until the gambler had owned up to cheatin' him."

"He stood up to Bat Masterson?"

"For all of ten seconds. Because that's about when Mysterious Dave Mather came out of nowhere. He walked up behind Floyd and put a pistol to the back of Floyd's head and splattered his brains over the wall and the ceiling. I'll never forget all that blood that got on me, or the awful look in Floyd's eyes. I still see his face in my nightmares."

"Mather shot him in cold blood?"

"Without so much as a word or a warnin'," Rafe confirmed. "It happened so fast, none of us had a chance to warn Floyd."

"But how could Mather get away with it?" Jess was appalled. "It was murder, plain and simple."

"When you kill someone and you're not wearin' a badge, they call it murder, and they string you from the gallows or a handy tree. When you have a badge pinned on your chest and you kill someone, they call it doin' your job, and they pat you on the back." Rafe lifted his reins. "But I've wasted enough time jawin'. The important thing is, don't make the same mistakes Floyd did. Dodge is no place to put your mettle to the test." He rode toward the head of the herd.

Jess Donner waited until the trail boss was too far off to hear him, then declared aloud, "That was right considerate and all, but I don't need a mother who wears spurs."

For the rest of the day, all Jess could think about was Dodge. The Babylon of the Plains, as it was commonly called, even though it wasn't nearly as wild and wooly as it had been in the early days. Heck Myers claimed they planted a man every night back then, but Heck was about the liveliest liar north of the Pecos.

That night around the campfire, Dodge was the only topic. Bill Groate, the cook, was looking forward to buying supplies. "We're about plumb out of sugar and we only have enough flour to last us a week. I swear, this is the eatingest outfit I've ever had to feed."

Peeler Watson, the wrangler, put his stomach at risk by scoffing, "With the size of the portions you serve, it's a miracle we're not skin and bones."

Jess expected Groate to explode. The old man had the temper of a mossy horn, and once fed Heck Myers nothing but wasp's nest bread for a week after Heck recklessly made a crack about the quality of Groate's sourdough biscuits.

"I've never yet met a cavvy man who can tell fact from fiction," Groate said while taking a pie from a Dutch oven. "And if you're down to skin and bones, how come your middle jiggles when you walk?"

The general mirth brought a flush to Peeler's pockmarked features but he had the good sense not to dig himself into a deeper hole. "Aw, I was only joshin'. You're the best bean master I've come across or I wouldn't always ask for seconds."

"For that," Groate said, with a grin, "you get the first slice of pie while it's fresh and hot."

"What about me?" Heck Myers threw in. "I'm always praisin' your meals to high heaven."

"High praise from you is no praise at all," Groate said. "And for havin' the gall to beg, you get the last slice."

"I bet there will be plenty of pie in Dodge," Steve Ellsworth said. "I aim to belly up to the trough and not stop until my mouth falls off."

Tom Cambry gave an exaggerated wink at the other hands. "Which in his case should be about five minutes. Four, if the girl just lies there."

Their hoots and whistles rose to the stars.

Jess's were among the loudest. He loved this life, loved the freedom and the friendships. He even loved the hardship, although, like everyone else, he grumbled about them.

They were making so much racket that they almost drowned out the arrival of one of the nighthawks. Ben Fetterman didn't bother to dismount. He rode straight over to where Rafe was sitting and bent low to excitedly impart information.

Rafe shot to his feet as if poked by a pitchfork.

Hitching at his gun belt, he moved close to the fire so they all could see and hear. Then Rafe motioned for quiet. "Break out your hardware, boys. We've got trouble."

Chapter Two

Four riders had appeared from the northeast. Moving in single file, their mounts at a walk, they circled the herd. Not once, but twice. It was at that point Ben Fetterman hurried to camp to inform the foreman, and now Rafe Adams, with every hand except the cook and the wrangler, was looking to catch the night riders unawares.

"What can they be up to?" Steve Ellsworth whispered to no one in particular. "It can't be rustlers. Not this close to Dodge." The entire way from Texas he had lived in secret fear of cow thieves. Not that he was a coward. It was just that he had never shot anyone, and honestly didn't know if he could.

"Whatever they're about, it can't be good," was Heck Myers' assessment. "Or else they wouldn't be skulkin' around in the middle of the night."

Jess Donner was about to offer his opinion when Rafe Adams twisted in the saddle to say softly but sternly, "Hush, you lunkheads!"

"Isn't he in a mood?" Stu Wilkins whispered. His

Eastern accent stood out even more than Jess's Southern drawl. The only hand who hailed from New York City, Stu was considered an oddity. Not because of where he spent the first fourteen years of his life, but because he liked to wash regularly.

Jess Donner knew the question was directed at him but he didn't answer. Rafe had told them to be quiet and the trail boss didn't brook disobedience. But then, Stu Wilkins did like to prattle on so—usually about how New York City was the greatest place on earth, and how much he missed it. Nearly everyone in the outfit wished he would pack up and go back, but Stu couldn't. Apparently he had run afoul of the law and headed west one step ahead of a spell in jail. Or so Stu liked to hint.

Suddenly Rafe Adams drew rein. Everyone instantly followed suit. Several had revolvers in their hands. Others held rifles.

Jess palmed his own pistol. Many of the boys were partial to Colts, but not him. He favored a Smith & Wesson .44 caliber. Known as the Frontier model, it was a new double-action model, meaning he could fire it without having to thumb back the hammer. What he liked most, though, was the nickel plating. During the day he would sometimes take it out to admire how the sunlight turned the nickel to burnished silver.

Ben Fetterman rose in his stirrups and pointed. Rafe looked, then turned and put a finger to his lips. The cowboys all froze, and thankfully none of their animals elected to whinny.

Try as he might, Steve Ellsworth couldn't see

anything except the dark. He never could see well at night. His mouth went dry and he licked his lips to moisten them. Some outfits lost hundreds of head to brand artists, who would stampede the cows using a variety of tricks.

Suddenly shapes materialized out of the night. Four riders, in single file, moving slowly, their eyes on the herd. They did not notice the cowboys until Rafe Adams worked the lever of his Winchester and commanded, "Hold it right there!"

At that, Tom Cambry hollered, "Surround 'em, boys!" And before the four riders could so much as spit, the outfit had them ringed and covered.

Jess Donner leveled his Smith & Wesson at a chunk of sinew with a bushy beard and eyebrows that reminded him of woolly caterpillars.

"What's the meanin' of this?" asked a shrew-faced man, who in the moonlight appeared pasty white with surprise. "Why all the artillery?" By his accent, he was another son of the South.

"Who are you and why are you sneakin' around our herd?" Rafe demanded, kneeing his mount closer. The barrel of his Winchester was fixed on the center of the shrew-faced man's chest.

"Sheath your horns, saddle stiff," the man said. "We're not breakin' any laws. You had no call to jump us."

"A cowman always has call when rustlers are involved," Rafe said flatly. "Beside which, I'm top screw and responsible to the owner if any of these cows go missin'."

Jess Donner glanced at the remaining two. One

was in his forties or fifties and sat as stiff as a board. The last was no older than he was, and carried a pearl-handled Colt, butt forward, on his right hip.

"I respect a gent who takes his job seriously," the shrew-faced rider said, "but if I told you the truth, you wouldn't believe me."

"Try me," Rafe said.

"We're lookin' for my dog."

It was so preposterous that Steve Ellsworth and Heck Myers both laughed, and Stu Wilkins said in his Eastern twang, "Sure you were. And I've got a cat stuffed down my pants."

Rafe simply said, "It won't wash, stranger. Be honest with us and maybe I can talk the men out of searchin' for a tree and treatin' you to a hemp social with you as the guest of honor."

"You're not on the open prairie, cowpoke," the man snapped. "You're in Ford County now. There's a law against lynchin' folks. String us up and you're liable to be strung up yourselves. The sheriff doesn't like it when someone takes the law into his own hands." He smiled thinly. "In case you haven't heard, Kansas is gettin' real civilized."

The young one with the pearl-handled Colt snarled, "Too goddamn civilized, if you ask me, Grat. A man can't even wear his gun on the streets anymore."

"No one asked you, Rusty," the shrew-faced man growled. He seemed unhappy at having his name mentioned. "So shut up while I handle things."

"Dodge County or not," Rafe said, "that business

about your dog is too thin. I propose to disarm you and turn you over to that sheriff you're so fond of."

The one called Rusty sat straighter. "Take my pistol? I'd like to see anyone try." His right hand was on his hip, inches from his expensive Colt.

No one expected Grat to do what he did next—namely, to whip around in the saddle and lean out and smack Rusty, open-handed, across the shoulder. "Let me handle this, damn it!" Raw fury twisted Rusty's features, but although his hand leaped to the butt of his revolver, he didn't draw it.

Grat supplied the explanation why. "Little brother or not, do as I say." To Rafe he said, "As for you, I was doin' you a favor by lookin' for my dog as quietly as we were doin'. Otherwise, we might have spooked your herd."

Rafe was no one's fool. "What's your dog doin' so far from town?"

Grat pushed his short-brimmed hat back on his head. "We were on our way into Dodge when Lucky ran off. He does that a lot. If I had any sense, I'd shoot him and put him out of my misery. I came after him, and when we spotted your cows, I knew he must have caught their scent. He could be in among them right this moment, lookin' for a calf to chase. That's what he likes to do, chase calves."

The cowhands visibly tensed. The last thing they needed was a stampede. Lightning had caused one about four weeks ago and it took the men days to round up the strays.

Grat had gone on. "Since you don't seem to appreciate my good manners, I might as well do this the easy way." With that, he stuck two fingers in his mouth and a shrill whistle pierced the starlit plain.

Almost instantly there was an answering yip, and half a minute later a long-haired mongrel came loping up and sat next to Grat's horse. It looked eagerly up at him, its tongue lolling, its long tail swishing back and forth.

"Well, I'll be," Tom Cambry declared.

Rafe slowly lowered his Winchester. "I reckon I've misjudged you, mister. You and your pards are free to go."

The man with the bushy beard wasn't satisfied. "That's it? You poke guns at us and don't have the decency to say you're sorry when you're in the wrong? That's not very Christian of you. I've got half a mind to pull you from that nag of yours and pound on you from now until Christmas."

"You're sure welcome to try, mister," Rafe coldly responded, "but I don't pound easy."

"Now, now, Baxter," Grat said to the rider with the beard. "We can't blame these cowpokes for bein' cautious. If we were in their boots, we'd likely do the same." He reined around. "Be seein' you, gents. Heel, Lucky, heel."

No one uttered a word until the foursome and the dog were out of sight. Then Heck said, "That was plumb embarrassin'."

"I don't buy the dog story," Tom Cambry said.

"Me neither," Rafe Adams said, "but they didn't actually do anything other than nose around, so I had to let them go. Still, we'll keep two extra guards

on the herd at all times tonight. See to it, Tom." He
rode for the wagon.

As *segundo*, it was Cambry's job to carry out the
foreman's orders, and he did so without delay.
"Heck, you and Stu take the first watch. Steve and
Jess will relieve you at midnight."

"There goes my beauty rest," Heck said.

Stu chortled. "You'd need a month of solid sleep
just to look half human."

The cowboys drifted hack to camp. Jess and Steve
were at the rear, Steve still holding his rifle.

"Well, that was interestin'—about the only excitement we've had on this drive other than the
stampede."

"Like excitement, do you, bunkie?" Jess asked.

"Show me a man who doesn't," was Steve's retort. "Back in Texas, the most excitement we had
was watchin' the corn grow. I about died of boredom. So I left to see the world."

"All you've seen the past couple of months are
cows and grass. I wouldn't call that much of an improvement over corn."

"I swear," Steve said in mild reproach, "if you
ever start lookin' at the bright side of things, the
shock will kill me."

"Do you ever get a hankerin' to go home?" Jess
Donner asked.

"Now and then," Steve admitted. "I have a sister
I miss a lot. And my grandma is about the sweetest
woman who ever drew breath. But whenever the
urge comes over me, I get to thinkin' about all that

corn and workin' a plow twelve hours a day and the urge goes away."

Rafe and Tom were huddled by the cook wagon when Jess and Steve arrived. Steve told the wrangler, Peeler Watson, they would need their night horses from the remuda in about four hours. The two spread out their tarpaulin on as flat a spot as they could find. They each had two blankets. Jess liked to use an old coat for his pillow; Steve liked to use his boots. Within minutes of lying down, both were fast asleep.

"Good kids, those two," Tom Cambry said, and swallowed a mouthful of hot coffee. "Another couple of years and they'll do to ride the river with."

"They're hard workers," Rafe conceded. "But Jess has a temper and the other one tends to think the grass is always greener over the horizon." He accepted a tin cup from the cook.

"At least they don't talk your ears off, like Stu Wilkins," Bill Groate griped, "or spew tall tales like that Heck character."

Rafe smirked. "You're a fine one to complain about tall tales. What was that marvel you fed them the second night out—about your days up in Montana and tamin' a griz to eat out of your hand by feedin' it honey and then teachin' it to wear a saddle so you could ride it on your days off?"

"I might have exaggerated," Groate said with a grin.

"And the Grand Canyon is no bigger than a water trough," Tom Cambry said dryly. "But don't stop tellin' your whoppers on my account. It will give me more to write about someday."

The cook scratched his stubble. "Oh, that's right. You're a scribbler. But no one will buy this yarn of yours. Who wants to read about a bunch of dumb cowpokes?"

"Folks back east," Tom said. "They can't get enough of stories about the West, about scouts, law-dogs, outlaws—you name it. They think life out here is glamorous."

"But we're talkin' cowboys," the cook said. "We spend our days breathin' cow farts and our nights listenin' to cow belches. Ain't no glamour there."

Rafe was staring off across the prairie. "I reckon I'll take a swing around the herd before I turn in. I've got a bad feelin' in my gut about Grat and his friends, and I've learned to trust my feelin's."

"I'll tag along," Tom offered. "I'm not tired yet anyhow."

The cattle lay in a broad irregular circle on a plain of dry grass. Many were chewing their cuds. The starlight played over a phalanx of horns, glistening dully as if wet.

"Well, we did it," Tom said. "In a few days you'll meet up with Carruthers and we'll be paid, and then it's back to Texas."

"Is it?" Rafe said.

"Where else?" Tom asked. "Or has someone put a bee in your bonnet? I've noticed how your eyes light up whenever Montana is mentioned."

"They call it Big Sky Country," Rafe said. "They say a man can start little and work himself big in no time. We could buy a couple hundred head and start our own ranch."

"Is Texas short of land? Why not buy a small spread there and build it up? We know the country. That's a plus."

"Montana isn't China."

"Now don't go gettin' contrary on me. All I'm sayin' is, why live somewhere we don't know when we can live somewhere we do? We don't know the rivers. We don't know the lay of the land. Half of Montana is Blackfoot country, and they're as salty a tribe as the Comanches ever were."

Rafe snorted. "You must live in terror of fleas."

"There you go again," Tom said in exasperation, "mistakin' common sense for bein' yellow. But if you go on to Montana with Carruthers, you go alone. I was born in Texas. I'll feed Texas maggots when they plant me."

"We could always come back when we're old and gray."

"Who are you foolin'?" Tom asked. "Ten years after we're settled, you'll probably drag me off to Alaska. Hellfire, if cows ate snow, we'd end up at the North Pole. Steve Ellsworth isn't the only one who likes to take a gander over the horizon."

"So that's a definite no?"

"Short of clubbin' you with a rock, yes."

They both abruptly drew rein when shots cracked faintly to the north. Three, four, five in swift cadence, followed by a deep and somber silence.

"That couldn't be more than a mile away," Tom

observed. "You don't suppose Grat shot his ornery dog?"

"It could be anyone," Rafe said. "But we'll take turns stayin' up so one of us is awake at all times." He let out with a long sigh. "I can't wait to reach to Dodge. Things should be a little more peaceful there."

"You hope," Tom Cambry said.

Chapter Three

From Mulberry Creek the outfit saw plumes of smoke from a train many miles to the north. Plenty of fine grazing bordered the creek but Rafe Adams pushed the herd on to the Arkansas River and crossed it a mile above the Babylon of the Plains. The water was low, the crossing easy.

Once on the other side, the cowboys were surprised when Rafe announced they would push on to Duck Creek, another five or six miles.

"I knew it!" Jess Donnor grumbled to his bunkie. "He's not fixin' to let us go in. He'll keep us out here and we'll miss all the sights."

"When did your brains leak out your ears?" Steve Ellsworth responded. "Whether he lets us go in now or we go in ourselves in a couple of days, we *will* go in. Or have you forgot that Dodge is where he's to meet the buyer?"

"I haven't forgot nothin'," Jess said indignantly.

"Then quit spoutin' acid like an old biddy," Steve

chided. "You'll get to see your precious Dodge. I just hope she's all you seem to think."

Jess said, "You've heard the stories, same as me."

"All that matters are the painted cats," Steve said dreamily. "More than Denver and Kansas City combined, they say."

"Oh, hogwash. Dodge ain't half as big as either of those places. I doubt there's more than a few hundred girls in the whole town."

Steve's eyes lit up. "A few hundred! Think of it! I could dance with a different girl every minute and not come back to the first for a month of Sundays."

"You say the silliest damn things."

"There's nothin' silly about women," Steve said. "Their hair, their smiles, their ruby lips. The way they move." He put a hand to his chest. "God knew just what He was doin' when He made 'em."

"And you claim my brains have leaked out?" Jess chortled and slapped his thigh. "Damn, if you ain't smitten. You sure have missed your callin'."

"How do you figure?" Steve asked with more than a trace of irritation. His fondness for females was well known, and a constant source of amusement.

"Why, here you are, nursemaidin' cows, when it's as plain as the big nose on your face that you would much rather be nursemaidin' two-legged fillies. If you ask me, you should have your own dance hall."

Steve looked at his friend in amazement. "Why, that never, ever occurred to me! But you sure have struck gold. I should, shouldn't I?"

"Oh brother," Jess said. "I was only joshin'."

"But don't you see?" Steve gestured excitedly in the general direction of Dodge. "It would be perfect! My grandma used to say that the good Lord put us here for a purpose. That each of us has a callin'. Well, my callin' is to run a dance hall so I'll be surrounded by beauties twenty-four hours of the day."

"Just when I think you can't get any more ridiculous . . ."

"What's so ridiculous about it?" Steve bristled.

"For one thing, you're not old enough," Jess said. "I can ever recollect hearin' of a seventeen-year-old dance hall owner. For another, buyin' one has to take a lot of money, of which you have next to none." Jess shook his head. "No, as divine callin's go, this one seems to be off the mark."

"Why, you block of wood," Steve snapped. "I didn't say I had to go out and own a dance hall tomorrow, did I? Somehow or other I'll get up the money, and in five or six years you can come pay me a visit so I can laugh in your face and tell you that I told you so."

The outfit reached Duck Creek by one o'clock. The herd was taken off the trail and bedded down and the first guard posted. Rafe called the rest of the hands together and, after everyone had taken a seat, motioned for quiet.

"Well, boys, we did it. I was hired to bring this herd to Dodge. As all of you know, these cows aren't bein' shipped east. They're bound for a big ranch up in Montana. The buyer, Mr. Carruthers, is supposed to meet me sometime over the next several days, and I have the full authority of the owner, Mr.

Henry, to sell them for a prearranged price. That's when you get paid."

"It's been so long since I had spendin' money," Heck Myers remarked, "I can't recollect what it looks like."

Stu Wilkins couldn't resist. "The coins are pink, except the twenty-dollar gold pieces. They're purple. The bills are chartreuse."

"What the hell is chartreuse?" Bill Groate wanted to know.

"Ah, probably some color he made up," Heck said, "like the time he claimed that in New York City they have trains which ride on air."

"I never said air, you ignorant clod," Stu took exception. "The trains ride on elevated rails above the streets."

An argument threatened to erupt until Rafe Adams threw withering looks at Heck and Stu. "Now then, where was I? If I've kept track of the days right, Mr. Carruthers should already be in Dodge. If not, then we have to sit tight until he shows up."

Jess Donner groaned.

"What I propose to do is leave five hands here at a time. Four on guard and one with the wagons and the remuda. The rest of you can indulge yourselves."

Several hasty yips greeted the news.

"But what will we do for spendin' money?" Heck asked. "All I have in my pockets are spiderwebs."

"I have enough left from the expense money Mr. Henry gave me to advance each of you ten dollars on your pay," Rafe proposed. "It's not much, I grant you, but it will tide you over until the sale is made."

Peeler Watson commented, "Sounds fair to me."

"Just remember," Rafe said, "Boot Hill is fertilized with fools who took Dodge too lightly. Don't make the same mistake. Check your guns when you go in. Don't drink yourselves booze blind. And whatever you do, don't get tangled up with anything in skirts." He bestowed another pointed look, this time on Steve Ellsworth. Then he announced, "I'm leavin' for town in ten minutes. Groate, you can bring the wagon in and pick up whatever we'll need to tide us over until the sale is final. Templeton, you and Larn have first watch. Pernell and Tim the second. Donner and Ellsworth the third." He smiled broadly. "The rest of you, dig out your war bags and put on your finest toggery. Dodge, here we come."

Whoops of delight rose to the sky and those who were going scrambled to get ready. A line formed at the washbasin. Steve Ellsworth took so long, some of the others heaped less than flattering words on his lineage and his general fitness as a human being.

"Insult me all you want, boys," Steve took the abuse in stride as he wrestled with a stubborn cowlick, "but it's the hombre who looks the best who attracts the prettiest fillies."

"In that case," Jess Donner said, "any sage hen on your arm is bound to be ugly enough to scare a buffalo."

"Now, now," Heck said, with a wink at the listeners, "I've heard that females go crazy for a man with peach fuzz on his chin. The more fuzz he has, the more kisses they lavish." He deliberately paused, then snapped his fingers and added, "Wait a minute. Was that fuzz or money?"

"Either way," Jess said, "the only way he'll ever get a gal to pucker up is to pay her triple the goin' rate."

Their mirth was punctuated by a growl from Ben Fetterman. "If you yearlin's don't mind, some of us are pressed for time. I have to be back before dark, so hurry it up."

Steve turned from the mirror with a frown, his cowlick victorious, and jammed his hat on his head. "I swear. I would shave my head if bald men didn't look so ridiculous."

"In your case it would be an improvement," Stu Wilkins said.

Rafe was in the saddle waiting. "Remember my advice. I don't want to have to plant any of you, hear?" A tap of his spurs and he was off, Tom Cambry, as always, at his side.

The older hands stayed up with the trail boss but the four youngest hung back, nerves taking their toll.

It was Heck Myers who proposed, "Since none of us has been to Dodge before, what do you say to all of us stickin' together?"

"Are you afraid a gambler will cheat you out of your paltry ten dollars?" Stu Wilkins asked.

"You boys can fritter away your money however you want," Steve Ellsworth said. "I'm spendin' all my time in dance halls."

"There's a shock," Jess Donner said.

"Well, I still think it's a good notion," Heck insisted, "for the first couple of hours, anyhow, until we know what's what."

Jess shrugged. "Fine by me. But I'm not doin' anything until I've visited the barber and had a bath."

Rafe Adams did not strike out direct for town but led them south to a bridge that spanned the Arkansas River.

"What was the sense of this?" Steve wondered. "We took six steps back to take one step forward."

On the other side of the Arkansas reared scores of buildings abuzz with activity, like a giant beehive. Before they could fully absorb the sight, Rafe Adams reined around and trotted back to them. "Are you forgettin' something, boys?"

Heck's brow creased in puzzlement. "We're not naked and we're heeled. That's all that counts."

"What about your spendin' money?" Rafe reminded them, and proceeded to dole out the ten dollars each had coming. "Remember what I told you a while ago. It wouldn't please me no how if I had to notify your next of kin."

"My mother wouldn't care less," Stu Wilkins said. "There were fourteen of us, stuffed into a tenement no bigger than the cook wagon. She probably threw a party when I left."

"My ma might cry for all of four or five seconds," Jeff Donner commented. "She always said I was the worst of her brood, and that I have more devil in me than angel."

Rafe Adams stopped counting to say, "Well, don't get killed anyway, just to spite them. If you need me, you'll find me at the Wright House. That's where I'm supposed to meet Mr. Carruthers. If he hasn't shown up yet, I'll cool my heels in the lobby."

Jess sat staring at the gold coins in his hand as the foreman departed.

"Thinkin' of all the whiskey you can buy?" Steve asked.

"No, I was thinkin' about the rest of the money due us. Seventy dollars is more than I've had at any one time my whole life long."

"All sixteen years of it," Stu said.

"You know what I mean," Jess said stiffly, and clinked his coins. "I'm not about to fritter this away. No gamblin' for me, gents."

Heck Myers chuckled. "We sure are bundles of fun. I vote we find us a bench to warm and feed the pigeons."

"We could always visit the library if they have one," Stu Wilkins suggested.

Heck scrunched up his face. "I'm amazed New Yorkers can get dressed without help. There's plenty to do besides playin' cards and guzzlin' coffin varnish. Wait and see."

Rafe and the others had already crossed the bridge. Steve Ellsworth spurred his buttermilk into the lead but as he came to the near end of the bridge he abruptly drew rein and motioned for the others to do likewise.

A lone rider was coming toward them from the other side. He rode a *grulla*, wore a wide-brimmed black hat, and sported a pearl-handled Colt, butt forward, on his right hip. He was as young as they were, and had long, stringy brown hair that hung to his slender shoulders.

"What's the attraction?" Heck Myers asked. "I thought you were girl crazy."

"Don't you recognize him?" Steve whispered. "That's the one called Rusty from a couple of nights ago.

"Are you sure?" Stu asked.

"*I'm* sure," Jess confirmed his bunkie's opinion. "That snotty look of his, and that Colt. There's no doubt in my mind."

Steve gnawed on his lower lip. "I wonder if he'll recognize us?"

"I doubt it," Jess said. "It was fairly dark and Rafe did all the talkin'. Most likely he doesn't know us from Adam."

They fell quiet as the *grulla* neared their end of the bridge, the clomp of its heavy hooves louder with each step. The slim rider in the black hat stared straight ahead until he was abreast of them, when he suddenly reined sharply around and rested his right hand on his Colt. "Explain yourselves."

"How's that?" Heck Myers asked.

"What in hell are you four starin' at?" Rusty growled. "You've been lookin' at me like I have feathers."

Stu proved once again that Easterners let their mouths do their thinking. "It's a free country, the last I heard. A man can stare at anyone he wants."

"Sure he can," Rusty said, "so long as he doesn't

mind havin' his eyes shot out." To emphasize his point he patted his Colt.

"Bluster and balderdash," Heck said. "Gun us this close to town and you'll be behind bars by midnight "

"Maybe I would, maybe I wouldn't," Rusty arrogantly replied. "Beelzebub, here, can outrun most any horse this side of the Rockies."

"You named your horse after the devil?" Steve Ellsworth said.

"What of it?" Rusty was quick to take offense. His dark eyes narrowed and he regarded them suspiciously. "Don't I know you four peckerwoods from somewhere?"

"Not us," Heck said. "This is our first time to Dodge."

"I'm sure I've seen you before," Rusty insisted. "It will come to me. In the meantime, girls, have fun." Sneering, he cantered westward.

"Friendly cuss, ain't he?" Steve said. "For two bits I'd have punched him."

"And he'd have plugged you for free," was Heck's assessment. "Be thankful he didn't recognize us. I figure he'd be all too happy to carve new ones at our expense."

"Carve new what?" Steve asked.

"Are you blind?" Heck Myers rejoined. "New notches. There were seven on those fancy pearl handles of his. He's a killer, that one."

"So?" Jess Donner said. "It's not as if we'll ever see him again."

Chapter Four

The Babylon of the Plains was everything the cowboys expected it to be, times ten over. They crossed the bridge and drew rein in wonderment at the whirlwind of commerce.

The railroad tracks ran smack through the center of town. On those tracks sat a puffing monster. The engineer was leaning out the engine window to watch travelers board. Several were gaily dressed ladies with sweeping dresses and hats wider than any the cowboys had ever seen. Other women were more primly attired in plain homespun and bonnets. There were men in new suits, farmers in faded work clothes.

Businesses bordered the main street: saloons, dance halls, gambling dens, a dry goods store, the Beatty and Kelly restaurant, a place that billed itself as a Tonsorial, a freight office, a barbershop, and more.

"Notice anything?" Heck Myers asked.

"That engine sure is big," Steve Ellsworth said. As a boy he had always been fascinated by trains.

"Not that," Heck said. "Almost all the saloons and such are on the south side of the tracks. Why should that be?"

"It's done that way on purpose, son," someone said, and out of the shadows strode a nattily dressed man in a bowler and a vest. He smoked a cigar. A gold watch chain gleamed in the sun. He made it a point to open has jacket so they could see the badge pinned to his chest.

"The marshal!" Stu Wilkins blurted, and almost reined around. He had to remind himself he was west of the Mississippi River now. It was unlikely the law was looking for him. The two dollars and forty-seven cents he had stolen from the church collection plate so his mother world have money to buy food wasn't exactly the sort of crime that put a man's face on a wanted poster. But it did shame his mother so bad he couldn't stand to look her in the eyes.

The dapper man removed his cigar and smiled. "No, son. I'm a deputy. One of five, should any of you decide to go on a spree." He looked them up and down, taking their measure. "You might think of me as the welcoming committee."

"We're not here to cause anyone trouble," Jess Donner said.

"That's nice to hear, son. Because if there's one thing that gets my dander up, it's idiots who spray lead when there are women and children about to take a stray bullet." The lawman focused on Steve. "Ever seen a woman hit by a heavy-caliber slug?"

Steve gulped. "No, sir, I sure haven't."

"It's not a sight for the squeamish. A few months back a Texas crowd came in and wouldn't follow the rules. They got drunk and rowdy and along about midnight they started riding up and down Front Street, spraying lead at every window and door. To hear them laugh and holler, they thought it was hilarious." The deputy pointed at a tall building. "But one of their shots went through a window of that hotel and struck a woman trying to sleep. Hit her in the elbow. Now you might not think that's so serious, but then you didn't see her crying and thrashing in her own blood, and you didn't hear Doc Samuels tell her and her poor husband and children that she will never have the use of that arm again."

"Land sakes!" Steve breathed.

"Exactly, son. So you can't hardly blame the law here in Dodge for keeping a tight lid on things, can you?"

Heck shook his head and said, "No, sir. What are the rules you mentioned? I wouldn't want to break one by accident."

The deputy smiled again, more warmly this time, and lowered his right arm. In doing so, his jacket slid back, exposing the well-worn butt of a revolver. "They're pretty simple. First and most important, no gunplay. None whatsoever. We catch you spraying lead promiscuously on the streets, we will shoot you dead where you stand. Savvy?"

The four young cowboys nodded.

"To keep that from happening, the town council passed an ordinance against the carrying of firearms north and south of the deadline—"

"The what?" Stu Wilkins interrupted. He had never heard the term before.

The deputy nodded at the railroad tracks. "You're staring at it. It used to be, guns were permitted south of the tracks. But the mayor has been cracking down on that sort of thing, so now all hardware has to be checked until you're ready to leave."

"We'll be sure to do that," Steve assured him.

"That's good to hear," the lawman said. "I'd hate to have to kill you." He turned to go. "Have a good time in Dodge."

"Wait," Heck said. "Anything else we should know?"

The deputy tapped ashes from the end of his cigar. "North of the deadline it's Sunday every day of the week. It's where the respectable folks live, and they don't like rowdy behavior. No yelling. No throwing rocks through windows. That sort of thing." He paused. "South of the deadline anything goes. Get as drunk as you want. Be as loud as you want. Just don't let that go to your head and resort to your revolvers." He touched his hat brim and melted into the shadows.

"That was Bat Masterson!" Heck whispered excitedly.

"How would you know?" Jess Donner was skeptical. "You've never laid eyes on Masterson or you would have bragged about it by now."

"He had a mustache, didn't he? And Masterson has a mustache."

"Why, your skull is plumb empty," Jess said in disgust. "Take a gander around you. Every hombre over twenty has hair on his lip."

Heck was unswayed. "Well, I've seen Wild Bill, and that deputy had the same cold eyes."

Jess, Steve, and Stu all twisted in their saddles, and Steve said, "You saw Wild Bill Hickok? The deadliest shot who ever lived?"

"This should be a good one," Jess commented. "To tell the truth, boys, I was gettin' worried. He hasn't told a whopper in so long, I was afraid he'd forgotten how."

"Scoff all you want," Heck Myers said, "but I did so bump into Hickok. It was down in Dallas about ten years ago when I wasn't no bigger than a foal. There he was, standin' on a street corner, wearin' that red sash of his with two pistols stuck in it, and him glarin' at everyone like he was mad at the whole world. It gave me shivers just to look at him, I don't mind admittin'."

Steve Ellsworth made a sound reminiscent of someone being strangled. "Why, you lyin' sack of bones. Everyone knows Hickok never got to Texas. He had so many enemies down there, he'd have run out of bullets before he went two blocks."

"Next he'll be claiming he's met President Arthur or John J. Sullivan," Stu Wilkins said.

"It's true, I tell you," Heck insisted.

"And that horse yonder has gold coming out its backside." Jess Donner clucked to his own. "Come on, boys. That barbershop yonder is fixin' to get our business."

They were almost to the train engine when, without warning, it belched a cloud of steam, hissing like a riled rattler, and Stu's chestnut reared and whinnied. He had to grip his saddle horn to keep from being thrown. It was a credit to how skilled a horseman the former New Yorker had become that he quickly brought his mount under control and patted its neck while saying soothingly, "There, there, big fellow. Everything is all right."

Jess was glaring at the engineer. "I bet that grinnin' ape did it on purpose. I should climb up there and pistol-whip him."

"And have that deputy take exception?" Steve said.

No one had paid any attention to their near mishap, leading Heck Myers to mention, "It must happen a lot. None of these folks paid us any mind." He suddenly pointed. "Hey, look! There's the Long Branch! The most famous saloon ever built. Why don't we stop in for a drink before we get all city slicked?"

"The barbershop first," Jess refused to change his mind. "Or haven't you noticed that we draw as many flies as our horses?"

"That's harsh," Steve said. "I take more pains than any of you to keep clean, and you darned well know it. You can't tell me I stink."

"Me either?" Heck declared. Lifting his left arm,

he sniffed his armpit, and coughed. "The barbershop it is, then."

A tiny bell tinkled as they entered. Only one customer was present, getting a shave. The three barbers were black, as was the shoeshine boy in the corner. The oldest of the barbers, a heavyset man with gray hair at the temples and a friendly smile, greeted them with, "Welcome, young sirs! Welcome! My name as Franklyn. Come and have a chair."

Jess Donner studied the prices posted on the walls. "Fifty cents for a bath? Why, I could buy a box of cartridges for that much."

"Prices are high in Dodge, sir, I agree," Franklyn said. "But a man has to earn a living. Or a lady. There's one who runs a boardinghouse a couple of blocks from here, and she offers baths, too. Only hers cost sixty cents."

Steve ran a hand across the fuzz on his chin. "We want the works. A trim and a wash, and shine our boots while you're at it. When I walk out of here, I want the ladies to admire how gorgeous I am."

"Sometimes I am embarrassed to be around you," Jess Donner said.

Franklyn winked at Steve. "We'll make you as gorgeous as we can." He moved toward a door at the back. "Whichever of you gentlemen wants a bath, follow me."

They had to take turns since there was only one tub. To decide who went first, they flipped a coin. Jess and Stu both called the coin right so they got to call it again and only Jess correctly called heads.

At this, Steve stepped to the tub. "I don't want you boys thinkin' poorly of me, but I refuse to bathe in your dirty water. I want to go first and I'm willin' to pay ten cents to each of you for the privilege."

"Make it twenty cents," Stu Wilkins said.

"That's sheer robbery," Steve griped.

Jess was starting to strip. "You're the fussbudget. If you want the cleanest water, pay up."

"It's a fine state of affairs when one's own pards fleece him," was Steve's retort, but he paid them their twenty cents, and then hurriedly stripped and climbed into the washtub. "Brrrrrrr!" he squeaked, shivering. "This water ain't hardly warm."

No sooner were the words out of his mouth than the boy appeared carrying a bucket full of bubbling water which he upended into the tub.

Steve let out a yip and shot to his feet, then covered himself and plopped back down, only to yip anew.

"Have you ever seen such a baby?" Jess Donner asked the other two. "Makes you wonder if he ever gave up breast-feedin'."

"That would explain his fondness for the fairer sex," Stu said.

Steve was red in the face and huffing and puffing like the train engine. "Dang. Now I know how crawdads feel when we boil the little critters for supper."

"Get scrubbin'," Jess said, passing him a used bar of lye soap. "Some of us want to take in the town before next summer."

Franklyn took a long-handled brush from a peg

and held it out to Steve. "For scrubbing your back, sir. We like folks to get their money's worth."

Steve plucked a handful of hairs from the bristles. "Who used this last? A bear?" He ran the brush up and down his back a few times, and grinned. "A gent could get used to this high life." He dipped the brush so low that the handle was under the water, and a dreamy expression came over him. "Now that's pure heaven."

"Someone kick him," Jess said.

"I'm not usin' that brush now," Heck Myers declared. "I shudder to think what it's touchin'."

The barber chairs were empty and waiting when they were done. Once again they flipped a coin. Once again Steve Ellsworth lost. He offered to pay them to let him go first but Jess, Heck, and Stu flatly refused.

"Some friends you are. Here I am, in the closest town to heaven on God's green earth, with more dance halls than you can shake a quirt at, and I have to wait to make the rounds."

"We figure we're doin' those girls a favor," Jess said as Franklyn spread an apron over him. "The way you dance, Dodge is about to suffer an epidemic of busted feet."

"How would you like your hair cut?" Franklyn asked. "A lot of young gentlemen like it parted in the middle and greased down. Or maybe you would like it soap-lock style. That's real popular, too."

"What's that?" Jess asked.

Franklyn indicated a hatless young man walking

by the front window. "There's one now. I did him just yesterday."

The man's hair was cut long in the front and short in the back and combed so the hair fell below the ears.

"That's not for me," Jess said. "Make mine short all over. A shave, too, if you please, and don't spare the lilac water."

Franklyn picked up a scissors and comb but had only begun when the bell over the door tinkled and a black boy of fourteen or fifteen burst inside.

"Pa! Have you heard the news? A exhibition came in on the train. They're posting flyers." He waved a sheet of paper.

"Calm down, Thad," Franklyn coaxed. "I haven't seen you this excited since that giant from Belgium put on a show."

Thad began reading the flyer aloud, pronouncing each word slowly and carefully. " 'Come one, come all, to the Collection of Curiosities. The most exotic animals known to man. A tiger from fiercest India. A king of beasts from darkest Africa.' "

"Nothing much special about that," Franklyn interrupted. "I've seen lions and tigers, and leopards, besides."

Thad wasn't done reading. " 'Behold the mystery man of the woods, the orangutan. The marvel of the century, a genuine unicorn. And the wonder of wonders, a mermaid.' " He waved the flyer. "Can we go see them, Pa? Please?"

"I'd like to see the mermaid my own self," Steve

Ellsworth spoke up. "Folks say they're downright beautiful."

You should ask her to dance," Jess suggested.

Ignoring the barb, Steve gazed happily out the window at the passersby. "Dodge is my kind of place, sure enough. I bet no one ever gets bored here."

"That's true, sir," Franklyn said. "But there is one thing a lot people get that's a lot worse than being bored."

"What would that be?" Steve asked.

"Dead."

Chapter Five

Rusty Vanes came to an oasis of trees in the prairie. The aroma of brewing coffee and sizzling bacon made his stomach growl. He threaded through the cottonwoods to a clearing, where two other horses were already picketed, and dismounted. "Hope you have extra for me."

Grat Vanes was hunkered by the fire, flipping juicy strips of bacon with a big fork. "You always did have a knack for showin' up just at mealtime, little brother."

On a blanket nearby, cleaning his rifle, sat Ira Baxter. A hulking, bearded man, he sneered and said, "Eat and gamble—that's all he ever does."

About to squat by the fire, Rusty stiffened. "I would be sparin' with the insults, if I were you." He had never liked Baxter and never would.

"Or what, boy?" Baxter said without the slightest trace of fear. "You'll pull on me?" His bearded face split in a grin. "That'll be the day. Those seven notches of yours don't mean diddly when you've bucked out as many men in gore as I have."

"So you keep remindin' us," Rusty said, thinking that the jackass would never know how close he came to being gunned down.

Baxter glanced at Grat. "I'm startin' to think that lettin' him join us wasn't the best notion you ever had."

"You eat regular, don't you?" Grat speared another strip of bacon. "And with the belly you've got, that should count for somethin'."

"Funny man," Baxter said. "But there's more to life than eatin'. Money, for instance. You promised me we'd have more than we'd know what to do with. But so far all we've done is swipe a few cattle now and again for stake money and grub."

"We're playin' it smart," Grat said.

"How do you figure?"

"By only stealin' a few head we take less risk and don't draw attention to ourselves," Grat explained. "It gives us spendin' money to tide us over until somethin' better comes along."

"When will that be?" Baxter asked.

"How would I know?" Grat was growing angry. He resented being badgered. "I can't predict the future, can I?"

"You sure as hell can't," Baxter said, "or those cowboys wouldn't have come close to catchin' us the other night. If it wasn't for your dog, we'd have done strangulation jigs." He put a hand to his throat. "And I ain't hankerin' to have my neck stretched."

"Who is?" Grat coldly snapped. "Why do you think we always take Lucky along? In case somethin' like that happens."

At the mention of his name, the mongrel, sprawled a few yards away, looked up expectantly.

"We do what we can for now," Rusty said.

"What's this 'we' stuff?" Baxter responded. "Your brother has the brains in your family. You can't even write your own name."

"What does my scrawlin' an X have to do with anything?" Rusty bristled. "Writin' ain't important. It's not like a man can earn a livin' at it."

"I don't call what we're doin' earnin' a livin'."

Rusty was silent, then he sullenly said to Grat, "Remind me again why we need this joker?"

"Another gun is always handy to have," his brother answered. Checking the coffee, Grat nodded. "Almost ready."

Baxter was inserting cartridges into the chamber of his Winchester. "You might need to find yourself another extra gun before too long. Jed lit out on us yesterday, and I've been thinkin' about movin' on to greener pastures, too."

"I would take it as a personal favor if you stick around," Grat said. "Findin' someone to take your place won't be easy."

"Sure it will," Rusty said. "There are more curly wolves in Dodge than you can shake a stick at. Any one of them would do."

Grat placed three battered tin plates on the ground and beside them set three equally battered tin cups. "Not all curly wolves are equal. Some aren't worth a lick. Others are half-rabid and will bite the hand that feeds them."

"Even so—" Rusty began.

"Findin' someone we can trust, someone who won't shoot us in the back to take what little we have, is like lookin' for a needle in a haystack. You might not think highly of Baxter here but him and me were partnered up long before you joined us. I trust him."

"Thanks," Baxter said.

Rusty squatted and watched his brother pour coffee. "I reckon you know best, Gratton. But if this big bear doesn't quit teasin' me, he's liable to find he's bitten off more than he can chew."

"That'll be the day," was Baxter's next remark.

Grat put the pot down and swore. "That'll be enough, the both of you! Havin' to listen to all this bickerin' is givin' me a headache. It reminds me of my wife."

"That's right," Baxter said. "You were married once. Susie, wasn't that her handle? Whatever happened to her?"

"She got what was comin' to her," Grat said sourly. "The nag always did have the disposition of a contrary mule. Forever on me about this or that. Sayin' how she didn't like how I dressed, or how my table manners weren't elegant enough, and how I was never goin' to amount to a hill of beans. One day she nagged once too often, and that was that."

"You didn't," Baxter said.

"No, that wouldn't be right, a husband killin' his own wife," Grat said. "So I had Rusty do it."

"The brat shot her?"

"Right between the eyes," Rusty bragged, and laughed. "You should have heard her squeal when I drew my Colt."

"You killed a woman?"

"So?" Rusty said. "Men, women, children—they all bleed the same. What difference does it make?"

"It just ain't done, boy," Baxter said. "Lord knows, I've broken the law more than most. But I'd never murder a kid, and I sure as hell wouldn't lay a finger on a female. Nothin' will get you hung quicker."

"I shot her when I was only eight and I'm still here," Rusty said. "You only get your neck stretched if you're stupid enough to get caught, and I aim to be around a good, long while."

Baxter switched his displeasure to Grat. "I'm surprised you let him do it. Don't you remember what happened to that clerk who took a club to that whore in Bixby? All he did was bust her face and break an arm and a leg, and they hung him so fast, he was dead before she stopped bleedin'."

"He did it in front of a bunch of drunks in a crowded saloon in a minin' camp with no law," Grat said. "It's a wonder he lived long enough to hang." Grat placed two strips of bacon on a plate, added a heaping spoonful of scrambled eggs, and gave it to Baxter.

"Still, women are off-limits. This troubles me, pard. Troubles me plenty. I don't much like ridin' with someone who can stoop that low."

"Listen to you!" Rusty scoffed. "When did you

get religion? Or is it just that you've grown yellow all of a sudden?"

The lever of Baxter's Winchester rasped, and he pointed the muzzle at young Vane's chest. "That's about all the sass I'm ever goin' to take from you, brat. I've warned you before about that mouth of yours but you just don't listen."

"Apologize," Grat said to Rusty.

"Like hell," Rusty spat.

Grat slowly rose. "If you don't, he'll blow out your wick. Sure, you're kin, and Ma would forever hold it against me if I let anything happen to you, but you can't go around talkin' to folks like you do and not expect to add lead to your diet. So do as I damn well tell you or I'll come around this fire and box your ears in." Balling his fists, Grat took a couple of steps to the right, which put him between Baxter and Rusty.

"You're in my sights," Baxter warned.

"Sorry," Grat said, and took another long stride.

Too late, Baxter saw the pearl-handled Colt in Rusty's hand.

Rusty was grinning from ear to ear. The Colt boomed and Baxter was whipped half-around, his right arm shattered. Baxter clawed for his revolver with his other hand but the Colt cracked a second time, coring his wrist and leaving a walnut-sized exit wound. Gritting his teeth against the pain, Baxter clutched his arms to his middle and spewed obscenities.

The dog rose and slunk off, its tail between its legs.

Grat stood with his arms folded, and said with the barest hint of regret, "I'm truly sorry, Ira. But you shouldn't have pointed your rifle at him. A brother always counts for more than a pard."

Baxter struggled to stand, the sleeves of his shirt red with blood. "Damn both of you to hell!"

Rusty came partway around the fire. "Oh, I reckon you'll learn what it's like down there long before we do." He slowly extended his arm.

"Wait!" Baxter cried. "Now you just hold on there, boy! I've learned my lesson! Let me ride out and we'll forget this ever took place!" Gasping from fear as much as from exertion, he made it to his knees.

"Ain't he a peach?" Rusty asked his brother.

"Please, Grat," Baxter pleaded. "We've been pards for years. You can't let him do this to me."

"There was a time I'd agree," Grat said, "but your company ain't what it used to be. In the old days you didn't gripe nearly as much. I wasn't joshin' when I said you remind me of any wife. In time I might have shot you my own self."

Baxter's eyes watered and he choked out, "You bastards! You're nothin' but worthless saddle trash. You'll gets yours one day!"

"Maybe," Grat said, "but you won't be the hombre dishin' it out."

"I should say he won't," Rusty said, and fired again, into Baxter's right hip.

An inhuman howl keened from the stricken outlaw's blood-frothed lips. Flopping wildly about, Baxter gurgled and sputtered until exhaustion claimed him and all he could do was gaze furiously at his killer, and groan.

"Pitiful, just pitiful," Rusty said. "I've seen frogs with more sand."

"Finish it," Grat said.

"What's the hurry? Remember that Injun we carved on? The old crippled half-breed who used to come around beggin' for scraps?" Rusty placed his other hand on his belt knife. "I'm fixin' to do the same to Ira, here."

"No," Grat said.

"No?"

"He *has* been my pard a good long while."

Rusty frowned and kicked at the soil. "Hell! You're always spoilin' my fun. But to prove how good a brother I can be, how's this?" He shot Ira Baxter through the forehead and Baxter flopped onto his back and was still.

"I appreciate that," Grat said.

Baxter lay with his head in a spreading red pool. His mouth hung open, revealing half a dozen yellow teeth, and his tongue jutted out. Blood seeped along his crooked nose and down over his chin into his beard.

Rusty was replacing the spent cartridges. "Damn, he's ugly."

Grat squatted beside the body, hiked up Baxter's right pants leg, and slid a dagger from a brown sheath.

"What are you fixin' to do with that pigsticker of yours?"

"Waste not, want not. Isn't that what Ma was always sayin'?" Grat removed Baxter's hat and gripped the front of Baxter's black hair. He tugged a few times. "I know a gent in Dodge who pays fifteen dollars for Injun scalps. His son and daughter-in-law were part of a wagon train bound for the Oregon Country, and were butchered and scalped. The old man has hated Injuns ever since." Grat sliced the dagger's tip a quarter of an inch into Baxter's flesh. "He has a whole wall in his parlor decorated with Injun hair he's collected."

"But Baxter ain't no redskin," Rusty said, then caught himself, and cackled. "Oh. I get it. But won't the old geezer be able to tell the difference?"

"Hair is hair. We'll smear some grease in it so he'll think it's bear fat and I'll trim the scalp so that he'll believe it came from a young buck." Grat carefully slit the skin along Baxter's hairline.

"How many scalps have you sold him?"

"Two others besides this one. One was a lice-ridden scalp I won in a poker game. The other was from a drunk who wandered down by the river. I killed him, then cut him into pieces and threw them in the water."

"Gratton, you think of everything," Rusty complimented him.

"There are two kinds of peope in this world," Grat said while inserting a thumbnail under the skin and prying upward. "Those who are breathin' air and those who are breathin' dirt. Since our lungs work better with air, it pays to stay one step ahead of everybody else, like I was with those cowboys the other night."

"I'll be!" Rusty exclaimed, and snapped his fingers. "That's where I saw those them before!"

"Saw who?"

"Four leather pounders I ran into at the bridge outside of Dodge. I thought they were familiar. They were with the saddle stiffs who took us by surprise. And from the looks they were givin' me, I'm sure they recognized me."

"What does it matter?" Grat cut into the flesh around Baxter's right ear. "We never stole anything. They caught us before we could."

"I wouldn't want them spreadin' word around that they suspect we're cattle thieves," Rusty said. "Not when they know our first names."

Grat stopped carving and grew thoughtful. "You're right. That wouldn't do. It might set folks to wonderin' how we always have money when we don't have jobs. Maybe we'd best ride in and check on them."

"Fine by me," Rusty said eagerly. "I wouldn't mind beddin' all four down, permanent-like."

"That's always been your trouble, little brother," Grat mentioned as he pulled at Baxter's scalp to test how loose it had become. "You're too damned bloodthirsty."

"And damn proud of it," Rusty Vanes said, and laughed.

Chapter Six

By late afternoon, with the sun baking the Kansas prairie, a collective lethargy gripped Dodge. Most of the town's populace was indoors awaiting the cool of evening. Horses dozed at hitch rails. Dogs lazed in the shade. The train had chugged westward, belching great coils of smoke, and the streets were quiet.

From Franklyn's barbershop emerged four freshly clean and combed young cowboys, eager to see the sights.

"The first thing for us to do," Steve Ellsworth said, "is to visit every honky-tonk in town. I want to find the prettiest girl there is and dance with her until my feet fall off."

"I want to go see the traveling exhibition," Stu Wilkins said. "I've never set eyes on a mermaid before."

Heck Myers shook his head. "Are you two men or imitations? First we find us a saloon where the coffin varnish hasn't been watered down and we drink until the whiskey leaks out our ears."

Jess Donner stepped to the edge of the sidewalk. "You're all wrong. The first order of business is to find new clothes. I'm not goin' anywhere in these rags." Of all of their clothing, his was in the poorest shape. His paper-thin pants were torn in several places; his shirt had holes under the arms and a tear in the side, where a horn had nearly gored him the night of the stampede.

Studying him, Steve said, "I reckon you're right, pard. No self-respectin' gal would dance with anything so mangy."

"There's always the exhibition," Stu urged.

"Which won't be open until tonight," Heck said. "Didn't you hear that boy read the flyer? They're at the edge of town settin' up right now and won't be ready for the public until sunset. Your silly mermaid will have to wait, city boy."

Stu was adjusting his hat in a window. "What's so silly about her, you country bumpkin?"

"A mermaid is part fish. You might as well make love to a bass as get excited over one."

"And you call me silly?" was Stu's retort. "I want a woman big enough to hold in my arms."

"Some bass grow over five feet."

At this, Jess Donner and Steve Ellsworth stopped and turned, and Steve asked, "Since when?"

"Since always," Heck said. "Everyone knows that, in some ponds and lakes, bass are as big as we are."

"Here it comes," Jess said.

"When I was little, an uncle of mine caught a bass as long as he was tall," Heck related in all earnestness. "The blamed fish nearly swamped his boat when he finally got it out of the water."

"Next he'll be sayin' it was a bass that swallowed Jonah," Jess said.

"What happened to this wonder?" Steve asked.

"My uncle had it mounted over his mantel, and people would come from miles around to see it."

Jess shook his head. "I'm ashamed to be seen in public with you. Go fish in Duck Creek. Last year someone pulled a bass out of there the size of a bull. It was so big, they had to bring it into town in a buckboard."

"You're just makin' that up," Heck said.

Rolling his eyes at the clouds, Jess commented, "I would shoot you but bullets cost money." He surveyed Front Street from end to end. "The general store is our best bet for clothes. All those with me, feel free to tag along."

The proprietor was a short, balding man absorbed in a *Harper's Weekly*. He lit up like the full moon when he saw the four men come in. "Why, howdy, my fine young gentry of the plains. What might Paddy O'Roarke do for you today?"

"You're Irish," Steve said.

"Nothing gets past you, does it, laddie?" O'Roarke observed, then proudly declared, "Yes, I'm a former resident of the Emerald Isle. I came to this great country because they have more food than famine, and I haven't missed a meal since." He smiled and winked. "Texans, I'll wager."

"Two of us born and bred," Heck bragged. "The other two are imports."

Jess was examining a shelf piled high with shirts. "Did I hear you right, mister? You came to America because you were hungry?"

"Aye, laddie. There's nothing quite like an empty belly to motivate a man to seek greener pastures."

"I need a new shirt and pants," Jess said, "but I don't have a lot of money so the cheapest will do."

O'Roarke came around the counter. "I admire a man who knows his own mind. Very well. See these fine white shirts? Made by New York Mills, and one will only cost you two dollars and fifty cents."

About to sniff a pair of socks, Stu said, "In New York City I could buy three shirts for that much."

O'Roarke gestured at the front window. "Take a look outside, laddie, and tell me if it's the Atlantic Ocean you see, or a sea of grass? What goes for a dollar there goes for three here."

"Why, that's robbery," Heck said.

"No, it's called profit," O'Roarke corrected him. "And it's no different than taking a steer worth four dollars in Texas and bringing it here to sell for forty."

"I'll take one of those shirts," Jess piped up.

Stu wagged the socks. "And I'll take a pair of these."

"That will be fifty cents."

"Is that fifty cents each? Or fifty cents for the pair?" Stu shook his head in amazement at the price. "Extravagance is wasted where feet are concerned."

Heck mumbled something, then said aloud, "Spoken like a true New Yorker. When it comes to footwear, cowhands spare no expense. Why, my boots alone cost more than I've ever spent on anythin' except my saddle."

Steve noticed a small pink umbrella and opened it. "What in tarnation is this? The rain would leak right through."

"It's called a parasol," O'Roarke said. "All the rage with the ladies. And it's to ward off the sun, not a deluge. It protects their delicate complexions."

Giving the parasol a twirl, Steve chuckled. "What will they think of next?" He closed it and put it down. "Land sakes! There's a wooden woman in the corner. And what is that she's wearin'?"

"The woman is a mannequin," O'Roarke revealed, "and she's rigged with a hoop skirt and a bustle. I've found that women are more prone to buy if they can see how the garments will look on them." He walked over and patted the mannequin on the backside. "The lass doesn't have much of a face, but to her credit she doesn' nag a man to death like some I've known."

Soon the four cowboys had made their purchases and were back on the boardwalk. Only Jess bought a shirt and pants. Stu settled for socks and a shirt. Heck was satisfied with the clothes he had on but he did treat himself to some dried apricots. Steve purchased two items: a bottle of lilac water and a pink parasol.

"Why in blazes did you buy that thing?" Jess

asked. "It's for females, and you're two breasts shy of bein' called 'miss.'"

Steve brandished the parasol as if it were a cavalry saber. "My ma used to say that the way to a man's heart is through his stomach, and my pa would always answer that the way to a woman's heart is to go broke buyin' her presents. I aim to give this to the first dance hall beauty who strikes my fancy."

"Good idea," Heck said, "except that dance halls have roofs."

"The ladies have to step outside sometime, don't they?" Steve patted his prize. I figure she'll be so flattered, she'll give me special treatment. Maybe a walk in the moonlight. And who knows? True love could blossom."

"I take back what I said," Jess responded. "Go ahead and use that thing. The heat is gettin' to you."

Someone tittered, and the four cowboys turned. Two lovely young women in bright dresses and stylish hats were eyeing them. One was a stunning redhead with a parasol of her own, the other a dark-skinned woman with lustrous black hair that cascaded to the middle of her back. Rose-scented perfume wreathed them, and their smiles were dazzling.

"God in heaven!" Heck blurted.

Stu recovered his wits first and, after removing his hat, gave a courtly bow. "My apologies, ladies, for my uncouth friends. It's not that they always walk around with their mouths hanging open. Where they come from women are scarce."

The redhead twirled her blue parasol and grinned playfully at Steve Ellsworth. "My goodness. I'm jealous. Your parasol is so much prettier than mine."

Steve's lips moved but no sounds came out.

"Looks like a cat has his tongue," the black-haired lovely said to her companion. "Why is it cowherders are always so shy?"

The redhead sashayed up to Steve, touched the tip of his chin with a red fingernail, and peered deep into his eyes. "Are you willing to trade, kind sir?"

"Ma'am?" Steve squeaked.

"A trade. My parasol for yours. I like pink better than blue." She held hers out to him. "That is, if you don't mind."

Steve stared blankly at her parasol. "Pink or blue?"

"He's quick, this one," was the raven-haired beauty's opinion, and the two women laughed merrily. "Poke him with your hatpin, Franny, and wake him up."

"Franny?" Steve mewed.

"Francine Brice," the redhead confirmed. "But everyone calls me Franny." She touched his chin again. "Mercy me, but you have the most adorable baby whiskers. What's your name, cowboy?"

Clearing his throat, Steve found his voice. "Stephen Raphael Ellsworth, at your beck and call, ma'am." He removed his hat and nervously rolled the brim. "Meetin' you is the best thing that's ever happened to me. I hope you'll honor me by goin' out to supper with me this evenin'."

The dark woman grinned and nudged Franny. "From shy to gallant in the bat of an eye. Better watch this one. He's a regular lover."

Steve turned the same hue as a beet just plucked from the ground. "I'm not any such thing. My intentions are strictly honorable!"

"Too bad, cowboy," the dark woman replied. "The honest ones don't get ahead in this world."

"Be nice to him, Chelsea," Franny chided. "Can't you see he's fresh off the farm?"

"I lived on a ranch," Steve took exception. "And I've been on my own for over six months now." He thrust the pink parasol at her. "Here. Take this if you want. Keep it and yours, both."

"Are you sure cowboy?" Franny asked.

"The handle is Steve," Steve reminded her. "And yes, I'm sure. I was savin' it to give to the prettiest girl in Dodge, and here you are."

"Why, how sweet." Franny accepted his gift and twirled it in her left hand. Her lively green eyes lingered on his. "Tell you what, Steve. Come to Rankin's Dance Hall tonight after eight p.m. and I'll reserve a dance for you. My treat."

Heck was openly admiring Chelsea. "The two of you are dance hall girls? Who would have thought it?"

"Something wrong with that?" Chelsea asked. "It beats working at a saloon. Men can't take liberties."

"I didn't mean anything," Heck apologized. "I don't think less of you because you dance for a livin' any more than you would think less of me because I push cows."

"Aren't they adorable?" Chelsea giggled and hooked her arm through Franny's. "But we have somewhere to be."

"I can't thank you enough," Franny offered in parting to Steve. "I sincerely hope you will look me up later."

"You can count on it," Steve said.

"Enough of this." Chelsea tugged on Franny's arm and they strolled past. "Why do you always encourage them so? He's a *cowboy*, for crying out loud. Rankin will throw a fit if he finds out."

"I don't care what Lem Rankin likes or doesn't like," Franny snapped. She said more but too softly for the four men to hear. Farther down they turned into a millinery shop. Franny glanced back and waved.

"Did you see that?" Steve Ellsworth said. "There went the woman who is goin' to be my wife."

"Oh brother," Jess said.

"I'm serious. Did you see how she looked at me? How she touched me, not once but twice?" Steve's eyes glazed dreamily as he put his hat back on, backward. "She's the gal of my dreams."

"Why do we put up with him?" Heck asked the other two, then snatched Steve's hat and jammed it back on Steve's head the right way. "This from an hombre who can't even dress himself."

Jess Donner was moving toward the Long Branch Saloon. "I don't know about the rest of you but I could use a drink."

After the hot glare of the sun, the cool interior was a welcome relief. A long, polished bar ran along the right wall. Behind it were several paintings and a magnificent set of bull horns. On the rear wall, overlooking the card tables, hung an exceptionally large elk rack.

"Nice place you have here," Jess said to the bartender, a stocky man who wiped a clean cloth across the bar top as they bellied up.

"What's your poison, gents? Whiskey, rye, bourbon, beer, ale—you name it, we have it."

"Whiskey all around," Jess Donner said.

The bartender nodded, then glanced toward the entrance and suddenly stepped back wearing a worried expression.

The deputy who had greeted the four men at the edge of town was stalking toward them with his hand on the butt of his revolver. "And here I thought you had more sense than most. I guess what I told you went in one ear and out the other. Or else you're hankering to visit Boot Hill."

Chapter Seven

The four cowboys were rooted in bewilderment, except Stu Wilkins, who jerked his hands into the air and became whiter than snow.

Heck Myers asked, "What is it we did that has you so riled, Deputy?"

Halting, the lawman took his hand off his revolver, revealing it to be a Remington with black handles, worn high on his hip and angled so that the butt was tilted for a quick draw. "You honestly don't know? How much have you had to drink?"

Jess Donner caught on before the rest. "We forgot to check our hardware."

"We did?" Steve Elsworth glanced down at himself "I swear. We're dumber than stumps. We're mighty sorry, Deputy. We sure didn't do it on purpose."

"What with our baths and haircuts and all, we plumb forgot," Heck Myers hastily explained.

"You're not drunk?" the lawman asked.

"No, sir, we sure ain't," Steve said. "We were just about to order our very first drink since we rode in."

The bartender stepped the bar. "I haven't sold these pups any liquor yet, Trace. And can check their weapons for them, if it's all the same by you."

"Do it," the deputy said, and whirling, he was out the door before Stu Wilkins let out the breath he had not realized he was holding.

"Damnation!" Heck breathed. "For a second there I thought for sure he would draw on us."

"He must like you," the bartender said. "That there was Trace Morgan. They say he's killed more men than you can count but the particulars aren't well known and no one is fool enough to ask for the details."

"Could be bluster," Jess Donner commented. "A lot of man killers haven't killed half the tally the newspaper claims."

"Go on thinking that about Morgan and you'll push up daisies if you buck him," the bartender said. "I was over to Rowdy Joe's last month when two freighters who couldn't teach a hen to cluck created a commotion. One had his pocket picked, and they stood in the middle of the dance floor, waving pistols they hadn't checked and threatening to clean out the place if the money wasn't returned. They fired a few shots and one hit a girl in the leg." He swiped his cloth at a speck of dust. "Trace Morgan was the first tin star through the door. He didn't ask why they were upset. He didn't tell them to drop their six-shooters. He took one look at that girl bleeding all over the floor, drew his pistol as slick as you can imagine, and shot them both so quick, I swear, if I'd blinked, I'd have missed it."

"Curled up their toes, did he?" Heck Myers asked hopefully, thinking of the story he could tell to future listeners.

"No, as a matter of fact," the bartender said. "He shot them both in the legs. The exact same spot where they shot the girl. Mighty fancy shooting, if you ask me."

Heck was undoing his gun belt. "Too fancy for my peace of mind. Here, you can have my hog leg, and welcome to it."

Only Jess delayed, saying as he placed his on the bar, "I surely don't like not bein' heeled. I've been totin' a six-gun since I was twelve, and it doesn't feel natural."

"Being cooped up in a coffin wouldn't feel natural either," Steve Ellsworth observed. "Why invite trouble? Hand it over and keep your horns sheathed until we head back to camp."

"Take this," the bartender said, handing Heck a stub of paper on which he had scribbled the number seventeen.

"What's it for?"

"So you can reclaim your artillery. You don't expect me to remember which is who's, do you?" The barman gestured at the rows of bottles. "Now then. Weren't you gents about to order?"

An empty table suited them better than the bar, and the four men sat sipping their whiskey with care, as if every drop were precious. Except for

Heck, who downed his in two gulps and broke into a coughing fit.

"It sure is quiet here," Stu Wilkins said. Somehow he had thought Dodge would be like Brooklyn on payday.

"I'm beginnin' to think Dodge ain't all folks have been sayin'," Jess said. "Why, my grandma would find it restful."

"Care for a game of cards, gentlemen?"

The speaker was a nicely dressed individual in a black suit and bowler, who was all by himself at the next table, idly riffling a deck of cards.

Steve wagged his hand. "No offense, mister, but my pa always warned me that playin' poker with a professional card sharp is the same as givin' money away."

"Me, a professional?" The man chuckled. "Believe it or not, I work at the bank. My name is Harris. I co-own this establishment, but after the recent trouble, I'm thinking of selling out." He rather sadly surveyed the customers. "You're right about the quiet. The nights are busy enough, but during the day it's so dull, you can hear yourself think." Tapping the deck on the table, he urged, "How about that game? You can set the stakes. I'm not out to fleece you, only to while away the time."

The cowboys looked at one another, and when Steve Ellsworth nodded, they switched tables. Harris dealt, and as they were inspecting their hands, Stu Wilkins inquired, "What was that about trouble?"

"Where have you boys been that you haven't

heard about the Dodge City War?" the banker marveled. "It was in all the papers." He proceeded to relate how two factions fought for control of Dodge.
One faction wanted to clean it up. The other wanted
things to go on as they were. "At one point, a self-
styled peace commission made up of Bat Masterson,
Wyatt Earp, Luke Short, and other celebrated killers
descended on Dodge to set matters aright."

"Hellfire!" Heck declared. "And we missed it? I'd
give my right ear to meet Masterson, Earp, or Short
in the flesh. All three are as famous as it gets."

"Just think of the whoppers you could tell," Jess
said.

Harris stared glumly about the room. "It hasn't
been the same since, though. The mayor and the
council have cracked down on the sporting girls,
and it won't be long before they close the dance
halls, too."

"That's loco," Steve said. "What reason would us
Texans have for comin' here?"

"It isn't just to sell cows," Heck Myers said. He
slid a coin to the center of the table. "I'll open for a
nickel."

Twilight shrouded Front Street when the four
men ambled outside. Jess Donner patted a bulging
pocket and crowed, "I'm almost three dollars to the
better. Let's fill our bellies and have us some fun."

"If there's any fun to be had," Heck said glumly.
"From the sound of things, Dodge has become
downright tame. I'm so disappointed, I'm tempted
to get booze blind."

Steve nodded at a sign. "That there says the Wright House is one block over. The food is supposed to be as good as any, and the trail boss is there, besides."

Catering to the tastes of anyone who had anything to do with cows, the Wright House was famed for its quality. Rafe Adams and Tom Cambry occupied high-backed chairs facing the entrance.

"Well, look at what the cat drug in," Tom said. "Some mothers have lost their toddlers. Do you reckon we should change their diapers and send them back out to play?"

Jess was not amused. "Is this the thanks we get for comin' to keep you company?"

"What have you been up to?" Rafe Adams asked.

"We're havin' a contest to see who's the first to die of boredom," Heck Myers answered.

"It can't be that bad," Rafe said. "Dodge is the wildest town since Sodom and Gomorrah."

"Not anymore it ain't," Stu told him. "Take away the cows and the dust and it could pass for Philadelphia on a Sunday."

"Any sign of the buyer?" Heck asked.

Rafe shook his head. "He hasn't checked in yet or wired word that he'll be delayed. All I can do is twiddle my thumbs until he shows up. In the meantime, what do you say to a full-course meal on me?"

"Twist my arm and I might be persuaded," Heck said.

The dining room was packed. Now that the sun had gone down, Dodge was stirring to life. They had to wait ten minutes for a table. A waiter handed them menus, and one look had Jess Donner licking his lips in anticipation.

"Will you look at all the kinds of food! This has eatin' drag dust beat all hollow. I thought I would have a thick steak but roast beef smothered in gravy sure sounds temptin'."

"They have five different pies!" Steve was astounded. "I reckon I'll pass on the main course and have a big slice of each."

Jess ran a finger down the menu, moving his lips as he read. "What's this turtle soup? And who in their right mind would eat kidneys covered in wine sauce? I thought this place was partial to the cow crowd."

"Cattle buyers, too," Rafe said. "Many from back east, where fancy eatin' is an art. My cousin wrote me that fish eggs are as popular as anything."

"They call it caviar," Stu Wilkins said. "I've never had any myself, but it's served at all the better restaurants in New York City."

"Leave it to Easterners to eat somethin' that comes out the hind end of a fish," Jess Donner said. "I wouldn't eat any on a dare."

The waiter returned with piping hot coffee and a bowl of sugar and cream, then took their orders. When the food came, the men dug in like starved wolves, and as Heck had to admit, "This chuck beats everything. I could take to city life if I ate three meals like this a day."

Rafe mentioned that thirty-one herds had come up the Western Trail that month. "Which sounds like a lot, but some of the townsfolk are worried. It's less than in previous years."

"The other outfits probably went to Newton or Abilene," Heck guessed, his mouth crammed with pot roast, "where a man can find a willin' dove when he wants one."

"What would you know about doves?" Jess asked. "The only female you've ever kissed was your sister."

"Why, you consarned smart-aleck. If you weren't my friend, I'd hit you with my chair."

"Name one time you've been with a woman," Jess challenged.

Heck resumed chewing. "A gentleman never talks about stuff like that."

In the act of spooning sugar into his coffee, Tom Cambry winked at Rafe Adams. "Somethin' tells me these four goslin's have never broke in a feather bed."

Heck, Jess, and Steve went on eating as if they had not heard his remark, but Stu Wilkins said, "I have." He did not elaborate.

"It's just as well Dodge has run the easy ladies out," Rafe said. "You four would be flat broke when they were done with you."

"But I'd be smilin' for a week," Heck said, summing up the sentiments shared among the four young men, "and rate it worth every cent."

Steve was almost done cleaning his plate. "All this talk of lovemakin' has me itchin' to visit Rankin's."

"The dance hall?" Tom Cambry said. "Better

watch yourself. The sidewinder who owns it is as shady as they come. His girls are pickpockets."

"Not all of them," Steve said. "I met one today who is as sweet as honey and as pure as an angel. One look in her eyes and you just know she could never do wrong."

"He's in love," Jess said.

"I like her, yes," Steve admitted. "She must like me, too, or she wouldn't have taken my pink parasol."

Tom's eyebrows met over his nose. "Your what?"

"He was plannin' to open a parasol business in Texas," Heck said. "Once the other hands saw how cute he looked, and how it spared his delicate skin from the sun, everyone would want one. He could give up cows and make his fortune."

Steve hissed like a kicked snake. "That's shy of the truth by about ten miles." He pushed back his plate. "Since I refuse to sit here and be teased, I'm off to go see my cow bunny."

"Yours?" Jess scoffed. "I hope the other fifty men she dances with tonight take that into account."

"You're hopeless, all of you," Steve said. "You have no sense of romance." He made for the door.

Jess Donner pushed back his plate and stood. "I'd better tag along to keep him out of trouble."

"What about you two?" Rafe Adams asked Heck Myers and Stu Wilkins.

"It's the exhibition for me," the former New Yorker said. "I've always enjoyed visiting museums and the like, and this should be a treat."

"Count me in, then," Heck said. He helped himself to a toothpick and pried at his teeth. "I just hope to God somethin' happens to make this night interestin'."

Front Street was thronged. Townsmen, frontiersmen, and cowboys were on the prowl for entertainment. Splashes of gay color testified to the presence of more than a few women.

"Looks like things are pickin' up," Heck said.

Stu was on the tips of his toes. "I don't see Steve or Jess anywhere. I guess we'll catch up with them later."

An immense canvas tent had been erected in the vacant lot at one end of Chestnut Street. Painted in giant yellow letters on the front were THE COLLECTION OF CURIOSITIES and, underneath, T. Q. SNELL, MANAGER. A long line of people waiting their turn to buy tickets stretched for fifty yards down Chestnut.

"Step right up, ladies and gentlemen!" a hawker cried. "Witness the marvels of the era for fifty cents! That's right! A paltry price to pay for an experience you will never forget! Shudder with fear at the savage orangutan! Tremble at the terrible teeth of the tiger! Gasp at the beauty of the mermaid! And prepare yourselves for the sight of the only known unicorn in captivity!"

"Steve should be here," Stu said. "He wanted to see the mermaid, too."

"He probably figures half a woman can't compete with a whole one," Heck said. "Makin' love to a mermaid would be like making love to a bass."

"Don't start with that again."

Heck glanced over his shoulder. More and more

people were lining up. He suddenly stiffened and leaned to the right, then to the left, and shook his head.

"Didn't the food agree with you?" Stu asked.

"I'd swear I just saw Rusty and Grat, those two hombres from the other night. The hothead was starin' right at me. Then he up and disappeared."

"Maybe you were mistaken," Stu said. "With this many people, a few faces are bound to look familiar."

"I suppose. After all, what would those two want with us?"

Chapter Eight

Rankin's Dance Hall was at the south end of a street lined with honky-tonks and saloons. It was the biggest, the brightest, and the loudest. Out front stood a towering slab of muscle with his arms folded across his barrel chest and a much smaller man with a thin mustache and glittering dark eyes who collected the twenty-five cents it cost to go in.

"I thought we only had to pay for dances," Steve Ellsworth said as he fished coins from his pockets.

"You thought wrong, sonny," the small man said. "But it's well worth the extra expense. Our girls are beauties. And friendly as can be."

Jess Donner was not at all pleased. "It's the same as robbery, if you ask me. Do we get our money back if we don't have a good time?"

The slab of muscle unfolded his brawny arms and in a gravelly voice asked, "We're not going to have trouble with you, are we, cowboy?"

"I don't like your tone," Jess said.

Balling fists with knuckles the size of walnuts,

the big man started toward Jess but the small man put a hand to the other's chest.

"Easy now, Moose. He's not worth creating a scene. And we don't want the law called, do we?"

"I guess not, Tilly," Moose said sullenly.

Tilly fixed his beady eyes an Jess and Steve. "Keep in mind we reserve the right to throw out anyone who acts up."

"We're only here to dance," Steve Ellsworth assured him.

Jess, though, hitched at his belt and said, "I'd like to see someone try to toss me out of somewhere I wanted to stay."

Again Moose took a step and again Tilly stopped him. "Simmer down. It's plain he's not armed, and without a gun these cow pushers are all bluster."

Steve gripped Jess's arm and pulled him toward the door. "Don't you dare spoil this night for me. We're here to find the love of my life, not get thrown behind bars."

"They insulted us," Jess said. "Only my friends can do that and get away with it."

"Since when did you become a badman?" Steve demanded, and then they were inside and he stopped short as his senses were assaulted by a whirlwind of sights and sounds.

The dance floor was lit up brighter than the sun. Scores of couples swirled in zestful rhythm to the music, the women smiling politely, the men either nervous or so liquored up they were whooping and hollering and pounding the floorboards as if trying to break them. Loudest of all were the cowboys, each seeming to try to outdo the others.

"Land sakes," Steve breathed.

As bright as the dance floor was, the light did not extend to the many booths that lined the side walls and the rear. The booths were mired in shadow, lending the illusion of privacy in a building packed to the rafters. Shadowy shapes were cheek to cheek and hand in hand.

"I've died and gone to heaven!" Steve Ellsworth exclaimed. He had to shout to make himself heard above the band on a platform at the front. "Isn't this the grandest place you ever saw?"

To Jess it was a nightmare. He had only tagged along because Steve was his pard and his bunkie. He had imagined a nice, quiet place where couples danced to slow tunes while everyone else stood sipping drinks and talking. He had not imagined such total bedlam.

The four musicians were playing so loud, their music assaulted the ears. The piano player, in particular, was pounding the tinny keys with such force, it was a wonder he didn't break them.

The slope of the ceiling had a lot to do with the din, as it amplified every note.

Girls were everywhere, dancing, chatting, waiting to be asked. Blondes, redheads, brunettes—every shade and mix ever known. Girls in yellow dresses, girls in green dresses, girls in bright blue dresses, girls in red dresses. Fair-complexioned girls and dark-complexioned girls. Girls with shapely figures and girls with figures less so. Girls with ample bosoms and girls with no bosoms at all. Girls with long legs and girls with short legs. Girls, girls, girls.

The perfume was enough to choke a man's lungs. It filled the air to where the eyes watered.

"Look at all the females!" Steve said in rapturous wonder, and breathed deep of the fragrance.

Jess liked women as much as the next fellow, but being around this many made him vaguely uneasy.

"Do you see Franny anywhere?" Steve yelled in Jess's ear. Finding her in that maelstrom of colors and movement would be akin to finding a needle in a very large haystack.

"Just look for a pink parasol," Jess said dryly.

"We'll rove the room," Steve proposed, but they had only taken a couple of steps when a pair of giggling girls materialized before them.

"Howdy," the tallest said in a Southern accent similar to Jess's. "I'm Margaret and this here is Ethel. Would you care to dance?"

Margaret had sandy hair, an oval face, and a button nose, but no lips at all and a chest as flat as a board. Ethel was a plump little thing whose most attractive features were her blue eyes and watermelons her print dress could scarcely contain.

"No, thanks, ma'am," Steve said politely.

"Please," Margaret coaxed. "We don't get paid if we don't dance and it's early yet, so we haven't had but two dances."

"Please," Ethel mimicked. She had a high-pitched voice more befitting a ten-year old.

"You wouldn't want to hurt our feelin's, would

you?" Margaret pressed them, with a wink and a chuckle.

"I'm lookin' for someone," Steve said, seeking to soothe them. "Maybe you know her. Francine Brice?"

Margaret and Ethel swapped glances and Margaret said, "What do you want with her? She's Mr. Rankin's favorite, and hardly ever dances. Besides, I don't think she's here yet."

"You cowboys must be rich," Ethel said. "Franny will cost you twenty cents a dance. We only cost ten. So how about it?" Grabbing Steve by the hand, she pulled him out into the bright glare. "Come on. You'll have fun. I promise."

"How about you?" Margaret asked Jess. She reached for his hand but he swung his arm behind his back.

"I'm not much of a dancer."

"You're not very friendly, either."

Jess had no desire to hurt her feelings. And since he was there, he might as well make the best of it, so he asked, "How much does it cost to talk?"

"That's all you want to do?"

"Why not? It can be as much fun as dancin' but it's a lot less sweaty." Jess sidled toward the platform. "Over here where it's out of the way."

"No," Margaret said, and snagged hold of his sleeve. "A booth is better. We can hear each other without havin' to shout."

Out on the dance floor, Ethel placed one of Steve's hands on her hip and clasped his other firmly in her warm fingers. "I'm all yours, cowboy. Just don't step on my toes. I hate that more than anything."

"I ain't much at shakin' a hoof. You'd be safer stompin' with someone else." In order for her to hear him, he had to lean so close, his mouth nearly brushed her ear.

"I don't want anyone else. I want you. You're cute," Ethel said, and took a step to goad him into moving. "Come on. We look silly standing here like a couple of statues. Any minute a pigeon will drop poop on us."

Steve was so startled, he brayed like a mule.

"It wasn't that funny," Ethel said.

"I just never heard a girl say poop before."

"Don't you have sisters?" Ethel asked while side-stepping to avoid another couple careening among the dancers. A towheaded cowboy with a wisp of a girl in a bear hug was thumping the floorboards with the frenetic abandon of a bull gone amok. "Poor Sally. She always gets the wild ones."

Steve was doing his best but he was slow and awkward and moved his feet with extreme care so as not to accidentally tread on her black shoes. "I've never danced but once my whole life," he apologized. "Sorry I'm so terrible at it."

"Relax. Leave it to me," Ethel said.

Before Steve could ask what she meant, Ethel did the most incredible thing; she assumed the lead but did so in a way that made it seem as if he were still leading. Every step she took flawlessly anticipated and matched his. The two of them flowed across the dance floor, avoiding other couples with impressive ease.

"Goodness gracious, you sure are somethin'," Steve said in her ear. To his surprise, Ethel blushed.

"It's nice to hear a compliment someone means."

The song came to an end and they stood at arm's length until Steve asked, "Would you like to dance again?"

"Sure."

The band launched into a slow tune and Ethel snuggled close. Beads of sweat sprinkled Steve's brow as he began to waltz. His chest brushed her bosom and he quickly said in her ear, "Sorry. I didn't mean to do that."

"It's all right," Ethel said. "With you I don't mind. You're so polite and nice. You're special."

"I am?" Steve's voice sounded strange. He licked his lips to moisten them and swallowed a few times. "I reckon you say that to all the men."

Ethel drew back, hurt in her blue eyes. "No, I don't. The last man I said it to was Danny, my beau, over a year ago. I thought he cared for me, but he was struck by gold fever and ran off to Colorado to pan for ore. He never even bothered to say good-bye. Just up and left me."

"That was wrong of him," Steve said.

"Jobs are scarce for girls like me," Ethel had gone on, her mouth next to his ear, her breath fanning his neck. "I refuse to stoop to selling myself, and I'm not much of a seamstress, so this was the best I could do."

"What about your folks?" Steve heard himself ask.

"My father is a clerk. He barely makes enough to feed a goat. My mother scrubs floors for a living and earns even less." Ethel placed her cheek on his chest. "I get by the best I can. Please don't hold it against me."

Swallowing hard, Steve made bold to slide his hand a few inches higher on her back. He was unbearably hot and his heart was thumping wildly in his chest. "I would never do that."

In a cramped booth along the north wall, Margaret smiled and said in Jess's ear, "It looks like your friend and Ethel have hit it off."

Fidgeting uncomfortably on the narrow seat, Jess remarked, "My pard tends to put all you females on a pedestal." Margaret's arm and leg were brushing him and he shifted to make himself more comfortable.

"Is something the matter?" Margaret asked. "You can't sit still for two seconds. Don't you cotton to my company?"

"We're too cramped," Jess said. "I can't hardly breathe without breathin' on you."

"I don't mind," Margaret said. "It's been weeks since I talked to a son of the South." She placed her hand on his. "That makes you special."

Jess hesitated. "Truth is, I've never been much at conversation. One look at a woman and my tongue is tied in knots."

"Be serious," Margaret said, squeezing him. "A

handsome man like you must have girls fallin' over themselves for the pleasure of your company."

"Now who's joshin'?" was Jess's reply. "You're paid to tell that to every gent you dance with."

Suddenly pulling back, Margaret jerked her hand away. "That was cruel. How can you think so poorly of me? What have I ever done to you?" She bowed her head. "And here I thought you were different than most. I could just cry."

Her shoulders shook, and Jess heard a muffled sob. "Are you blubberin'?" Afraid someone would hear her, he groped in the dark and found her hand. "Quit that."

"What do you care?" Margaret asked, sniffling.

"I didn't mean that as an insult."

"Sure you didn't. I don't mean anything to you or you wouldn't accuse me of bein' so heartless."

"I didn't accuse you of anything," Jess said angrily. He tried to raise her chin but she resisted. "Everyone knows dance hall girls are taught what to say and how to act so us men will spend every last penny we have."

"There you go again," Margaret mewed, and burst into great racking sobs, her hair over her face, her whole body quaking. "And here I thought you were so sweet. I could just die."

Several nearby dancers were staring at the booth. Jess shifted so his back was to them and said much more softly, "Please, Margaret. Stop your bawlin'. Maybe I'm wrong."

"Maybe?" Margaret repeated, and sobbed louder than ever.

Jess's skin was prickling as if from a heat rash and his thoughts were a jumbled riot of confusion. "All right. All right. You're a decent lady and I should be horsewhipped. Happy now?"

"You're just sayin' that."

Jess noticed a man in a suit coming toward their booth. Suspicious bulges under each arm hinted at shoulder rigs. Instinctively, Jess dropped his hand to his hip, and frowned.

"Is there a problem here?" The man wasn't much over twenty, if that, and wore his insolence with pride.

"What's it to you?" Jess was tensed to spring should the need arise.

"I work here. It's my job to see everyone is on their best behavior."

Just then Margaret sniffled and said, "Everything is fine, Vince. Honest."

Vince peered at her, then nodded. "I'll keep an eye on this one, just the same. If you need help, you only have to wave in my direction." To Jess he said, "Hurt her, cowboy, and you'll answer to Mr. Rankin."

"The gall," Jess said as the bouncer strutted off.

"Pay Vince Shamblin no mind," Margaret said. "He's tryin' to impress me. For months he's been after me but I've refused to give in."

"After you?" Jess said, and put a hand on her shoulder. "Why, the polecat. I should take the hideouts he wears and beat him over the noggin until he can't tell up from down."

"Why would you do that for someone out to

fleece you?" Margaret bluntly asked. Then she smiled and caressed his cheek. "Or can it be you're not as gruff as you pretend?"

"Aw, shucks," Jess said. The temperature seemed to have climbed twenty degrees. He rested his elbows on the table and his chin in his hands. "I'm sorry I made you cry."

"I'm fine. Truly I am." Margaret bent closer so her lips touched his ear. "Fact is, I'm happier than I've been in a coon's age."

"Oh, hell," Jess Donner said.

Chapter Nine

Heck Myers and Stu Wilkins were greeted by T.Q. Snell himself at the entrance to the giant tent. Snell wore a gaudy suit and a straw hat, and pumped their hands as excitedly as if Hank and Stu were long-lost relatives. "Welcome! Welcome! You're about to feast your eyes on the wonders of the age! I've scoured the world for the most marvelous oddities money can obtain and now share my treasures with one and all!" He had a booming voice and a thin mustache waxed and curled at both ends.

"I love oddities," Stu Wilkins said.

"Then you are in for a treat!" Snell assured him. "The Queen of England was so captivated by my wonderments, she knighted me as a peer of the British empire."

"Strange," Stu said. "I thought I read somewhere that she could only knight British subjects."

"I'm Yankee born and bred, and proud of it, son," Snell declared, then whispered conspiratorially,

"The queen made an exception in my case. She recognized greatness when she saw it." Laughing, he motioned for the two other men to go in.

"I wouldn't trust that jasper as far as I can throw his tent," Heck Myers commented.

"What do you know?" Stu rejoined. "You've spent your whole life in Texas. He's a man of the world. He's seen things you and I can only dream about."

"I know a natural-born liar when I meet one," Heck said, "and he wouldn't know the truth if it sank its fangs into his backside."

The interior of the tent was surprisingly dim. Plain brown blankets had been hung on rope strung from poles, creating a winding aisle, which the line of eager attendees followed until it brought them to the first exhibit. In a cage lay the tiger the flyer had advertised. Well on in years, it was a scrawny specimen with a scruffy coat. Its tail looked as if rats had gnawed down to the bone. The tiger sluggishly yawned, revealing that half its teeth were missing.

"Mighty fierce critter," Heck Myers said. "My aunt could beat it off with her broom."

"Still, it's a real tiger," Stud said, "and how often do you get to see one of those in living flesh?"

Heck was still not impressed. "If it's flesh I'm after, I'd rather see a naked female with all her teeth."

A matron behind them sniffed. "I say, young man, that was in terribly rude taste. Show some manners."

"Sorry, ma'am," Heck said, politely doffing his

hat. "I wasn't raised in a chicken coop, so I tend to forget that most hens pretend they have feathers."

"Why, that makes no sense whatsoever," the matron said. "Are you sure you're not under the influence of hard liquor?"

"Would to God I were," Heck replied.

The line moved on, and soon the two cowboys stood before the next exhibit. In a cramped cage barely large enough to contain it lay a maned lion so thin, its ribs showed through its hide. Its mane was falling out and yellow mucus dripped from its nose.

"The king of the beasts," Stu said.

"Some king," Heck spat. "Seems to me a mouse could lick it without half tryin'. I just hope it doesn't sneeze."

"He's sick," Stu said, stating the obvious, bending for a better view. "Why, he could die if Snell doesn't do something."

"He'll just send to Africa for another," Heck guessed.

The matron made her sniffing sound again. "What is that awful stench? It's worse than at the tiger cage."

"These contraptions don't come with outhouses, ma'am," Heck said. "I wouldn't look too close if I were you."

The next cage was home to the Mystery Man of the Woods. As broad as a buckboard, the orangutan was on its haunches in a far corner, one hand wrapped around the bars. It stared at the spectators with flat, listless eyes.

"That has to be the fattest monkey alive," was Heck's opinion.

The orangutan chose that moment to grunt and pick at itself.

"How disgusting!" the matron complained. "No decent woman should be exposed to so vile a creature."

"Now, now, my dear," said her husband. "There's no denying nature. Animals will be animals."

"Ain't that the truth," Heck agreed.

A murmur ran down the line. Someone mentioned that the unicorn was the next attraction.

"I can't wait," Stu said, rubbing his hands like a boy about to be treated to candy. "Unicorns were common in Asia once. My sixth-grade teacher told me so."

"You got as high as the sixth?" Heck said. "I had to drop out in the fourth. My pa couldn't do all the work by his lonesome. But I still learned to read and write, which made my ma awful proud. She always liked to say that learnin' letters was as important as learnin' to shoot." He paused. "Women come up with the silliest notions, don't they?"

The line had slowed. Stu took that as a good sign and said, "I bet the unicorn will be something to remember for the rest of our lives."

"I felt that way about my first pair of boots."

A bend was ahead. Stu tried to see past it by craning to the right but there were too many people. "Darn it. I really want a look. My teacher told me unicorns are as white as snow and as big as a stallion."

"I never heard of them before today," Heck admitted. "But I have heard of skunk apes."

"Excuse me?" Stu said.

"Three-toed skunk apes. They live mainly in brush country and swamps from Texas to Louisiana. There might be some in Florida, too, if my uncle had his facts straight."

"Is this another of your yarns?"

"Honest to goodness," Heck said. "Back in the old days, when the first white settlers came to Texas, skunk apes were all over the place. One was shot down in Galveston, and another somewhere I can't rightly recollect at the moment. They were always breakin' into barns and kitchens and helpin' themselves to food. My uncle told me that one stole a fresh-baked cherry pie from a neighbor of his."

"You're impossible."

Heck shrugged. "Don't believe me if you want but I'm tellin' the truth. Ask Steve. He's heard of 'em too."

"But why are they called 'skunk' apes?"

"Why else? They have white stripes down their backs."

The two men reached the bend and beheld an enclosure. A waist-high fence had been erected, and in the center was the animal everyone was gazing at.

Stu rose onto the tip of his boots. "I still can't see it. It must be lying down."

"Either that or it's an awful small stallion," Heck said.

Someone swore, and the group ahead moved on, several people shaking their heads and others muttering. Stu eagerly rushed to the fence and gripped the top rail.

"Well, I'll be switched," Heck remarked. "There's a sight you don't see every day—or any day at all."

The occupant of the enclosure was a medium-sized goat with a stringy beard. It glared at Heck and Stu as if it dearly desired to butt them, but it was restrained by a rope around its neck, tied to a thick stake. It was dull brown in color, and completely unremarkable except for a single horn growing from the center of its forehead—not even a true horn: two separate horns had entwined together and fused.

"Why, it's nothing but a fake!" Stu exclaimed, smacking the rail in frustration. "We've been hoodwinked."

"There's a shock," Heck said.

"It's a freak," Stu continued. "Like a two-headed snake or the rabbit I saw once with five legs. It's not a unicorn at all." Stu straightened and glared about. "I ought to punch T. Q. Snell in the nose."

"Go right ahead. But if you get tossed in the hoosegow, don't expect me to pay your fine."

A sign over the next exhibit billed the occupant as the Madagascar Cannibal.

Stu stared, sighed, and closed his eyes. "How could I fall for this? I'm from New York City."

"It's nothin' but a midget prancin' around in rooster feathers," was Heck's assessment.

"Peacock feathers," Stu amended. "I saw one once at a zoo."

The Grecian Siren was a corpulent woman attired

in an outfit that elicited considerable comment from those filing past her. "Scandalous, simply scandalous!" the matron declared. "She's hardly wearing anything at all!"

"This whole show is a fake," Stu said. He hardly looked at the Burmese python or the Saharan Tortoise. Then whispers came down the line that the mermaid was next.

"Cheer up, pard," Heck said. "This is the marvel you've been waitin' for."

"The way this has been, it will he a guppy with hair glued on its head," Stu forlornly said. "I've wasted our money on frivolous silliness."

"Not hardly," Heck said. "When I tell the others about this, for once I won't have to make things up."

The moment came. Stu uttered a tiny whine and said in embarrassment, "Shoot me and put me out of my misery. Steve and Jess will never let me hear the end of this."

Heck was scrutinizing the Wonder of the Age. "I'm no expert on mermaids, mind you, but that's the ugliest critter I've ever laid eyes on. Any notion what it is?"

"As near as I can tell," Stu said, crestfallen, "it's the top half of a baboon sewn onto the bottom half of a seal."

"You don't say? I like the eyes. But why are they purple?"

"I think they're buttons."

There were more exhibits but Stu refused to look at them, even when Heck exclaimed, "I'll be switched! I didn't know there was such a thing as rabbits with horns!"

The exit was located near the entrance, and T. Q. Snell was on hand to thank everyone for coming and to urge them to visit again soon.

Stu swore and started toward him but Heck gripped Stu's arm and wouldn't let go. "Not until you simmer down. It's your own fault for bein' so gullible. And look around you. It's not as if you're the only one that old geezer buffaloed."

"I'm supposed to know better. I'm half-sophisticated."

"Stupid is stupid no matter where you're from," Heck said, and pulled Stu toward Chestnut Street. "Come on. What you need is a drink or three. Then we'll go find Steve and Jess."

A brisk northwesterly breeze rustled the trees. Overhead, a multitude of stars sparkled in the firmament. Somewhere out on the prairie a coyote yipped, causing several dogs in town to bark.

"Yes, sir," Heck said. "My grandma would love a peaceable place like Dodge. She could sit around with the other biddies and watch the grass grow."

Stu walked in a slouch and dragged his feet. "To think we could be dancing with pretty girls right now."

"You never know how a horse will be until you ride it," Heck philosophized. Stretching, he adjusted his hat. "The thing to do now is persuade Jess and Steve to go see the exhibition."

Stu glanced up. "Whatever for? It's a waste of

money. They wouldn't like it any better than we did."

Heck grinned wickedly.

"Oh, I get it." Stu grinned, then chuckled, then indulged in a belly laugh. "Why, Jess would be so mad, he'll beat us with a stick."

"Not if we run real fast," Heck said, "and it would be worth it to see the look on his face when he comes out of that tent."

"You're terrible."

"And danged proud of it." Heck began to laugh but abruptly stopped and spun. They were at the intersection of Chestnut Street and Fourth Avenue, and Fourth was filled with folks either going to or coming from the Collection of Curiosities. "Did you see him?"

"See who?" Stu asked, scanning the flow of humanity.

"That Rusty character. I'd swear he was just watchin' us."

Stu hopped up and down a few times. "I don't see him anywhere. Maybe you were mistaken. With this many pilgrims—"

"I saw him, I tell you."

Stu shrugged. "So what if you did? Did you ever think he went to see the exhibition, too? It's nothing to fret about."

"I suppose." Heck faced toward Front Street. "Let's go find our pards. The name of the place they're at is Rankin's, as I recollect."

"I believe so, yes," Stu confirmed, taking two steps for every one of the lanky Texan's.

Front Street was jammed. The wild night life for which Dodge was famed was in full raucous bloom. Every saloon, every gambling house, every dance hall was brightly lit. Loud music wafted from a dozen buildings. Merry laughter tinkled on the air, punctuated by the occasional squeal of a woman or the oath of a man.

"Now this is more like it!" Heck declared. "A honky-tonk town could get into a person's blood if he wasn't careful." He glanced back.

"How about a drink before we visit Rankin's?" Stu proposed. "I could use one after that mermaid."

"The mermaid, hell," Heck said. "I'm still tryin' to recover from the Grecian Siren." He looked over his shoulder and came to an abrupt stop.

"What is it now?" Steve asked.

"You'll think I'm loco."

"That goes without saying. But try me anyhow."

"There's a dog following us."

Chapter Ten

The walls of Rankin's Dance Hall shook to the frenetic drumming of scores of boots and shoes. Cowboys whooped and hollered. Texans occasionally gave voice to Comanche war cries, demonstrating to all and sundry that their reputation for wild antics was well deserved.

At a small booth in a secluded nook along the north wall, one cowboy sat as still as still could be. He had not uttered a sound for almost two minutes. His hands folded on the table, Jess Donner gazed at the mad whirl of forms and felt another pair of warm hands cover his.

"Thanks for tellin' me about your family and your life and all," Margaret said. "I've gotten to know you a whole lot better."

"There wasn't much to it." Farm life, to Jess's way of thinking, wasn't very exciting.

"If my folks were still alive I sure wouldn't be doin' this for a livin'," Margaret mentioned. "My father would have walloped me black-and-blue for steppin' inside a place like this."

"Don't you have other kin?"

"Back in Kentucky. An uncle who came to visit us twice the whole time I was growin' up. Him and my pa never could get along. And an aunt who was lucky enough to marry above her station and now looks down her nose at the rest of her relatives as somehow bein' inferior."

"No sisters or brothers?"

"Afraid not," Margaret said. She was pressed against his side, her mouth less than an inch from his ear so she could be heard. "Nor many friends, either, except for Ethel."

A second later Vince strode past their booth. He glanced sharply at her and gestured but did not stop.

"What was that about?" Jess Donner asked.

"He's lettin' me know I'm not earnin' my keep. If I'm not out dancin', I'm to make sure the customer keeps orderin' drinks. Lem Rankin says any girl who can't earn him five dollars an hour isn't worth her weight as a worker. The girls who have been here longest teach the new hires the tricks of the trade, everything from false flattery to pickin' pockets."

Jess looked at her. "Why are you tellin' me this?"

"I'm not rightly sure, other than I've taken a powerful shine to you."

Their faces were practically touching; Jess could feel her breath on his cheek. "I reckon I should order a drink, then."

"I'll go you one better," Margaret said. "That is, if you're willin' to meet me when I get off at two a.m. We could eat and talk some more." She quickly added, "Only if you want to."

"That sounds fine," Jess said. He slid to the end of the seat. "I should go now so you don't get into any trouble."

"You're so considerate," Margaret said.

But Jess did not stand up. For over a minute they stared into each other's eyes. Then Jess said softly, "Lordy, it's hot in here. I'm about to burst into flames."

"Me, too. I've never felt like this before."

"Maybe we're comin' down with somethin'."

Margaret clutched his hand to her bosom. "Will you be here at two?"

"I'll shoot anyone who tries to stop me." Jess started to bend his mouth to hers but suddenly drew back and pushed to his feet. "I need some air. Two a.m. it is." He hastened toward the double doors, not once looking back, and as he stepped out into the welcome coolness of night, he raised his head to the heavens and shook like a man who had just awakened from a particularly vivid dream.

"You're blocking the door, friend," someone said.

Five city dwellers were about to go inside. Jess walked past them to a tree and sat with his elbows on his knees and his chin in his hands. He was not there long when spurs jangled and Steve Ellsworth plopped down next to him.

"Well," Steve said.

"Well," Jess responded.

"I saw you makin' for the door. I was still out on the dance floor with Ethel. That gal is the best dancer ever born."

"You can go dance some more if you want," Jess said. "No need to stop on my account. I'll wait here."

"No need. She wants me to meet her when she gets off at two o'clock."

Jess raised his chin from his hands. "Margaret made the same arrangement with me. It appears we have dates."

They were quiet a while. Steve plucked a blade of grass and stuck it between his front teeth, then pulled it out and threw it down. "What exactly is goin' on here?"

"I'm not rightly sure."

"Me either. Do you reckon we did the right thing?"

"I don't know. My brain went numb. I never knew a woman's perfume could do that."

"Ethel had the same effect on me. When I was holdin' her, I couldn't hardly breathe without havin' to remind my lungs to inhale and exhale."

"There should be more windows in that place— that's for sure."

Again they were quiet. Then Jess said, "I can't decide if I'm fallin' in love or comin' down with the flu."

"Ethel sure is sweet," Steve remarked. "So light on her feet, you would swear she was dancin' on air. She has this cute way of puckerin' her mouth that makes you think of strawberries."

"Whatever happened to your other true love?"

"Huh?"

"You've forgot your pink parasol already?"

"Oh. Her. I didn't see Franny Brice anywhere. It's just as well. A man shouldn't hog all the best women."

They sat and watched people come and go, mostly cowboys liquored up and eager to wear down their bootheels. Finally Jess stood. "It can't be later than ten, so we have four hours yet until the girls get off. Let's explore more of Dodge."

At the end of the block Steve Ellsworth abruptly stopped. "I wear a ten-dollar hat on an empty head. We have a problem, pard. We're supposed to relieve the watch at midnight. If we don't show up, Rafe will drown us in the Arkansas."

"We could go to the Wright House and ask him to switch us with someone else."

"Even if he agreed, which I very much doubt, all the hands are scattered to hell and back, takin' in the sights the same as us."

"Then we need to find Pernell and Tim and ask them to take our shifts. Or else a couple the other boys."

Steve was not optimistic. "Can you see anyone givin' up a night on the town so we can spark fillies?"

Mulling over their predicament, they were almost to Front Street when a sign caught Steve's eyes. " 'The Lone Star Saloon,' " he read aloud. "And listen. The piano player is playin' 'Yellow

Rose of Texas.' Let's lubricate our gray matter and maybe the solution will come to us."

Wall-to-wall cowboys made reaching the bar a challenge. Poker and faro devotees filled every table. Doves in too-tight dresses circulated freely. Between songs, lusty mirth and the clatter of chips rose to the low rafters.

"Right hospitable of these Kansans to provide a taste of Texas," Steve Ellsworth said. "All we need now is for a tumbleweed to blow in the door."

The red-eye was the real article. Steve smacked his lips and declared, "I'm gettin' plumb homesick."

At the other end of the bar a commotion started. A cowboy who couldn't be much over eighteen was unsteadily trying to climb on the bar. His friends were attempting to stop him. Shrugging them off, he caught his knees on the edge and reared erect. "I am a curly wolf from the Pecos country," he shouted, "and it is my night to howl!"

A cowboy at a table spat a stream of tobacco juice and declared, "Why, that longhair is totin' a pistol."

The drunken cowboy was, indeed, wearing a revolver, a Cooper double-action Navy, which he unlimbered and cocked. "Let's show 'em how we celebrate, Texas style!"

"Get down from there, Pesos Bill!" the barman said, and reached for the cowboy's legs, only to have his hand kicked and the revolver waved in his face.

"Back off, barkeep!" the cowboy warned. "I am hell on wheels when I am riled, so don't rile me."

Throwing his head back, he yipped lustily and fired a shot into the ceiling.

All talk ceased and the piano player let up on the ivories as every eye swung toward the cowboy, who screeched like a Kiowa and fired a second shot.

"You roostered clunk!" someone hollered. "Shed that shootin' iron before the law shows up."

The cowboy took a few unsteady steps. "I'll thank you to mind your own business. I don't give up my persuader for anyone or anything." He twirled the Cooper and nearly dropped it. "You are lookin' at a genuine man killer!"

"We're lookin' at a coffin warmer!" an older man responded. "Hop down before it's too late!"

But the cowpoke refused to listen. Shifting the revolver from one hand to the other and back again, he cocked it and took aim at the front window.

"Don't!" the barman cried. "Glass doesn't come cheap!"

Once more the Cooper thundered and the window dissolved in a shower of shimmering slivers. Those nearest to the window had to scoot out of the way to avoid flying shards. The cowboy on the counter rocked with glee.

"Please get down, Pecos," the barman tried anew. "A deputy is sure to hear all the shooting, and the last thing I want is gunplay in my establishment."

"I eat tin stars for breakfast!" the cowboy bawled. "Raw or cooked, it makes no never mind!"

"He's a walkin' whiskey vat," Steve said to Jess. "And if he ain't careful, he'll spring a leak."

No sooner were the words out of his mouth than the door crashed open and in barreled Trace Morgan and another deputy. They took in the situation at a glance and shouldered toward the bar.

"Put down the pistol, son," the other deputy said. "I place you under arrest for disturbing the peace and violating the firearms ordinance by discharging a fireram withthin the town limits."

"Like hell," the cowboy said, and trained his revolver on them. "Back off and let a man have his fun."

Trace Morgan stopped. Those is front of him scattered right and left. "You were lucky you didn't hit a bystander with your antics. Hand over the black-eyed Susan, boy, and come along peaceably."

"Who are you callin' a boy?" the cowboy demanded. "I've made wolf meat of plenty of hombres."

"Sure you have," said the other deputy. "But we can't let you stretch your string here. It's our job to arrest troublemakers."

Trace Morgan extended his left arm. "Be reasonable. Give me the gun and no one need be hurt."

For a few moments it appeared Morgan's appeal had worked. The Pecos cowboy stared at his Cooper, then hefted it. "I reckon I'm not bein' too sensible, am I? It's all the tornado juice. Sure makes a man's head spin." He put his other hand to his temple and smiled.

An onlooker picked up his cards and remarked, "These young ones today, every last one is paperbacked."

Overhearing the insult, the cowboy stiffened and steadied his hand. "Who said that?" he angrily demanded. "Stand up and take the blame, you coyote, and I'll show you what sand is."

Trace Morgan took a slow step. "Don't listen to him, Texas. Listen to me. I respect a man who knows when he's stepped over the line and has the sense to admit his mistake. Toss the lead chucker to me."

"I've changed my mind," the cowboy said. "The two of you can toss yours to me."

"That's not going to happen," Trace Morgan said. "I'm asking you for the last time to quit the shenanigans and climb down."

"No," the cowboy said, and then, without any forewarning or threat, he squeezed the trigger.

The slug ripped into the plank between Trace Morgan's legs. Morgan's answering shot was so swift, the two boomed heartbeats apart. One instant his right hand was empty, the next instant it held the black-handled Remington.

Struck squarely in the chest, the cowboy was smashed back by the impact. His arms pinwheeling, he fell against a shelf. Bottles crashed to the floor with him, some shattering, others spilling their contents.

"My liquor!" the barman wailed.

"That ends that," Steve Ellsworth said.

But he was mistaken. Trace Morgan was moving toward the right end of the bar, the other deputy toward the left. Neither saw the cowboy roll onto his stomach and push into a crouch. He was bleeding profusely but that did not stop him from screeching in raw fury and unfurling. He spotted the other deputy, who ducked just as a slug tore into the top of the bar.

"I'll kill you! Kill you both!"

By then Trace Morgan was behind the bar. "Try me!" he shouted, and when the cowboy spun, Morgan banged off two swift shots that blew off the top of the cowboy's head, hat and all.

Like wax on a burning candle, the cowboy from the Pecos country melted to the floor and was still.

Sudden and total silence descended except for the ticking of a large wall clock.

Jess Donner drained his glass in a single gulp, wiped his mouth with his sleeve, and remarked, "You know, I'm beginning to understand why they make us check our six-shooters."

Chapter Eleven

The girls at Rankin's Dance Hall were allowed a ten minute break every two hours. A small room at the back was reserved for that purpose, but most of the girls preferred to go outside for a much-needed breath of fresh air.

Shortly after Jess Donner and Steve Ellsworth left, Margaret and Ethel went out and stood off by themselves.

"Ten minutes is too damn short," Ethel complained, as she always did. "Rankin should give us half an hour. My feet are killing me."

"We won't need to put up with this much longer, sugar," Margaret said, placing a hand on her friend's shoulder. "Pretty soon we'll have five hundred dollars socked away, and then it's on to New Orleans and a life of our own!"

"Not so loud," Ethel cautioned, with a sharp glance at the building. "If anyone finds out what we're up to, we're in big trouble."

"Worrywart," Margaret said.

"You would worry, too, if you had more sense. The last girl who tried to skip out on Rankin had both her legs broke. The year before, a girl who was always sassing him took it into her head to flee to Denver. Rankin had her tracked down and brought back, and cut out her tongue." Ethel trembled. "I don't know about you but I'm fond of my body parts."

"New Orleans is farther and bigger," Margaret said. "We'll change our names and find respectable jobs. Rankin's goons can hunt for us until doomsday but they'll never find us."

"God, why did I agree to your crazy idea?" Ethel wondered.

Pulling the heavyset girl into the shadows, Margaret shook her, hard, and hissed in a whisper, "Don't you dare get cold feet now! We're too close! Another hundred dollars and we'll be set."

"And the closer we get, the more scared I am," Ethel admitted. "We're taking an awful chance."

"Some rewards are worth any risk," Margaret insisted. Her features and tone softened and she gave Ethel a reassuring tender squeeze. "Besides, I thought you wanted it this way. Just the two of us, together. Free to do as we please. No more dance halls. No more spendin' hours every night bein' manhandled by drunk cowpokes. No more beasts like Rankin lordin' it over us."

"Sure, I want all that."

"Then show some grit. To give up when we're so danged close is plain foolish." Margaret lowered her voice even more. "I can't take much more of this. I'm so sick of it, I would slit my wrists rather than go on."

Ethel poked her. "Don't talk like that. You know I don't like it when you talk like that."

"How else should I talk? Should I lie and say I enjoy workin' my tail off twelve hours a day, every day of the month except the second Sunday? Should I say I love how Rankin tricked me into signin' a contract that gives him sixty percent of all the money I earn? And how wonderful it is that I've been his to do with as he pleases for four years, or suffer the consequences?"

"No, no, but—"

"There are no buts," Margaret said harshly. "There is no silver linin' to our predicament. We are slaves, plain and simple, to a soulless brute who would maim us for life, or worse, if we dared demand our freedom." She gazed sadly into the boughs above. "How could I have been so stupid? A hundred times a day I ask myself that question."

"You're not the only one," Ethel said. "The only girls who have it easy are his favorites, like that witch Franny. The rest of us might as well go around in chains."

"There you have it," Margaret said. "So don't you even think about changin' your mind. We are in this for keeps. As soon as we have the five hundred, we sneak out on the next train east."

"Another month should be long enough," Ethel said. "Provided we're not caught. Rankin has rules against girls socializing with cowboys after hours."

"How else can we get the money?" Margaret argued. Just then a swarthy figure emerged from the dance hall. "Careful, hon. There's that nosy Vince. We'd best get back to work."

Linked arm in arm, the two young women smiled at one another and walked toward the dance hall but Vince held out a hand, stopping them. "The boss sent me to fetch you."

"Both of us?" Pure fear spiked through Ethel and she might have fallen if not for Margaret.

Vince nodded and held the door for them. "After you, ladies." He said the last contemptuously.

"Did Mr. Rankin say what this is about?"

"No, and I didn't ask, since it's none of my business. Now let's hustle unless you want him mad. I've been searching for you for five minutes, and he's not in one of his better moods."

Once past Vince, Margaret and Ethel looked at each other out of the corners of their eyes and Margaret puckered her lips. They turned left, avoiding the main dance floor, and walked along a dark hall until they came to a closed door with the word PRIVATE painted in bold black letters. Vince knocked and a gruff voice bid them enter.

It was like walking into a whole different world. Plush wine red carpet covered the floor. A mahogany desk and a pair of fine chairs were to one side. A long sofa ran the length of the opposite wall. Two young men stamped from the same mold as Vince rose as the door opened.

At the desk sat the king of his domain, Lem Rankin. He had a great moon face and a great moon belly and eyes that bulged like those of a great obscene toad. Thick lips and a wide nose completed the portrait of the most notorious dance hall owner in all of Kansas. At the moment he was peeling an orange with a folding knife. "Come in, girls. Come in," he greeted them in his great rumbling voice. "We need to have us a little talk." Rankin indicated the chairs.

"This is an honor, sir," Margaret said as she sank down. "The last time I was in here was when I signed my contract."

Rankin stuck a piece of orange in his mouth and sucked it noisily, extracting the juice, before he chomped a few times and gulped the piece down like a toad gulping a fly. "I'm glad you brought that up, Miss Sanger. You do remember the terms of that contract, do you not?"

"Of course," Margaret said.

"And you, Miss Heatherton?" Rankin asked Ethel. "Do you remember the terms as well?"

"You spelled them out to me quite nicely," Ethel said.

"Did I?" Rankin removed another slice and dangled it before his thick lips but did not take a bite. "Then perhaps you can explain why the two of you are not doing as you were told."

"Sir?" Margaret said.

"Don't play the innocent with me, Miss Sanger. You were a common tart in rags when I took you in off the street and offered you the comforts and protection of my establishment, and now you don't have the decency to repay my kindness as required." Rankin sucked the slice of orange into his mouth with a loud slurp. "Were I a cruel man, I would have you beaten on general principle."

Ethel sat straighter in alarm. "What have we done?"

"You know damn well." Rankin thrust a pudgy finger at her. "And frankly, Miss Heatherton, I expected better of you. I've always thought you had more sense than your girlfriend."

"How do you expect us to understand if you keep talkin' in riddles?" Margaret asked in rising exasperation.

"Very well. I'll talk plainly. Both of you were taught how to pick pockets. Both of you are required to pick a minimum of ten dollars a night and turn it over to the floor manager." Rankin cut into the orange. "But our records indicate the two of you have missed a few quotas of late. That just won't do."

Margaret smiled and said, "Some cowboys have empty pockets. You can't blame us for that."

"On the contrary, Miss Sanger," Rankin said. "I can blame you for anything I want. If the day is too hot, I can blame you. If there's a speck of dust on my desk, I can blame you." His voice had been rising angrily as he spoke, and now he thundered, "If I come down with indigestion, *I can blame you*." He nodded at the two men on the sofa and they came over on either side of Margaret's chair and seized her arms.

"Please, no, Mr. Rankin," Ethel pleaded.

"Stay out of this, Miss Heatherton. Your attitude does not need adjusting. Miss Sanger's does."

Rankin motioned, and Vince walked up to the chair and without hesitation slugged Margaret in the stomach. He did not put his full weight into the blow but it was enough to double her over and leave her sputtering for air and gasping in pain.

Tears trickled from Ethel's eyes but she did not say anything.

"Is more discipline required?" Rankin asked Margaret. "How many times must I remind you which of us is lord and master?" He set down the orange and the folding knife. "Pay attention. I will only say this once. You will meet your quotas or I will give you cause to rue your laziness. Is that understood?"

"Yes, sir," Ethel said.

Rankin put a hand to his left ear. "I can't hear you, Miss Sanger."

Margaret was sucking in deep breaths and nodded her assent.

"Good." Rankin leaned back in his chair, tapped a thick finger on his desk, and thoughtfully regarded them. "Let me add a warning, my dears. I hope, for both your sakes, that you are not up to something." Ethel started to respond but he held up a hand. "Spare me your feeble protest. No one would slack off as you two have done unless you were."

Clenching her teeth, Margaret sat up and said, "That's plain silly, Mr. Rankin. We know better than to buck you."

"Do you, Miss Sanger? I wonder." Rankin tapped his finger several more times. "Let me enlighten you. Perhaps you have heard the expression 'I have seen it all before'? I truly have. More girls than I care to count have tried to break their contracts with me, and every one, without exception, has reaped a result they did not desire. I trust you won't repeat their mistakes."

"Never," Ethel said, but Rankin did not appear to hear her.

"Every stratagem you can conceive has been tried. From pretending to be crippled to out-and-out flight. It has gotten so, I can recognize the signs before a girl does whatever she has in mind. And you two, my dears, are showing some of those signs."

Ethel blanched. "We are?"

"You spend all your time in each other's company. You're too secretive. You're resentful toward the floor managers. And you talk about me behind my back," Rankin recited. "You don't press our patrons to buy drinks as hard as you should. Lastly, and most disturbing, you have slacked off on picking pockets."

"We'll meet our quotas from now on," Ethel said.

"I hope so. I truly do. Believe it or not, I do not derive pleasure from inflicting pain. I have many faults, I readily admit, but that is not one of them." Rankin picked up the orange and the folding knife. "Perhaps one of you would be so good as to refresh my memory. What is my cardinal rule of business?"

Ethel answered him. "Everyone who walks in the front door should leave broke or close to it."

"Precisely." Rankin grinned. "So you will forgive

me when I become perturbed when you ladies do not hold up your end."

"It won't happen again."

Rankin bent toward them. "It better not. I only issue a warning once. After that, whatever befalls you is on your heads, not mine." He dismissed them with a wave. "Escort them out, Vincent, and keep a close eye on them, if you please. Despite their assurances, I am not entirely convinced they have my best interests at heart."

Ethel waited until they were on the dance floor and Vince had left them, then whispered, "I told you! But you wouldn't listen! Now look at the trouble we're in!"

"Nothin' has changed," Margaret said, rubbing her stomach.

"Are you insane? Didn't you hear him? He suspects, damn it! Forget about our plan. Forget about New Orleans. It's over."

Digging her fingernails into her friend's arm, Margaret hauled her over against the wall. "Listen to me. He doesn't know a damn thing. He was scarin' us, is all. Just as he does every girl he thinks is slackin' off."

"No, no, no," Ethel said. "We had a fine dream, but that's all it will ever be."

"Like hell!" Margaret snarled, and looked toward the hallway to be sure Vince was gone. "Dreams can come true. All it takes is dedication. I won't let anyone stand in our way, and I pray to God you won't, either."

"You'll get us crippled," Ethel said.

"I would rather be dead than live another month like this." Margaret had tears in her eyes. "I refuse to be in the palm of any *man* from now on. I will live my life as I see fit, or you can bury me now with no regrets."

"Don't talk like that."

"Then buck up. Remember our vows to each other. We see this through to the end, come whatever may." Margaret smoothed her dress and dabbed at her eyes and fluffed her hair. "Now let's go out there and act like his little speech has us scared half to death."

The double doors opened, and in walked a pair of young cowboys, one stocky, one thin, the stocky one with sandy hair and a reckless air, the other dark-haired and somber. Nudging Ethel, Margaret pranced toward them and forced a friendly smile.

"Gentlemen! Welcome to Rankin's. My friend and I would be honored if you would see fit to dance with us. Only ten cents, and I can promise you a time you will never forget."

"We're lookin' for our pards," said the stocky one.

"You have better odds of spottin' them out on the dance floor," Margaret pressed him, snatching his hand. "What do you say, cowpoke? Care to show me how nimble you are?"

"Nimble is my middle name." The stocky one grinned. "The rest of it is Heck Myers, and this here is my pard, Stu Wilkins. He's from New York but don't hold that against him."

"A pleasure to meet you," Ethel said.

Chapter Twelve

"This is a waste of time," Rusty Vanes growled. "First we follow that other pair from the exhibition to Fifth Avenue. Then you spot these two comin' out of the Lone Star Saloon and decide to follow them instead. I wish you would make up your mind."

"These two were closer to us the other night," Grat said.

"So?"

"So the closer they were, the more suspicious they might be."

Rusty stopped dead and stared at his brother. "Did you drink a bottle of stupid today? That made no kind of sense."

"Sure it did. Trust me."

"All they're doin' is goin' from saloon to saloon, drinkin' themselves silly," Rusty said.

"They've been to five already but they're not tiltin' into the wind," Grat disagreed. "It's not drinks they're after. They're huntin' someone."

"Us, maybe?" Rusty said, his hand drifting to his pearl-handled Colt.

They were two blocks behind the young cowpokes, far enough back that the cowboys wouldn't spot them among the steady stream of passersby. At times Rusty and Grat lost track of the pair, but they always kept Lucky in sight, and Lucky was too well trained to lose them.

"I doubt they're after us," Grat said. "We'll find out when we talk to them." And with that, he walked faster to catch up.

Rusty's spurs jangled as he put on a short burst of speed to overtake his brother. "Hold on. You're being stupid again. Why show ourselves?"

"How else can we find out whether they suspect we're rustlers?"

"Oh sure, they'll come right out and tell us," Rusty scoffed. "Why didn't I think of that?"

"I'll see it in their faces, in their eyes."

"You can read folks like they're books—is that how it is?" Rusty swore. Sometimes his brother aggravated him to no end.

"Have I ever led you astray?" Grat retorted with a smirk. He would never admit it, but he loved his little brother dearly, and was proud as could be of his ability with a pistol. It was his opinion that Rusty was one of the best. All the boy needed was the chance to show everyone.

"Other than the killin' and the stealin', you mean?" Rusty asked, and they both laughed.

"There's our cur, and there stand the cowherders." Lucky had stopped beside a post. Beyond the dog, in the middle of Front Street, were the two young cowboys. They had met up with four others. From the amount of gesturing going on, they appeared to be arguing.

"What do you reckon that's all about?" Rusty wondered.

"When I learn to read minds as well as I read faces, I'll tell you," was his brother's reply.

"Look. They're shakin' on somethin'. And now one is forkin' over money. He doesn't look too happy."

After another handshake and a few more words were exchanged, the young cowboys made off up the street. Grat whistled for Lucky, and the dog came running back. Together, the three of them shadowed their quarry.

"They're goin' into the Long Branch," Rusty stated the obvious. "Should we go in or talk to them when they come out?"

"I can't see their faces in the dark." Grat hitched his gun belt and stalked across the street. Lucky stayed by his side, as inseparable as his shadow.

Business was brisk, as it always was at that time of night, despite the crackdown on painted women. The cowboys had bellied up to the bar and ordered drinks. Grat nodded at Rusty and threaded through the boisterous crowd until he was only a few feet from the unsuspecting hands. "Whiskey, bartender!" he said much louder than he had to, but neither of the cowboys noticed him.

"They're deaf as well as dumb," Rusty said.

"Hush, you infant." Grat paid and savored a sip,

then sidled along the bar until he was beside the cowboys. The pair were gazing longingly toward the gaming tables. "Well, look who it is," he said genially, and nudged the one with freckles and wisps of chin hair.

The cowboys turned. Both of the cowpokes grew wary with distrust, and the one with slight buckteeth said, "You two again."

"You make it sound like we have smallpox," Grat said.

The one with the chin hairs was staring at Lucky. "Why has your dog been followin' us the past half hour?"

"He was?" Grat smiled and patted the mongrel's head. "Maybe Lucky remembers you from the other night. He wandered away from us earlier and I only just caught up with him a few minutes ago."

The pair of cowherders shifted their attention to Rusty, their dislike transparent. "We ran into your brother this afternoon," the freckled one said.

"Is that a fact?" Grat kept on smiling and studying them. He had lived by his wits for so long, it came as second nature. "Small world we live on."

"He threatened to shoot us because he didn't like the way we were lookin' at him," the freckled one mentioned.

Grat stared into his glass. He had to remind himself that Rusty was only a kid. "You must excuse him. His social graces ain't what they should be." To Rusty he said, "Apologize, please."

Rusty was incredulous. "Say I'm sorry to these two cow nurses? I hope I'm shot before I do."

In a steely undertone Grat said, "I wasn't askin', little brother. Remember your manners."

Rusty threw back his head and started to laugh but then stopped and spat, "If we weren't kin, I'd have bucked you out in gunsmoke a long time ago." He glared at the cowboys. "I'm sorry. But I don't much like bein' stared at."

Grat thrust a hand out. "Suppose we start over? I'm Gratton Vanes, and this here is my temperamental excuse for a brother, Russian. He likes to be called Rusty, though."

"Jess Donner," the bucktooth one said. "My pard is Steve Ellsworth."

"How long are you gents in town for?" Grat inquired. "If I'm not bein' too nosy, that is."

"Just the night," Steve Ellsworth answered, adding, "It's cost us nearly every cent we had to our name but we're hopin' to make hay out of our poverty." He chortled to himself.

"I'm not sure I savvy."

"Pay him no mind. He has a habit of babblin' nonsense." Jess Donner touched his hat brim. "Nice meetin' you again." Prodding Steve Ellsworth, he turned to walk away.

"What's your rush, cowboy?" Grat asked. "I was fixin' to treat for a round of drinks. It's the least I can do after that little misunderstandin' we had out on the prairie. What do you say?"

Steve drained his glass and pounded on the bar. "I say bring on the red-eye! We have cause to celebrate."

"The end of the drive?" Grat reckoned.

"Oh, more than that," Steve informed him. "Much, much more." He was in exceptionally fine spirits.

Jess Donner, however, maintained his wary attitude. "I reckon if my pard agrees, I might as well, too."

"Somethin' wrong with our money?" Rusty took offense and moved a pace out from the bar.

"Simmer down, damn you," Grat growled. "I swear, sometimes I think that Ma found you in a nest of rattlesnakes and brought home the egg to hatch."

Jess Donner's gaze drifted lower. "You two haven't checked your shootin' irons. I wouldn't want to be you if the deputies notice."

"I'd like to see a tin star take my lead pusher from me," Rusty boasted. "It will be the last thing he does."

Grat hastily said, "We're not fixin' to stay much longer, so there's no need." He ordered drinks to go around and paid from a poke he kept tied to a string and tucked down his pants.

"You afraid of losin' it?" Steve Ellsworth teased.

"Spoken like an hombre who has never had his pocket picked," Grat said. "I lost sixty dollars once to a fair-haired beauty I'd have sworn was a saint, and I promised myself then and there to never to be so trustin' again."

When the drinks came, Steve took a deep gulp. But Jess Donner merely turned his around and around in his hands. "Tell me something, Mr. Vanes. Why are you bein' so friendly?"

"Why not?" Grat rejoined. "Treatin' for drinks ain't a crime, the last I heard." Of the two, Donner was the sharpest, the one for him to watch closely.

"Why us?"

"I've already explained." Gratton shrugged. "Why make a mountain out of a molehill of politeness?"

"Just like your dog *happened* to stray near our herd? And like it *happened* to be followin' us tonight?"

Rusty tried to step past his brother but Grat held him back. "What are you gettin' at, cowpoke? To hear you talk, we're up to no good."

"All I'm saying is that I'll pass on the drink." Jess slapped his partner's arm. "And you should, too, hoss. Let's go watch a faro game a while."

"Hold it right there!" Rusty barked. "Where we come from, refusin' a drink is as rank an insult as heapin' abuse." He had his hand on his Colt.

"I'm not heeled," Jess reminded him. "Neither of us are." He took hold of the glass. "And just so it can't be said we refused your hospitality—" In two swallows he disposed of the whiskey and smacked the glass back down. "Now if you'll excuse us . . ."

"Sorry," Steve Ellsworth said. "He's havin' a bad night. He's fallin' in love." Ellsworth hurried after his friend.

His fingers clenching and unclenching, Rusty wheeled on his brother. "That was pointless."

"Think so?" Grat rested his elbows on the bar. "I learned what I needed to learn. Now we know."

"Know what exactly?"

"You were right. That bucktoothed kid doesn't trust us and might do some squawkin'. The sheriff might hear and get to thinkin' about the other herds that have lost a few head. We can't have that."

"I wish Ma were still alive to hear you say that. She used to complain I couldn't do right if my life depended on it." Rusty bent his head so no one else would overhear. "How do you want to handle this?"

"As much as I would like to gun them where they stand, we'll stick to them like their own clothes until the right time comes. Then you get to carve a couple more notches in your six-gun."

"I can't wait," Rusty said enthusiastically. Shooting Baxter earlier had whetted his appetite for bloodletting. "It's been pretty near a month since I got to go kill anyone. Not countin' those greasers, of course." He never stooped to counting the Mexicans and redskins he killed.

"You've always been more trigger happy than me," Grat teased.

"Says you. You're the one who turned up the toes of that old geezer we ran into when we were crossin' the panhandle."

"Our horses were wore out and he had a spare. When you're one jump ahead of the law, you can't afford to be kindly."

For the next hour they sipped and reminisced and joked, with Lucky curled contentedly next to Gratton's boots, unfazed by the hubbub and the ribald mirth of men in various stages of intoxication. Then, out of the blue, Rusty made a comment that stunned his older brother.

"Do you ever wonder what our lives would be like if we hadn't taken up the owlhoot trail?"

"What kind of talk is that?" Grat asked. "Sometimes life doesn't give us any choice. It was either steal or starve, and I'm fond of breathin'."

"You never think about it? About us bein' respectable instead of livin' by our guns?"

Grat swiveled and regarded his brother in frank disbelief. "What in hell has gotten into you? You're talkin' like a damned Bible-thumper."

"Spare me," Rusty said, and nodded toward the two young cowpokes. It's them, I reckon. I see them and I think it might be me had things worked out different than they did." He shook himself and swallowed more whiskey. "You're right. It's dumb. We are who are. Forget I ever said it."

"You puzzle me sometimes, Russian Bartholomew Vanes," Grat said. "I keep forgettin' you were a decent kid until Pa died. Now you're mostly prickle and lip."

"I said forget it," Rusty snapped. "When I get like this, hit me. I'd rather be free to blow wherever the wind takes me than shackled to law and order like those fool cowboys."

"That's more like it." Grat clapped his brother on the arm. "And it's not like we'll be scrapin' to make ends meet forever. Sooner or later a lot of money will fall in our laps and we'll be sittin' pretty. Wait and see."

"So you keep sayin'," Rusty said.

Another hour went by, and the young cowboys showed no inclination to do anything other than watch the card play.

"I swear, those two are duller than stumps," Grat commented. "They should be out makin' the rounds. Instead they've grown roots." He raised a hand to signal the bartender, then lowered it again and whispered in his brother's ear, "Careful. A tin star just walked in."

A deputy was to the right of the entrance, surveying everyone.

"That's Morgan, ain't it?" Rusty said. "What if he spots our hardware? I was serious about not turnin' over my pistol."

"We can always leave town," Grat said, shifting so several others were between him and the hawk-faced minion of the law.

By a curious quirk of coincidence, the bartender chose that moment to refill their glasses, and blurted, "Say! I didn't know you two were heeled. Hand those revolvers over or I'll give a yell."

Rusty's lips curled from his teeth in feral defiance. "Go right ahead, mister, but it will be the last peep you ever make."

The bartender looked from one to the other and then nervously glanced toward Deputy Morgan. "What do I care? But be on your best behavior."

Apparently satisfied all was well, the deputy was leaving.

Rusty glanced toward the two cowboys. "Why in

hell don't they do somethin'? I want to blow out their wicks and be done with it."

"Calm down," Grat said. "You'll get your chance. Before this night is done they'll be as dead as dead can be."

Chapter Thirteen

Jess Donner and Steve Ellsworth did not leave the Long Branch Saloon until shortly after midnight. The Vanes brothers made no attempt to follow them but Jess did not trust them. He led Steve west along Front Street, then ducked into an alley.

"This should do. We'll wait here a spell and make damn sure they're not out to fill us with lead."

"Why would they be?" Steve asked, stifling a yawn. "We've never done them any harm."

"Sidewinders don't need an excuse to be mean," Jess noted, and for several minutes they closely watched the doors to the Long Branch but the Vanes did not appear.

"See?" Steve said, stretching. "They're still inside drinkin' and mindin' their own business."

"Maybe they went out the back way," Jess ventured. He stared toward the far end of the alley, which was littered with crates and refuse.

"I swear, you were born suspicious of the sawbones who delivered you," Steve grumbled. "Let's forget about them and get on with the fun. Not that we can have much with nearly all our money gone."

"That damned Pernell," Jess groused. "Wantin' five dollars just to ride watch for us tonight. He should give up cows and take to robbin' banks and trains. He's a natural."

"Be fair. Tim and Pernell gave up the rest of their night in town to do extra work as a favor to us. We should be grateful, not mad. Which reminds me. We're only a block from the Wright House. We should tell the boss what we did or he'll be good and mad at us for takin' liberties."

"Rafe won't mind," Jess said. "But I reckon it wouldn't hurt to be polite."

At that hour the spacious lobby was next to deserted. A neatly coiffed man in an expensive suit and a lithe woman in a too-tight dress were snuggled arm in arm in adjoining chairs in a far corner. Nearer, his broad shoulders slumped in boredom, sat Rafe Adams. Tom Cambry was asleep, his head thrown back, lightly snoring.

"Howdy, boys," Rafe greeted them. "Had your fill of excitement?"

"Not by a long shot, boss," Steve Ellsworth said. "I take it Mr. Carruthers hasn't shown up."

Rafe shook his handsome head. "Tom and I have taken a room for the night. When you get back to the herd—" Rafe stopped and his eyes narrowed. "Wait a second. You two have second watch. Why are you standin' in front of me instead of singin' to the cows?"

Steve nervously shifted his weight from one boot

to the other. "We paid Pernell and Tim to take our shift."

Jess quickly made it a point to say, "We figured the right thing to do was to let you know so you wouldn't be upset."

"The right thing to do," Rafe said slowly, "was to ask my permission *before* you made your arrangement with them. That herd is my responsibility until the sale is completed, and I take my responsibilities seriously."

"We didn't mean no disrespect," Steve said. "We'll ride out to Duck Creek right this minute if you say so."

The two cowboys waited anxiously for the trail boss to render his decision. Rafe Adams was frowning but his gaze was kindly. "I take it there's a reason you parted with the precious few pesos you had to your name?"

"Yes, sir," Steve said. "Two of them. Their names are Ethel and Margaret, and they're the prettiest, finest, most wonderful women who ever drew breath. We met them at a dance hall and they've agreed to join us later."

Rafe removed his wide-brimmed hat and ran a callused hand through his shock of hair. "It's not my place to meddle in your personal life. But I've been up the trail more than a few times and seen many a hand snared by many a filly. Sometimes it works out. More often it's a case of whiskey lendin' a woman charms she doesn't possess."

"But we've only had three drinks all night," Steve

said. "We might not be completely sober but we're a long way from seein' visions."

"It's your life," Rafe said. "I'm just suggestin' that most men don't realize they've caught calico fever until after the 'I do's', and by then it's too late."

"So it's all right if we stay?" Jess asked.

Rafe nodded, then rose and arched his back. "But I want you back at camp by sunup. No excuses, hear?" He turned to Tom Cambry, whose snores now resembled the growling of a riled bear. "I should leave him here. But a moth might decide to make a home in his mouth." He shook the *segundo*'s shoulder but all Tom did was snore louder.

Jess caught Steve's eye and they hustled outside. Letting out a sigh of relief, he declared, "For a second there I thought he was goin' to make us ride herd. Now we have the whole night to ourselves!"

"And to our cow bunnies!" Steve said.

"They ain't ours yet," Jess corrected him. "We need to impress them. But how to do that when we're close to broke?"

"We can take them for a moonlit stroll down by the cattle pens," Steve suggested. "Or how about along the river, where it's nice and peaceful?"

Jess stepped to the edge of the sidewalk and sat near a hitch rail. "Oh, sure. They'll be giddy to have us grope them. You knothead, that's no way to conduct a romance."

"I suppose you have a better idea? Give them a bouquet of weeds? Or sing to them like we do the cows?"

A buckboard clattered by. Several riders trotted

eastward. From a saloon across the way came the merry laughter of a woman having a grand old time. A window in a house opened and a man emptied a washbasin.

"We need to do this smart or they'll look for greener pastures," Jess said. He dug into his pocket. "Let's pool our pittances. How much do you have left?"

After patting each of his pockets, Steve hunkered, his coins in his left palm. "One dollar and fifteen cents."

"It's that danged parasol you bought. Fritterin' away money like that should be a crime." Jess uncupped his hand. "But I'm not one to talk. What with the clothes and the drinks, I have two dollars and sixty-seven cents to my name. Why, we're plumb wealthy," he concluded in disgust.

"It's enough to treat them to a meal," Steve said. "Even a slice of pie if they're hungry enough."

"You have pie between your ears. But why not? Pie has won many a female heart, I hear."

Steve sat next to his friend and gloomily placed his chin in his hands. "If you have a better notion, I'm all ears." His forehead furrowed and he twisted. "Seems to me you're takin' this romance business mighty serious all of a sudden. Weren't you the one pokin' fun at me for thinkin' female critters were the best thing this world has to offer?"

Jess picked up a pebble and tossed it. "That was before I met Margaret. If she were any sweeter, she'd be a bowl of sugar."

"Thank God Heck and Stu aren't here," Steve

mentioned. "They'd laugh us to scorn for simpletons."

"They wouldn't laugh long," Jess said. He pushed his hat back and gazed down the street. "Damn them, anyhow!" he unexpectedly exclaimed, and surged to his feet.

'Who?" Steve said, scrambling to rise. "Heck and Stu?"

"No, the Vanes. I swear I just saw their dog watchin' us, but it's gone. Come on. We'll find out what they're up to once and for all."

Steve Ellsworth had to walk at twice his usual pace to catch up. "Are you sure it was Lucky?"

"If it wasn't, it was his twin." Jess was threading through the pedestrians with the alacrity of a buck bounding through a dense forest. "I'll kick the cur's ribs in, so help me, I will."

"Have you thought this through?" Steve nearly collided with a man hurrying the other way and hastily apologized. "I mean, the Vanes have pistols and we don't. Confrontin' them is headstrong."

Jess slowed and came to a stop next to the barbershop, which had long since closed for the day. "We would be askin' for windows in our skulls, wouldn't we? Maybe we should collect our artillery."

"And be thrown out of Dodge by the first deputy who sees us?" Steve shook his head. "I'm not about to spoil my chance of seein' Ethel again. I say we forget about the flea magnet and work out how best to impress our lady friends."

They walked slowly on, past a millinery with a

mannequin in the window, and past a billiard hall, where all the tables were in use. Next was a general store, shut and dark, with a variety of merchandise on display. Steve Ellsworth glanced at one of the items and snapped his fingers. "That's it! I know just how to woo them."

Jess looked where he thought Steve was looking. "You plan to give Ethel a pitchfork?"

"Lower, and to the right."

"A book?" Jess stepped to the window and peered intently at the cover. "I can't make it out but I think it's a farmer's almanac. Since when do women give a hoot about when it will rain?"

Steve tugged at his friend's sleeve and drew him over to a water trough so they were out of the way of everyone else. "The almanac reminds me of another book I saw once. It was my grandma's and she loved it somethin' fierce."

"Was it a cookbook?"

"I swear. You'll be a bachelor all your days." Steve sighed with impatience. "It was a poetry book. Written by a Lord George someone or other. She would sit in her rockin' chair and read that thing for hours. My ma would read from it a lot, too." He smiled in triumph. "There's the answer."

Jess gazed up and down Front Street. The only businesses open were those devoted to some combination of whiskey, cards, and music. "Where are we going to find a poetry book at this time of night?"

"We don't need to *buy* one," Steve said. "We'll write our own poems and recite 'em to the girls."

Jess stared, and stared, and stared some more. "Remind me to buy you a magnifying glass for Christmas."

"What on earth for?"

"So you can find your brain. We don't know enough words to fill a thimble and you want to string some together like pearls? The girls will brand us infants and our poetry horsefeathers." Jess dipped a hand in the water and applied some to his neck and forehead. "If that's the best you can come up with, we might as well court frogs."

"We could at least give it a try," Steve sulked.

A twinkle came into Jess's eyes. "Go right ahead, pard. I'm all ears. And I promise not to throw rocks."

Steve roosted on the water trough and scratched his peach fuzz. "Let me think. Poems generally end with words that sound that same, as I recollect. So how about this." He hesitated, then haltingly launched into, "The sun is out in daytime, the moon is out at night, when I see your lovely face, I think you're a sight."

"It could stand improvement."

Steve muttered something, then said, "All right, all right. Give me a minute. This poetical stuff ain't as easy as it seems." He scuffed a circle in the dust with the tip of his boot. "Here's one." He took a deep breath. "Daisies are yellow, parasols are pink, I made up this poem and . . . and . . . and . . ." Steve struggled to end the verse.

"It truly does stink?" Jess suggested.

"You promised not to throw rocks," Steve snapped. "If you can do any better, give it a try."

"This was your harebrained notion," Jess said, "but just to prove you're not the only fool in these parts, here goes." He thought a bit. "You're so pretty you put me in a daze, I'd like to spark you for the rest of my days."

"Not bad," Steve said. "Not bad at all. But the sparkin' talk might be too bold."

"Then how about another." Jess had one ready. "You're a rose and a lilac all rolled into one, and you smell as sweet as a cinnamon bun."

"I like that even better!" Steve declared, then became aware of an old man with a cane who was gaping at them in amazement. "Somethin' we can do for you, old-timer?"

The old man shook his cane at them. "You ought to be whipped, you danged abominations! Right out in the open, too!"

"What have you been drinkin'?" Jess asked.

"Don't sass your elders, boy!" The townsman was shaking with fury. "Dadgummit, if I was ten years younger, I'd beat the devil out of both of you. A good caning cures more ills than castor oil."

Jess looked at Steve. "The world sure is full of lunatics."

The old man moved on while heaping imprecations under his breath. At the corner he turned and shook his cane again, then was lost amid the ebb and flow of humanity.

"Now where were we?" Steve asked.

Before Jess could reply, a loud whoop cut the

night and up bounded Heck Myers and Stu Wilkins. Both were showing all the teeth they had, and then some. Heck clapped Jess and Steve on the back, and whooped a second time.

"We've been searchin' all over for you two. What a night we've had! Wait until you hear! We've met us some females!"

"That's right," Stu Wilkins said, cheerfully bobbing his chin. "A pair of angels who couldn't get enough of us."

"They liked us so much," Heck said, "that they've agreed to meet us later on, after they get done with work." He spun in a circle and chortled for joy. "Real bosoms-and-legs women!"

"We had the same stroke of luck," Steve revealed. "And we're meetin' our gals later, too."

"How about if we all get together?" Heck proposed. "It would be great fun, and I'm sure Margaret and Ethel wouldn't mind."

The color drained from Jess Donner's face and he opened and closed his mouth a few times before saying, "Who?"

"Dance girls over to Rankin's Dance Hall. We went there lookin' for you and instead made their acquaintance." Heck stopped crowing to ask, "What's the matter? You two look sick to your stomachs."

"If you only knew," Steve Ellsworth said.

Chapter Fourteen

A subtle but profound change came over Jess Donner; his body went rigid and his features grew as hard as flint. "What did you say?" he asked in a voice that did not sound like his.

Heck Myers was laughing with giddy delight at his good fortune. "That I bet our gals won't mind if we hook up with you and your gals."

"No." Jess took a step toward him. "What were their names again?"

"Margaret Sanger and Ethel Heatherton."

Steve Ellsworth belatedly suffered the same reaction as his bunkie. "Can it be?" he bleated in shock.

"Maybe not," Jess said without conviction. "We never learned their last names. Maybe it's two others." He grabbed Heck's arm. "Quick. Describe these fillies of yours and don't spare the details?"

It was Stu Wilkins who did so, adding, "We're to meet them at three o'clock. They get off at two but they have an errand to run before we can get together."

Jess Donner sat on the corner of the water trough and uttered a strangled sort of laugh. "Just when the world is rosiest, the thorns rip your innards out."

Steve Ellsworth walked in a small circle, his fists clenched at his sides. "I liked her, too!" he groaned. "I honest to God liked her!"

Bewildered, Heck Myers asked, "Liked who? What's gotten into you? You should be happy for us, not actin' like your best horse broke its leg in a prairie dog hole."

"You're so dumb you couldn't teach a hen to cluck," Jess said in disgust. "Haven't you figured it out yet? The calico queens we're to meet are the same calico queens you're meetin'."

"No," Stu Wilkins said.

Heck gestured in confusion. "How can that be? They couldn't make dates with all four of us."

"*Think*, you gosling!" Jess snapped. "Use that noggin of yours for somethin' other than a hat rack."

"What do you—" Heck began, then stopped. "Can it be? Can it really and truly be?"

Steve Ellsworth was still pacing in small circles, repeating over and over, "I liked her! I really liked her!"

"First the exhibition, now this," Stu lamented. "I should stop claiming to be intelligent."

Stunned silence descended except for Steve's muttering until Jess Donner shook himself and grimly stood. "I reckon every man is entitled to a spell of silliness now and then, and we've had ours.

The question is, what are we goin' to do about it? Whatever those two fillies are up to, it's plain they're not virtuous."

"Well, they do work at a dance hall," Stu pointed out, and received three glares the likes of which made him take a step back. "All I'm saying is that dance hall girls are a trifle loose with their morals."

"I thought Ethel was different," Steve said.

"Is that who you were to see?" Stu sadly sighed. "Me, too." He glanced south, in the general direction of Rankin's. "Maybe we're being premature. Maybe we should give them the benefit of the doubt. It could be they think they're doing us a favor by being nice to four lonesome cowboys."

"What they did is rank," Jess said. "Margaret led me on like a guppy on a leash, had me thinkin' she really cared."

Heck was the one who now appeared deathly ill. "She did the same with me," he said softly, "had me lappin' at her feet like I was a kitten and her toes were made of milk."

"What can their game be?" Jess wondered.

"Maybe it's innocent," Stu tried again. "They spend an hour with you, bid you good night, and spend an hour with us, then off to dreamland with no one's feelings hurt. After all, how were they to know we're acquainted?"

"That's right," Heck said, grasping at straws. "We told them we were huntin' for friends but we never mentioned your names."

"It's still rank," Jess said. "They've played a dirty

trick on us and I say we play a dirty trick right back."

"I thought she liked me," Steve Ellsworth repeated.

"Someone kick him," Jess urged. Swearing bitterly, he kicked the water trough, instead. "When will I learn? I swear, women are poison. They should be kept in bottles and sold over the counter."

Another silence afflicted them until Heck Myers smothered his hurt enough to say, "I'm with you, Jess. Doesn't Scripture say somethin' about doin' unto others as they do unto you? Let's teach these fillies a lesson in how to properly treat cowpokes."

Stu spread his hands. "But what can we do? Beating them up is out of the question."

"I'll say it is," Heck snorted. "Touch a female in these parts and folks treat you to a hemp social. No, it has to be somethin' sneaky. Somethin' they'll remember the rest of their days."

"A good dunkin' in the river would serve them right," Steve Ellsworth suggested. "Ruin their hairdos and they'll be as mad as wet hens."

"That's your notion of revenge?" Jess scoffed. "Why don't you tweak their noses while you're at it? Or is that too vicious for your tastes?"

"They're women," Steve said.

"Which is no excuse. I'm thinkin' we should rustle up some tar and a bucket of feathers."

Stu Wilkins was aghast. "Tar and feather them? That's too severe, if you ask me. And bound to get us in trouble."

"We have to do somethin'!" Jess insisted.

But they could not agree on what. For long minutes they heatedly debated, getting nowhere. Stu urged leniency. Jess was in a frame of mind to boil them in scalding water. Heck thought chucking horse droppings at them would suffice. Steve just walked in circles. They might have argued for hours if Stu Wilkins hadn't pulled out the pocket watch his mother had given him.

"It's fifteen minutes until two. Whatever we're going to do, now is the time to make up our minds." He added, "If that's possible."

Steve Ellsworth smacked a fist against his other palm and declared, "Let's march over there and give them a piece of our minds!" Without waiting for his friends to agree, he stormed down the street.

"He's fierce when his dander is up," Jess said.

By now the number of people thronging the streets was thinning. Drovers were heading back to their herds and bleary-eyed townsmen were heading home to face the wrath of their wives. Even the horses moving along the street seemed tired, and those tied to hitch rails were dozing. The saloons and dance halls were still open but the blast of music and revelry was subdued.

Steve Ellsworth's spurs were jangling nonstop. "If I ever look at a female again, I'm the one who should be tarred and feathered."

"As girl crazy as you are, that's liable to be tomorrow," Jess remarked.

"Poke fun. I don't care. I opened my heart to her and she treated it like chewin' tobacco. Now I will spit her out like she was set to do to me."

A side street they took lay quiet under the sparkling canopy of the firmament. They passed a frame house with a small yard and a white picket fence. Inside, a baby squalled.

Steve gestured savagely. "Here I was, thinkin' that Ethel and me might get a place like that, and raise us a passel of little ones."

"Me, too," Heck said.

Stu Wilkins, bringing up the rear, remarked, "You hardly know her and already you're married and raising kids? Is it the air or is it Texans?"

Twisting, Steve speared a finger at him. "Don't start with us. You and your sophisticated New York ways."

Stu sighed and idly glanced over his shoulder. "Is it my imagination or is there a dog following us?"

"Forget the mongrel," Jess said. "We'll deal with it later. This is more important." He tugged at his pants so they rode higher on his hips. "I wonder how many others they've pulled this trick on?"

"I wish I was back at camp," Stu said.

They turned right on Maple Street. Several booze-blind cowboys staggered by, singing off-key, their arms draped over one another's shoulders. A man in a bowler scurried toward the center of town, a black leather bag clasped in his hands.

"Why did God make women, anyhow?" Jess fumed. "They look so pretty. But fiddlin' with one is like fiddlin' with a steel trap. You never know when the jaws will snap shut and take your arm off."

"Women have their good points," Stu Wilkins

said, and almost bumped into them when all three stopped.

"Whose side are you on?" Heck Myers demanded. "We've been done wrong and you're defendin' the enemy?"

"All I'm saying is that it we shouldn't judge them without all the facts," Stu explained.

"Lord, spare me from bein' citified," Heck said, and resumed walking.

At the next corner they turned left. Rankin's was still over a block and a half away but Steve and Jess veered off the street and under a solitary oak at the edge of a grassy lot.

"Why are we stoppin'?" Heck asked.

"This is where we're to meet them," Steve explained. "They didn't want to do it at the dance hall."

Jess squatted and angrily ripped a handful of grass from the sod. "It's the Garden of Eden all over again."

"I have an idea," Heck said. "Stu and me will hide behind the tree so they won't suspect we're on to them, and pop out when you give the word."

Jess's laugh was brittle. "I like it. Better hide now in case they get off early."

Of them all, Steve was taking the situation the hardest. He was walking in circles again, a hand pressed to his chest as if he were stricken.

A lively melody, borne on the night air, did nothing to lighten their moods. Nor did they pay any attention to the dozens of festive souls who soon began to file from the dance hall. The music ended.

The flow became a trickle, then stopped. It was a while before the first of the dancers emerged, bundled in a shawl and hastening home or to a rendezvous. Singly and in pairs and groups, more dancers walked past without seeing the young cowboys in the shadows. Gradually their numbers dwindled. Several minutes went by and no one else came out.

"Maybe they're jiltin' us," Jess said.

The door opened again, framing two women in a rectangle of light. Arm in arm, they came down the street and when they were abreast of the oak they suddenly turned in under its leafy boughs.

"You're here!" Margaret said, stepping up to Jess and taking his hands in hers. "I was so afraid you would stand us up!"

"Not me," Ethel said, grasping Steve Ellsworth's arm. "I knew when I first set eyes on you that you were the man for me."

"Is that a fact?" Steve said. "What did you have in mind for tonight? Enjoy a meal? Go for a stroll? Or have us climb to the top of the church steeple and push us off?"

Ethel giggled and ran a finger along his chin. "Don't be silly."

"We would never hurt you," Margaret said. "Don't you realize how special you are to us?"

"I've heard that word a lot tonight," Jess interjected, "and it's plumb lost its meanin'. Or is it that you think anyone in britches is special?"

Margaret stepped back. "What's gotten into you? Earlier you were treatin' me like a princess."

"Your luster wore off—maybe from spreadin' it too thin." Jess turned to the oak. "Come on out, boys, and give Miss Sanger and Miss Heatherton great big hugs."

"What's this?" Ethel nervously asked as Heck Myers and Stu Wilkins stepped into the open. Her fingers flew to her ivory throat and she blurted, "Heck! What are you doing here?"

"I should ask you the same thing," Heck replied, "since I thought I was special, too." He stood beside Steve. "How could you do this? After we held hands and whispered sweet nothin's?"

"We've been found out," Margaret said.

"How many others did you agree to meet tonight?" Jess asked. "Another pair of yacks at four? And another at five? Maybe two more at six to buy you breakfast?"

Margaret drew herself up to her full height. "I don't like how you're talkin' to me."

"You liked it when we were in that booth. You liked it when you were spinnin' a yarn about my bein' the kind of man you had been lookin' for all your life."

"She told you that, too?" Heck despondently asked. "She must be related to T. Q. Snell."

Ethel moved to Margaret's side and took her hand. "We'd better be on our way. They would never understand in a million years."

"You're not going anywhere," Jess Donner informed her.

"No, you're surely not," a newcomer said, and out of the darkness came Grat Vanes. Rusty was on his right side, Lucky on his left. The brothers had their hands on their hips, close to their revolvers.

"Who are these two?" Margaret asked.

"We didn't agree to meet them," Ethel said.

"We're acquainted with these cowpokes," Grat said. "We couldn't help but overhear, and we think it's a downright shame what you did to these boys. But I guess it's fittin'."

"What is?" from Margaret.

"That all of you are goin' to die together."

Rusty Vanes slid his hand to his Colt. "Who wants to be first?"

Chapter Fifteen

Rusty Vanes coiled to draw his pearl-handled Colt and grinned in wicked anticipation.

The four cowboys from the Double C outfit turned to stone. Unarmed as they were, they would not stand a prayer.

Margaret Sanger, though, spoke right up. "Who in hell are you two? And what's this talk about killin' us?"

"Now, now," Grat Vanes said. "Is that any way for a lady to talk?"

Ethel backed her friend. "This is a private affair, mister. Go pester someone else with your silliness."

"Silly like a fox." Grat, too, was relishing the moment, and in no hurry to gun the cowboys down. "You see, ma'am, my brother and me aim to turn up the toes of these four babes in the woods. Thanks to you and your friend, I can arrange things so it looks as if they had a fallin' out over you lovelies, and everyone ended up killin' everyone else."

"You're serious?" Ethel said, aghast.

"I take killin' mighty serious, yes, ma'am."

Stu Wilkins, who was nearest to the tree, took a step toward it but stopped when Rusty Vanes shifted toward him. "The law will never buy that four unarmed men shot themselves, and two others besides."

"Only one of you needs to be armed." Grat patted his revolver. "All I need do is leave this near your bodies. I can always buy another."

"You're loco!" Steve Ellsworth declared.

"They're killers," Jess said, "and they have us right where they want us." He stepped in front of Margaret. "But there's nothin' that says we have to make it easy on them. If all four of us rush them at once, maybe we can wrestle one of their six-shooters away."

Rusty's grin widened. "Wishful thinkin', cowboy. But you're more than welcome to try."

Tension crackled like lightning. Heck and Steve began sidling to either side and the Vanes brothers were practically quivering with sadistic hunger when three more figures materialized out of the nights, all wearing suits and bowlers.

"What's going on here?" demanded Vince Shamblin.

With the quickness of a rattler, Rusty Vanes spun. "Get lost, mister. This doesn't concern you."

"That's where you're wrong, boy," Vince said, and indicated the women. "Margaret and Ethel are the property of Lem Rankin. Any harm comes to them and you answer to him."

"You say that like it should scare us," Rusty said mockingly.

But it had an effect on Grat, who urged, "Let's not be hasty, little brother. I've heard of this Rankin. He's a big man in Dodge."

"Doesn't matter to me," Rusty said. "He bleeds the same as everyone else, doesn't he? And we have this to do."

Margaret moved from behind Jess. "Vince! Thank goodness! These two were talkin' about killin' us."

The three men from the dance hall spread out, Vince with his arms crossed at chest height, his fingertips brushing the edges of his open jacket. "I don't care what they do to these cowboys. Mr. Rankin sent me to follow you and Ethel and bring you back if you were up to no good." He stared at Jess Donner. "This is the one you were with earlier, isn't it? You arranged to meet him after you were off."

"I did not," Margaret said. "We just happened to bump into him and his friends, is all."

Vince was blunt with her. "Liar. You know Mr. Rankin's rules. He was right to suspect you were up to something. You're coming back with me and explaining yourself to him."

"Please. It's not what you think."

"No one is goin' anywhere," Rusty Vanes said.

Vince faced him. His companions had their jackets open, their hands raised above their waists. "Stay out of this, boy. My boss doesn't like it when people meddle in his affairs. I'm taking these two, and there's not a damn thing you can do about it."

Rusty's voice was ice and menace rolled into one. "We'll see about that, you dandified peckerwood."

"Russian," Grat said, "don't make a mistake we'll both regret."

"No one talks down to me like he's doin'," Rusty said. "Have him say he's sorry and maybe then I'll let him leave in one piece."

"Say I'm sorry?" Vince scoffed. "It'll be a cold day in hell before that happens. This is your last warning, boy. Back off or the two of you will be on display at the undertaker's come morning."

"Care to bet?" Rusty asked. Grat cried out for him not to do anything but Rusty was past listening. He drew and put a slug into Vince Shamblin before Vince's twin pistols cleared their shoulder holsters. The impact jolted Vince back and his right revolver went off, kicking dirt at Rusty's feet.

The other two men on Rankin's payroll went for their guns. So, too, belatedly, did Grat Vanes. But Grat fired first, and hit one of them high in the shoulder. The other one, though, extended his arm to better his aim and shot Grat in the stomach. Grat folded but did not go down. He fired as the third man fired a second time and they were both hit but it was not Grat who pitched to the grass. The wounded man whirled and ran. Grat fired at his retreating back but he could not hold his Colt steady and was slowly oozing to his knees.

The whole time, Rusty and Vince Shamblin were exchanging shots. Vince was jarred onto his bootheels but both his guns belched lead and smoke and Rusty was spun halfway around. Rusty then

did what most gun handlers deemed rash in a gunfight. He fanned his Colt three times, slapping the
hammer with his palm while keeping pressure on
the trigger. The three shots sounded almost as one,
so swiftly were they fired, and Vince Shamblin was
flung to the earth, where he lay convulsing and spitting gobs of blood while more gushed from his
nose.

"Damn him!" Rusty swore, and grabbed at his
side. The lead had dug a quarter-inch furrow along
his ribs, breaking the flesh but otherwise sparing
him. He grinned and turned, and the grin instantly
faded. "Gratton!"

Grat Vanes was on his knees, swaying like a
sapling in a strong wind, his lower jaw stained dark,
his left right hand pressed to his stomach to vainly
stanch the flow. "Russian! I'm hit! I'm hit bad!"

Rusty was beside his brother in a bound and
clamping his arm around Grat's shoulders. "Let me
have a look. Maybe there's somethin' I can do."

"No," Grat said, taking deep, ragged breaths.
"Get us out of here before the law shows up." He
tried to stand and closed his eyes and groaned. "My
gut is on fire. I hurt somethin' awful, and my legs
won't work."

"Lean on me. I'll carry you." Rusty wrapped both
arms around his brother and hoisted him off the
ground.

Wait," Grat said, spittle dribbling from a corner
of his mouth. "What about the cowboys and the fillies?"

Rusty bent his neck, and blinked. "They're gone!

The whole bunch! They must have lit a shuck when the lead started to fly."

Off toward Front Street shouting had broken out, and from the dance hall came the loud slam of a door.

"Quick," Grat said. "Cut across this lot. It won't be long before we're knee-deep in tin stars."

Firming his hold, Rusty grunted and headed toward a line of trees. Once past them, he turned north, crossing yard after yard until he came to a shed. Moving around to the far side, he carefully lowered Grat onto his back.

"What are we stoppin' for?"

"You're bleedin' like a stuck pig," Rusty said. The lower half of his brother's shirt was soaked. "This movin' can't be good. Rest while I go fetch a sawbones."

"No!" Grat gripped Rusty's hand as his younger brother went to stand, and clung fast. "Don't leave me! I don't want to be alone."

"You need a doctor."

"Don't," Grat repeated, and his whole frame shook. "I'm done for, and I know it."

Rusty placed a hand on his brother's shoulder. "Don't talk nonsense. Once the bullet is out, you'll be back on your feet in two flicks of a mule's ears."

Grat shut his eyes. His face was startlingly pale, and a gurgling sound came from the hole in his stomach. "Listen to me, Russian, and listen good. I've been bucked out. You'll be on your own soon. Go somewhere and start over. Change your name. Find a job that pays half-decent."

"More nonsense."

"Damn it," Grat said, and had to stop to cough. He put his hand to his mouth and when he drew it away, his palm dripped blood. "I've never amounted to much. I admit that. But you're young yet. You have a chance to make somethin' of yourself, to be respectable."

"And do what?" Rusty asked. "Nurse cows for a livin'? Or clerk in a store ten hours a day sellin' dry goods? I can't think of anything that would bore me more."

"Better bored than dead."

Rusty shook his head. "Not me. I'd rather die young than have all the life wrung out of me. That's what jobs like those do. Workin' for a pittance to make some other polecat rich. Havin' to scrimp and save and never gettin' ahead. And never free to pull up stakes and go where the wind blows me. That's not livin'. It's a prison."

"Now who's talkin' nonsense?" Grat attempted to sit up but couldn't. "I can't feel my legs anymore. Do me a favor and prop me up so I can breathe a little easier."

As gently as he could, Rusty eased his brother off the grass and leaned him against the shed. "Will that do?"

"Thanks," Grat said softly. He was breathing with considerable effort. "Killin' Baxter sure brought us bad luck." He paused, and weakly gazed right and left. "Say, where did Lucky get to?"

"To hell, for all I care. That worthless mongrel probably ran off when the shootin' commenced."

"He's never been afraid of it before," Grat said. "I want you to take care of him after I'm gone."

"You can count on it," Rusty promised. "Now lie there and be quiet. I'm fetchin' a doc whether you want me to or not."

"Go ahead, then. But by the time you find one and make it back, I'll be as dead as Baxter and we won't get to say our good-byes." Grat slumped to one side and would have fallen but Rusty caught him and eased him back up. "Do you remember when we were kids and we'd go down to the creek in the summer and swim? Those were the happiest days of my life, little brother."

"You shouldn't gab so much."

"Or what? I'll die a few seconds sooner?" Grat laughed mirthlessly. "I think of those days a lot. How Ma would bake pies on Sunday. Pa playin' his fiddle in the evenin's."

"What I recollect most about Pa is the switchin's he gave us," Rusty mentioned. "I couldn't sit for a week afterward."

"We deserved them," Grat said. "Remember that time you hung a pig from the barn rafters just to see how long it would take to die?"

"Or how about the time we poured kerosene on one of the cats and lit it on fire? That was a sight, with it jumpin' and caterwaulin'." Rusty grinned. "Now that you bring it up, I sort of miss those days, too."

Yells from an adjacent street caused Rusty to spring erect with his hand on his Colt. He waited tensely, and when no one appeared, he hunkered down. "I thought for a second the law was on to us."

Grat was a while answering. "All the more reason for you to get out of Dodge. Take my poke. There's enough left to last you a spell."

"I'm not goin' anywhere until I settle accounts."

"With who?" Grat asked, and when his brother would not answer, he said, "Let it be, consarn you. Dump me at Boot Hill and get on with your life. Try not to make the same mistakes I have."

Rusty made a clucking noise. "Will you listen to yourself? You sound like a parson. I'm not changin' my ways, even if you sprout wings and a halo."

Footfalls sounded, and Rusty whirled, the Colt flashing clear. But it was only Lucky, who slunk up to Grat and nuzzled him as if apologizing for running off.

"Well, lookee here," Grat said fondly, and feebly patted the dog's head. "I knew he wouldn't desert me. He's the best pard anyone ever had."

"There have been days," Rusty remarked, "when I've thought you cared for this sack of hair more than you do for me."

Grat rubbed behind one of Lucky's ears. "Remember to feed him regular. And when his time comes, dig a grave. Don't leave him for the buzzards." He coughed, and couldn't stop. Suddenly he stiffened and thrashed his arms wildly about, his mouth opening and closing.

"Grat?" Rusty caught hold of an arm and tried to hold his older brother still but Grat bucked like a mustang, the whites of his eyes showing in stark fear. They focused on Rusty and Grat tried to say something, tried so hard his face clouded and the veins in his neck bulged. But all that came out was a tiny squeak. Then he was gone.

Rusty stared at his brother's contorted countenance. Lucky had tucked his tail between his legs and dashed off a few yards but now he nervously slunk back, whining pitiably. Rusty walked to a small woodpile near the front of the shed. Left over from the winter before, the wood consisted of trimmed logs about a foot and a half long. He hefted a few, selected one he liked, and returned.

Lucky looked up just as Rusty swung. The log caved in the top of the dog's head and the animal folded like a limp rag, its eyes rolling up in its head and its tongue lolling. But Rusty went on swinging again and again and again and again. When he finally stopped and cast the log aside, Lucky's skull was in splinters.

"Feed you regular, my ass." Rusty helped himself to his brother's poke and pocketknife, then unstrapped Grat's gun belt and strapped it around his own waist so that the second pistol, too, was buttforward. Patting the Colts, he ambled toward Front Street. "One down, and a heap more to go."

Chapter Sixteen

For all of five seconds after the gunfire erupted, the four cowboys were riveted in shock. The grisly sight of men being shot to ribbons chilled them to their marrow.

Then Margaret Sanger gripped Ethel Heatherton's wrist and fled into the night, north toward Front Street.

Their leaving galvanized Steve Ellsworth into life. "The women!" he blurted, and bolted after them, running awkwardly on account of his boots. Out of vanity, he had heels higher than most, which was fine for riding but turned him into an ungainly goose when he had to move fast on foot.

Heck Myers was the next to follow. Stu Wilkins, thunderstruck, gaped at the carnage being wrought, and might have stood there indefinitely had Jess Donner not taken him by the arm and propelled him after the others.

"Move, you turtle, before they put lead into you!"

Already, the women were barely distinguishable

in the darkness. They were as fleet as mustangs, much faster than Steve Ellsworth, who was so used to letting his horse take him where he wanted to go that within fifty yards he was puffing and panting and had a sharp pang in his chest.

Heck caught up with him and commented, "Has anyone ever told you that you run like you're constipated?"

"Has anyone"—Steve huffed—"ever told you"—he puffed several times—"that you talk"—he took a deep breath—"too much?"

"They sure have." Heck grinned. "But usually they spit it out all at once instead of soundin' like a horse in labor."

The women had disappeared. Steve came to a stop and bent over with his hands on his knees. "Lordy, I have an ache you wouldn't believe."

Heck glanced back. "Here come Jess and Stu. And the shootin' has stopped. I wonder who's still standin'?"

"I hope to God the Vanes brothers are dead," Steve gasped. "They're the worst hombres I've ever run across."

"Not me," Heck said. "This reminds me of the time I met up with Billy the Kid. Now there was a natural-born killer who—"

"Don't start," Steve said.

"But I really did meet him," Heck asserted.

"I mean it. I'll hit you."

Jess and Stu reached them and Jess asked, "Why did you cut out after the women like that?"

"It seemed the thing to do," was Steve's reply. "But they could be anywhere by now."

Shouts from various quarters arose in reaction to the gunfire, and several men went running by in the direction of the dance hall.

Steve cocked his head and listened. "The question is, what do we do now? If Grat and his brother are still alive, they'll come after us."

"I don't understand why they want us dead," Stu Wilkins said.

"That young one doesn't need an excuse," Heck declared. "He's snake-mean. Just like Billy the Kid that time I ran into him down in—"

"Save your fairy tales for later," Jess told him. Crouching low to the ground, he removed his hat.

"What in tarnation are you doing?" Heck asked. "If nature is callin', shouldn't you take off your pants first?"

Jess was peering intently to the south. "It's a trick my grandpa taught me. At night you can spot people better when you're down low like this. They tend to stand out against the stars."

"Do you see them?" Steve anxiously asked.

"I don't see anyone," Jess said, and rose, jamming his hat back on. "Let's collect our hardware. From here on out I stay heeled."

"Good idea," Steve said. "Then we can light a shuck for camp. We'll bring half the outfit back with us tomorrow and look up those Vanes."

"I'm not headin' back," Jess announced. "And I don't have others do my fightin' for me." He walked briskly toward the bright lights of Dodge's main thoroughfare. "I'll deal with them on my own."

More and more people were hurrying in the opposite direction. Word of the gunfight was spreading like a prairie fire.

Steve and the others quickly overtook Jess, and Steve demanded, "Who do you think you are? Bat Masterson? You've never shot anyone in your life."

"There's always a first time," Jess Donner said.

Heck Myers was at Jess's other elbow. "Hold on, pard. I'm as mad as you but you're not thinkin' this through. Even if you plug them and live to tell about it, you'll be a wanted man."

"It's us or them and I don't intend to breathe dirt just yet."

Stu Wilkins doubled his pace and twisted so he was facing the Southerner. "Killing another human being is a serious thing. It's a stigma you'll carry with you the rest of your life."

"I don't even know what a stigma is," Jess said, "and I don't much care." He stopped so abruptly that the other three were a yard past him before they, too, halted. "In case none of you have caught on yet, we have a problem. The Vanes have been shadowin' us since we struck town. They want to bury us. The reason doesn't matter. They'll come after us if they're still alive, and I, for one, intend to be ready for them."

"They won't follow us to camp," Steve said. "We'll be safe there."

"Will we?" Jess countered. "How do you know they won't bushwhack us? Or stampede the cattle and pick us off while we're busy roundin' up the herd?"

"You're guessing, at best," Stu Wilkins said. "It's better to be safe than sorry, so I vote we head to camp and stay there until Rafe gets back, then tell him what's happened."

Jess resumed walking. "I'm a grown man. I don't need someone to hold my hand and walk me through life." He slapped his thigh. "What I *do* need is my Smith and Wesson. I'd like to see that Rusty Vanes throw down on me then."

"You're scarin' me," Steve said. "The last time we shot at targets, you didn't hit but seven out of ten bottles, as I recollect. And that was back in Texas before we joined up for the drive."

"Your point?"

"You ain't no pistolero. You're a lowly cowpoke, just like me, and you have no more business chuckin' lead than you do performin' surgery. I vote we go find that deputy, Trace Morgan."

"What can he do?" Jess argued. "All the Vanes did was threaten us. And you can't be thrown in jail for that."

"It could be they're dead," Heck said. "It could be all this jabberin' is pointless and the dandies from the dance hall took care of our problem for us."

"I wouldn't count on it," Jess remarked. "Nice clothes don't make a man lethal. When we ran off, it looked to me as if those three were gettin' the worst of it."

Steve Ellsworth was scouring the block ahead. "With all this talk about the Vanes, we've plumb forgot Margaret and Ethel. What do we do about them?"

"Forget they exist," Jess said. "I don't want to be reminded of how big a jackass I've been. I was partial to that girl and she played me for a fool."

"The way that fellow was talkin', they must be in some kind of trouble with Rankin."

"So? They brought it on their own heads." Jess jabbed his friend in the side. "Forget about them. Worry about the Vanes. Livin' is more important than love any day of the week."

"That's your opinion. Without romance life would be dull. We might as well be born trees."

"You say the weirdest damn things," Jess said, and after that, no one spoke until they came to the railroad tracks at the end of Fifth Avenue.

Dodge was known as the town that never slept, and with good reason. Even though it was the middle of the night, the saloons and gambling dens were doing a thriving business.

"I wish you would reconsider," Stu said as they angled toward the Long Branch. "I can't help worry we'll end up behind bars."

"No one is twistin' your arm," Jess said. "Go on back if you want, all of you. I'll tend to the Vanes alone if I have to."

"There you go again," Heck said in mild reproach. "What sort of pards would we be if we turned tail? I don't agree with what you're doin', but I can be as boneheaded as you can."

The same bartender was wiping down the bar when the four men entered. He smiled a weary smile. "Welcome back, gents. I take it you've seen the sights? Would you like a last drink or are you still brimming with vigor and vim?"

"We want our revolvers," Jess Donner said. "We're fixin' to ride out."

Stepping to where a score of gun belts hung on pegs, the bartender scratched his chin. "Where are the numbers I gave you? I can't keep track without them, what with all the comings and goings."

Jess smiled grimly as he buckled on his nickel-plated .44. Sliding it from its holster, he verified it was loaded.

"I'm glad you boys showed some common sense," the bartender said. "A lot of cowboys refuse to give up their irons and stick them under their shirts or vests. The next thing you know, they're drunk and on a spree, and they decide to shoot up the town."

"There were shots a while ago," Steve Ellsworth mentioned.

"We all heard them," the bartender said.

By coincidence, the door burst open and a lean man in homespun ran to the bar and leaned on it, out of breath. "Three men dead, by God! I saw the bodies with my own eyes!"

"Anyone we know?" the bartender asked.

"Only one I recognized. He works at Rankin's, or did, until someone turned him into a sieve. But I never heard his name." The man slapped the bar. "Give me a drink, will you, before I keel over from exhaustion."

Heck Myers had turned to go but he was now as

interested as everyone else. "Were the three dead ones wearin' store-bought suits?"

The man arched an eyebrow. "What a strange question, youngster. Yes, in fact, they were. Which makes me think all three might be Rankin's gunnies, in which case whoever sent them to hell did the rest of us a favor."

"Watch your tongue, Caleb," someone warned. "Rankin has ears everywhere."

"Let his bullies lay a finger on me, and I'll sic the law on him so fast, his head will swim." Caleb accepted a glass of Scotch and downed half of it. Smacking his lips, he declared, "The old times are almost done for. Coyotes like Rankin can't ride roughshod over everyone anymore. Just ask Luke Short and his friends."

At that, a man with a perpetually hangdog expression, wearing a wide-brimmed brown hat, stepped forward. "I am one of those friends, and I would take it as a favor if you would not cast aspersions on him."

"That's Neil Brown!" someone whispered.

The name meant nothing to the four cowboys but it sobered Caleb lightning-quick. "No offense meant," he hastily said. "I wasn't one of those clamoring to run Short out of town."

"I suspect you've left the truth in the stall," Neil Brown said, "but you're not worth the price of a bullet. Just remember my advice." He headed for the gaming tables.

Jess Donner was in motion for the door. He looked both ways, and when he was satisfied no lawmen were in the vicinity, he walked east, sticking to the shadows as much as possible.

"Where to now?" Stu Wilkins asked.

"Mary Richter's boardin'house on First Avenue," Jess revealed. "Margaret wouldn't tell me where she's stayin', but I overheard one of the other girls say that the boardin'house is where most of them lay their heads at night. It's south of the deadline since the respectable ladies north of it want nothin' to do with their kind."

Steve was gnawing on his lower lip again. "What will we do when we get there? Storm the place and take the women captive? Or shoot out all the windows until they wave a white flag?"

"You're plumb ridiculous," Jess said.

"I just don't see what good it will do us," Steve brought up. "Sure, Ethel and Margaret did us wrong. But short of slappin' them silly, what can you hope to accomplish?"

"I aim to find out why."

Heck Myers scratched his head. "Why what? Why they treated us so shabbily? They're female, for cryin' out loud, and females have been breakin' hearts since Adam. Be thankful we found out before we were tricked into buyin' them a lot of fancy clothes and whatnot."

"Amen to that," Stu said.

But Jess was not dissuaded. "I want to hear her say it. I want to be lookin' in her eyes when she does."

Steve Ellsworth said, "What will that prove, pard? It seems to me you're clingin' to a rope that isn't there. Besides which, I thought you were after the Vanes brothers."

"We'll deal with them soon enough," Jess vowed.

The east end of town was quiet. First Avenue was dark except for a lantern on the porch of a two-story building not far from the Arkansas River. A sign in white block letters confirmed they had located the boardinghouse.

Stu said uncertainly, "Well, we're here. But it doesn't look like anyone is up and about. Either Margaret and Ethel are already in bed or they live somewhere else."

"Don't expect me to knock on the door and wake everyone up," Heck said. "There's nothin' worse than an angry female except a swarm of angry females, and I learned long ago not to go around pokin' sticks in beehives."

"Let's forget about this," Stu said. "If it's that important, Jess, look up Margaret in the morning."

"No," Jess said.

The next moment, from amid the dark belt of thick vegetation along the bank of the river, came a shriek of unbridled terror.

Chapter Seventeen

Margaret Sanger had witnessed gunfights before. Seldom a week went by at the dance hall that a tipsy cowboy didn't pull a concealed pistol and start shooting up the place for the general fun of it. Usually the bouncers were able to talk the cowpoke out of his revolver and none too gently escort the offender from the premises. But there were occasions when no amount of talking worked.

Of all the men Margaret saw shot, only one died in front of her eyes. Most suffered wounds of varying severity, which sometimes proved fatal later, since once infection set in, stopping the spread was impossible.

Margaret had seen women shot, too. Bystanders who did not have the sense to flatten themselves on the floor when gunfire erupted. One incident, in particular, was forever imbedded in her memory, and every now and again she suffered a recurring nightmare in which she was that woman.

It happened one night on Front Street. A couple

of gamblers got into an argument, and before anyone could blink, the pair jerked revolvers and
blasted away. They were only eight feet apart but
they missed each other, and one of the slugs struck
a girl of sixteen who had stopped to watch. It tore
through her stomach and left an exit wound the size
of a large apple. She lingered for five days in the
most intense agony, and spent four of them begging
to have her life ended.

A lesson learned, as Margaret liked to say. So
now, when Vince Shamblin and the kid with the
pearl-handled Colt clawed for their six-shooters,
she instantly whirled and ran, pulling Ethel after
her.

Ethel, though, dragged her heels. "Wait! Vince
won't like us leaving!"

"Run, damn you!" Margaret fumed. Vince was
the least of their worries. She realized that, even if
her girlfriend didn't.

Never much of a runner, Ethel panted to keep up.
Shots cracked behind them. Margaret veered to the
east, cutting across a yard.

"Where are we going?"

"To the boardin'house," Margaret told her.
"We're packin' our things and takin' the mornin'
stage to Denver. Until it leaves, we'll hide somewhere."

"Why hide?" Ethel asked. "And why Denver? I
thought you wanted to live in New Orleans once we
had enough money saved up." She looked back.
The shooting had stopped, and she saw vague figures but could not tell which side had won.

"The money we've socked away will have to do us," Margaret said. "And we're headin' to Denver to try and throw Rankin off our scent."

"Oh," Ethel said. She thought about that, and said, much louder, "Oh! We have to get out of Dodge before he gets his hands on us!"

"Now you're catchin' on." Margaret could run faster but she matched her pace to her friend's shorter stride. "Remember what he did to the last girl who tried to run off? She was on crutches for two months, and she walks with a limp to this day."

"But why not head for New Orleans?" Ethel would not let it drop.

"Because we've told a few of the other girls about how wonderful it would be to live there, and you can bet Rankin will question each and every one." Margaret had it all worked out. "He'll figure us to head east, not west."

"What if he has every stage watched? Not just the eastbound?"

Margaret didn't answer. There was no need. She thought about the girl whose legs had been broken in five places, and then about several other girls, girls who mysteriously disappeared, and she could not repress a shudder.

"And those cowboys? What about them?"

"You pick the damnedest time to be a bundle of questions," Margaret criticized. "What about them? We can't steal their money now. They're too suspicious." Margaret swore in a manner a freight driver would admire. "It's a shame. Four in one night might net us a hundred dollars or better." Dodge was the end of the trail drive for many outfits. Cowboys were paid all the back wages they had coming. Then the men strutted around town with their pockets bulging. Once they were drunk enough, it was easy to pick their pockets. Margaret was a master at it, and Ethel was almost as adept.

"Things sure have gone to hell," Ethel lamented. Secretly she had always known they would. No one ever escaped Lem Rankin's clutches. Absolutely no one.

"We're not bad off," Margaret reassured her. "We have some money. We have each other. All we need now is to be shed of Rankin."

"Easier said than done."

They were out of breath by the time they arrived at the boardinghouse. Margaret put a finger to her ruby lips as they went up the short flight of steps to the porch. She produced her key and slid it into the lock. Many homes in Dodge were left unlocked day and night but not the boardinghouse. Mary Richter, the landlady, was a prim and proper spinster who did not abide amorous shenanigans. She always kept the doors locked "for the purity of her renters," as she put it.

The parlor was empty, as it usually was at that hour. Nor was anyone astir in the kitchen. A stair creaked loudly when Ethel put her weight on it, and both women froze. Sometimes that was all it took to bring Mary Richter from her downstairs quarters, but not tonight.

Their room was on the second floor at the end of

the hall. "Hurry and pack," Margaret said, opening the closet.

They did not own a lot: a pair of dresses apiece, a few undergarments, and several items of cheap jewelry, including a necklace that once belonged to Ethel's mother and that she wore every hour of the day except when she was at the dance hall for fear a wild cowboy might accidentally break the chain while pawing her.

"I wish I had time to take a bath," Ethel remarked.

"Don't be ridiculous," Margaret said. She liked a nice, warm bath, too, but Ethel was fanatical about taking one daily, and would loll in a hot tub for hours if Margaret let her. "Is that all you can think of at a time like this?"

"I think better when I'm clean and refreshed."

"What is there to think about?" Margaret was folding her best dress, which she only wore on special occasions.

"Staying alive." Ethel opened the small pine dresser and removed her hairbrush and comb.

The ten minutes it took them seemed ten times as long. Margaret gave the room a last sweep to ensure they had not missed anything, then opened the door and motioned for Ethel to precede her.

"What do we do if Mary stops us on the way out? She might wonder what we're up to."

"It's none of her business," Margaret said. "But we'll thank her for her kindness, and tell her I have a sick brother I need to go visit in Kansas City."

"You come up with the most wonderful fibs," Ethel mentioned adoringly.

"Do I?" Margaret had a lot of practice. She had been living hand to mouth for four years, ever since her folks died. To survive, she had had to hone her mind to a razor's sharpness. "There's a restaurant that's open all night near the stage office. We'll go there."

They avoided the stair that creaked. Ethel held the door for Margaret and quietly closed it behind them. "We did it!" she whispered.

"We're not out of the woods yet," Margaret cautioned.

They descended the short steps and were halfway to the street when two shadows detached themselves from the surrounding darkness. "Going somewhere, ladies?"

Margaret and Ethel stopped cold, and Ethel fearfully blurted, "Charley Warner! What are you doing here?"

"What do you think?" Warner asked. "Mr. Rankin will be upset to hear you were leaving town without saying good-bye." Warner was a squat slab of muscle who always wore a fine suit and hat and three rings on each hand. But no amount of finery could disguise the brutishness that lurked under the veneer. When Rankin needed legs busted, when Rankin needed a girl taught a lesson, more often than not, Rankin gave the job to Warner.

The other man was Rufus Spenser, a rodent born with two legs instead of the usual four.

"We're not goin' anywhere," Margaret said, thinking fast.

Warner glanced at their bags and sneered, "Do tell. Then what is all that for? Ballast?"

"We've taken new rooms over on Chestnut Street," Margaret said. "Since we just got off work, we thought we would move now rather than wait for morning."

Charley nodded at Rufus, who moved behind them. "Strange that Mr. Rankin didn't say anything about you moving. Or have you forgotten that when one of his girls changes lodgings, they're to let him know a week in advance?"

"It slipped our minds," Ethel said.

Rufus laughed them to scorn. "Sure it did. A lot of things slip your minds, from what Mr. Rankin told me. Not too smart, either of you, but hell, you're just women." He gazed up the street. "Mr. Rankin sent Vince to follow you, then sent us here in case you gave Vince the slip. Which you must have done since I don't see him anywhere."

Margaret tersely asked, "What now?"

"We're taking you to the dance hall," Rufus Spenser said, "whether you want to go or not." He gave Ethel a push.

"Will you be gentlemen and carry our bags for us?" Margaret held hers out to Warner and smiled her most charming smile.

"You must have me confused with someone from the other side of the tracks," Warner said. "I don't open doors for women. I don't stand up when a woman enters a room. And I sure as hell won't tote your damn bags."

"You packed it, you can carry it," Rufus echoed.

Margaret turned, but Charley Warner stepped in front of her and gestured toward the Arkansas River. "Not that way. There's a shortcut, a footpath along the river. After you."

"I don't know of any path," Margaret lied. "You'll have to lead the way."

The tangled wall of undergrowth and trees at the end of the street was not as impassable as it seemed. The city was thinning the underbrush at public expense to turn the strip of woodland into a park, and a footpath now wound along the bank for over half a mile. During the day couples strolled along it arm in arm and children scampered and played. At night the path was generally avoided since more than a few muggings had occurred, and six months ago a woman had been assaulted.

The river gurgled softly, like a thing alive. Margaret had to strain to see. She concentrated on Warner's back, marking the distance between them, then glanced over her shoulder at Rufus, who trailed a few yards behind. She tried to catch Ethel's eye but Ethel's chin was drooped in despair.

"You know," Warner said, "I always figured you for one of the smart ones, Sanger. But trying to skip out is just plain dumb. I get tired of breaking the legs of idiots like you two."

"I should think you would enjoy it," Margaret said, unable to resist slinging a verbal barb.

"Oh, I do," Warner said. "But it's tiresome having

to put up with all the blubbering and screaming. Were it up to me, I'd slit your throats and be done with it."

"Is that what you did to Emily Conover?" Margaret asked. "The last anyone saw of her, you took her into Rankin's office."

"She was as stupid as you. She went to the law and begged for help. Told how Rankin tricks you girls into signing contracts, and makes you steal for him."

Ethel snapped out of her sorrow. "The marshal didn't do anything?" She was appalled. She had considered going to the law herself.

"Emily didn't tell Marshal Bridges. She told a deputy. I guess she didn't know that Mr. Rankin pays most of them to look the other way. The deputy earned a bonus by bringing her back."

Both sides of the trails were flanked by heavy growth. Margaret saw a bend ahead, and slowed. To keep Warner from suspecting her intentions, she said, "You haven't told us what happened to her."

"And I'm not about to. Being strung up isn't high on my list of things I most like to do." Warner walked around the bend and was momentarily lost to view.

Rufus, Margaret saw, was gazing toward the river. There might not be a better opportunity. Suddenly whirling, she threw her bags at his legs, grabbed Ethel, and darted into the underbrush, yelling, "Drop your bags and run!"

Too dumfounded to reply, Ethel clung to Margaret in abject fright. They went twenty feet, then bore due west. Another twenty feet, and Margaret crouched and yanked Ethel down beside her. "Not a peep!" she whispered, pressing a hand to Ethel's mouth.

Oaths blistered the night. Warner was plowing through the vegetation like a mad bull. "Find them! They can't be far." Both men stopped and Warner bent toward a thicket.

Every nerve in Margaret's body was tingling. She was deathly afraid, yet also immensely excited. She felt Ethel's fingernails slice into her palm.

"You go that way," Warner directed, pointing toward the river, and Rufus slunk off. After a few seconds Warner slowly advanced, parting high weeds and checking behind trees as he went. "You can't get away!" he bellowed. "Give yourselves up and there will be no hard feelings!"

Margaret would die first. She shifted on the balls of her feet to sneak off but a twig crunched under her left shoe.

Instantly, Warner spun and rushed toward them. He stopped after only a few steps and looked all about. "I know you're here somewhere! Come out now before you make me mad!"

Easing her left foot off the ground, Margaret crept westward. Ethel was glued to her side. Margaret figured that if they could circle unnoticed to the trail, they stood a good chance of reaching Front Street. She had lost sight of Rufus, though, and he could be anywhere. Avoiding a tree, she hiked her dress to step over a downed cottonwood.

Ethel went to do the same when suddenly something waved in the grass beside it. Something long and sinuous that coiled and hissed.

Lunging, Margaret flung out her hand to clamp it over her friend's mouth. Ethel had never made a secret of her fear of snakes. Her brothers used to taunt her by putting garter snakes in her bed when she was little; she would feel them sliding over her legs in the dead of night. So it was perfectly understandable that Ethel did what she did next; she threw back her head and screamed.

Chapter Eighteen

Stu Wilkins was startled by the scream. So startled, he stood stock-still as his three friends bolted toward the Arkansas River and the dark band of greenery along its bank. With an oath he lent wings to his feet. He was impressed by how quickly the Texans and Jess had reacted, as was often the case. Whether it was roping a steer that broke suddenly from the herd, throwing wild longhorns for the fun of it, or jumping a rattlesnake, their reflexes put his to shame.

Stu blamed his New York City upbringing. City life dulled people. Their clothes, their food—everything they needed was there for the taking. They might go hungry for want of money, but that was not the same as going hungry because they missed a shot at a buck or grouse. A city dweller might occasionally have to avoid a speeding wagon, but that was tame compared to having to stay on a bucking bronc or dodge an angry bull or evade a coiled rattler.

Frontier life tempered a man, honed him like a whet stone honed a knife. Stu had never admitted as much, but he envied his friends to no end. City boys tended to look down their noses at country louts, but Stu had learned firsthand that country louts were a lot more intelligent, and a lot hardier, than their city-dwelling counterparts gave them credit for being.

Now, flying fast after the other three, Stu heard a sharp cry from off in the trees. A woman was in trouble. Leave it to the Texans and Jess to rush her rescue with no thought to their own welfare.

Stu remembered a time in New York City, when he was only ten. A woman had been dragged into an alley by a pair of footpads. Her cries for help echoed among the buildings, but not one of the score or more of passersby went to her aid. Stu had glanced at his father, who was staring straight ahead and seemed oblivious to the world around them. The memory flushed him warm with shame.

A few more bounds and Stu caught up with Steve Ellsworth, whose higher-than-normal heels slowed him considerably. Heck was huffing, his arm windmilling. "Are you all right?" Stu asked.

"I can do without all this runnin', thank you very much," Steve responded. "If the Almighty wanted us to pretend we're antelope, he wouldn't have invented horses."

Stu was going to mention that the proper word was "create," not "invent," but he had learned that there were few things Texans liked less than having their mistakes pointed out.

The woodland loomed. Jess and Steve flew into it without breaking stride. So did Steve. But Stu slowed, unwilling to risk a busted leg. It was so dark he could barely make Steve out even though he was only a few yards in front of him. Undergrowth hemmed them in on either side. Glancing down, he realized they were following a trail, although how anyone knew it was there bewildered him.

Stu flew around a bend. The ground sloped gradually toward the river, and so did the trail. He was so intent on not straying off it that he nearly slammed into Steve, who had abruptly stopped.

In a clearing stood two men and two women. The men had turned like wolves at bay and each had one of the women by the arm and his other hand under his jacket.

Margaret Sanger was one of the women. Conflicting emotions tore through Stu; he recalled how she had pressed against him when they danced, and how she continually played with his ear with her finger. Then he recalled how hurt he had been to learn she trifled with his affections.

"What the hell do you cowboys want?" demanded the heavier set of the two men.

"We could ask you the same thing," Jess Donner said. "These ladies are acquaintances of ours."

Margaret tried to pull loose but the man holding her had a grip of iron. "Damn you, Warner," she snapped. Then, to Jess, she said, "They work for Rankin. Don't let them take us or you'll never see us again."

"Shut up," Warner said, and backhanded her across the face. She staggered and would have fallen if not for his hold on her.

"Don't you dare!" Jess growled, taking a swift stride. "If anyone manhandles her, it will be me."

"Get lost, cowboy. This doesn't concern you." Warner shook Margaret. "Mr. Rankin wants to see this bitch, and he's not someone you want to make mad." He nodded at his companion. "Let's go, Rufus. If these tarts try to run off again, we'll drag them back by their hair."

Jess and Heck Myers started to sidle past them, and Heck said, "Take your hands off Ethel." Heck was still mad at her but he would not stand there and let her be abused.

Warner did not like the odds. That much was plain. He backed toward a gap across the clearing, saying, "I've heard that cowboys are dumb but you four take the prize. What are these girls to you?"

"They're nothin'," Jess Donner spat. But in his heart of hearts, he was ice-cold with fear for Margaret.

"Then let it drop," Warner said. "They're not worth bleeding over." He nodded at Rufus, then at the trail.

Steve Ellsworth chose that moment to spring, his hand on his pistol, and in a ringing voice cried out, "Hold it! Not another step!"

Everyone froze. Stu feared that blood would be spilled, and some of it might be the blood of his friends. "Listen, mister," he said, moving toward Warner with his hands out from his sides to show he meant no harm. "Can't we talk this out? What's to stop you from telling Rankin you couldn't find these ladies?"

"Lie to the boss?" Warner said, adding a brittle bark of scorn. "Boy, he'd have me gutted like a fish and dumped in the Arkansas."

"He need never know," Stu said.

Rufus, who had been silent until now, swore lustily. "Where do you get off telling us what to do? It's our job to take these two back, and we're damn well doing it whether you like it or not." He twisted Ethel's arm and she yipped in pain.

Jess Donner had had enough. He drew his Smith & Wesson. They all heard the click of the hammer. "I'll only say this once, mister. Make yourselves scarce or dabble in gore. Your choice."

Stu's anxiety rose. Murder was a hanging offense, and frontier communities weren't shy about stringing up lawbreakers. He had to do something. Moving between Jess and Rankin's hired muscle, he said, "Put that away, Jess. We can work this out without violence."

"Says you," Jess retorted, making no effort to holster the Smith & Wesson.

Neither Warner nor Rufus let go of the women. Margaret and Ethel were standing as far back as the lengths of their arms allowed to avoid taking lead.

Smiling at Warner, Stu tried one more time. "Be reasonable. You're outnumbered. You can't hope to kill all of us and not be killed yourself. Inform Rankin we took the girls from you at gunpoint. He'll understand."

"Like hell he will," Warner spat. "He'll call us yellow. We wouldn't live to see the light of day."

Rufus was of the same mind. "I'd rather swap lead with the four of you than face the boss when he's mad. So light the fuse, if you want, and we'll all go to hell together."

Stu had tried his best, and went to step aside. "Suit yourselves. Die if you want to. I wash my hands of the whole mess."

Jess raised the Smith & Wesson. Warner's free arm rose, as if to shield his chest from the bullet. But suddenly Warner's arm snapped down and out, and a blade glinted dully in the starlight. In the blink of an eye he had Margaret in front of him and the knife pressed to the pale skin at the base of her throat. "See this? You've wasted enough of our time. Drop your guns or I'll slit her from ear to ear." To stress his point, Warner cut her just deep enough to draw blood.

Margaret cringed and reached for his knife arm but reconsidered. "Do as they want, Jess. It's no bluff. He would stab his own mother if Rankin told him to."

"Damn right I would," Warner bragged, and wagged the knife. "You've got ten seconds or I commence carving."

Stu, Steve, and Heck all looked to Jess, who slowly lowered his revolver. "This isn't over. We're comin' for you, and Rankin, too."

Warner chuckled. "Please do. There's nothing I'd like more than to splatter your brains all over creation." He began to back off. "What are you waiting for, Rufus? You go ahead. I'll make sure they stay put."

Margaret did not resist. She pretended to be resigned to her fate. But when they reached the edge of the clearing, she suddenly spun and raked Warner across the eyes with her fingernails. Bellowing in rage, he instinctively let go and pressed his hand to his face.

Jess Donner and the Texans charged. Stu joined them, unsure of what they intended to do but not wanting to be left out. Rufus tried to draw but Steve Ellsworth slammed the barrel of his Colt against the rat-faced man's temple and Rufus fell to his knees, his arms gone limp. A second blow pitched him to the earth unconscious.

Heck had his pistol out and tried to give Warner the same treatment but Warner somehow dodged and whirled and slashed at Jess Donner, who nimbly skipped aside.

Margaret ran past Stu, and Warner lunged, stabbing at her leg. Again he missed. Stu caught hold of Warner's wrist and declared, "It's over!" But Warner didn't agree. In a snarling surge of pure brute force, Warner tore loose.

A strange warm sensation filled Stu's belly, similar to the warmth brought on by a glass of good whiskey. He took a step back, or tried to. An equally strange lethargy had come over and his legs grew unaccountably weak.

Margaret and Ethel fled up the trail. Warner ran after them. Jess and Steve sped after him. Heck

Myers started to join the chase but stopped short as Stu's legs folded of their own accord.

"What's wrang, pard?"

Stu felt his friend's arms around him. "I think I've been stabbed."

Heck looked, and his Adam's apple bobbed. "The bastard!"

Not quite able to believe it, Stu tried to stand on his own power but couldn't. He had not seen the knife thrust; he did not feel any pain—only the peculiar warmth, which was spreading.

Heck bent and pried at Stu's shirt. "We're gettin' you to a sawbones, pronto."

"It's that bad?" Stu could not understand why he did not hurt. "If this is a joke, it's in poor taste." Again he tried to gather his legs under him but they refused to obey.

"Oh God," Heck said. He glanced up the trail and hollered, "Jess! Steve! Get back here!" But no answer was forthcoming. The faint crackling of underbrush explained why. "You'd best lie down," he suggested, and gently lowered Stu onto his back. "I won't be gone long. You have my range word."

An awful premonition came over Stu and he grasped his friend's hand. "Stay here." He was feeling worse, a lot worse—queasy and weak and dizzy all at once. "Please."

"I really need to find a doctor."

The warmth now filled Stu's chest and he could feel a moist sensation deep in his gullet. "Not like this," he said.

"What's that?" Heck leaned over him. "I couldn't quite hear you."

Stu opened his mouth to answer and was horror-struck when a warm liquid came coursing up out of his throat and he spewed blood all over himself and Heck's face and neck. He gagged, gasping for breath as more blood seeped from his nostrils. Frantic, he attempted to sit up but once again his body betrayed him. He was choking to death and could not do a thing to stop it.

Then Heck's arms were under him, and Heck propped him up. "Sweet Jesus! I'm gettin' you to a doc whether you like it or not."

Stu was too weak to resist or complain as Heck lifted him and headed back down the trail toward First Avenue. He could breathe but it took great effort, and his chin and chest were wet with blood. "First the mermaid, now this."

"All it will take is some stitchin' up, I bet," Heck said. "You'll be back on your feet quicker than you can holler howdy."

The stars disappeared. One second the night sky was filled with myriad shimmering pinpoints; the next it was black as pitch. Stu blinked but they did not reappear. "I'm not long for this world."

"Don't talk nonsense, pard," Heck chided.

Stu shut his eyes. He was tired, so very tired. All he wanted to do was curl into a ball and sleep.

"Don't you pass out on me, damn your hide! Just because you're from the East doesn't give you the right to give up." Emotion choked Heck's voice, and he stumbled.

Stu opened his eyes again, and now everything was black. The trees, the bushes, the whole world. He could not even see Heck. "It's like being in a tunnel."

"Hush, I said," Heck said sternly. "We're almost out of these woods. I seem to recollect there's a sawbones about two blocks west on Front Street."

"I've enjoyed being your friend." Stu had to speak with blood in his mouth; it sounded like the time he tried to talk under water when he was a kid. "You're a good man, Heck Myers."

"Damn you."

"Will you see that my mother gets the money I'm owed? Keep five dollars for yourself for going to the trouble."

Heck was moving faster. "There's the street! Hang on, you hear? You just hang on."

"Heck?" Stu said.

"If you don't shut up, I'll shoot you."

"One last thing. Would you ask Jess to kill the one who killed me? He shouldn't get away with it."

"Jess, hell." Heck's voice was strained. "I will buck out the son of a bitch myself, and I will give him your regards as I send him to hell."

"Like I said," Stu said, "you're a good man." He had a lot more to say, about how he had always looked forward to marrying a pretty girl one day, and raising a family, and being a better husband and father than his father ever was. About how sweet life tasted when death came calling. But he was too weak to talk. He smiled into the blackness, which was inside him now, and spreading. He could not feel his arms. Or his chest. Or anything else.

Chapter Nineteen

Jess Donner was mad at himself. So damn mad, he could scarcely think. Here he was, recklessly chasing a killer to save the lives of two women who had treated him and his friends as if they were nothing more than a child's playthings. A sensible man would let them reap what they had sown. A sensible man would not go up against a sidewinder like Lem Rankin.

But Jess couldn't help himself. God help him, but he liked Margaret Sanger. More than liked her, the truth be admitted. Those intimate moments in the dark booth at the dance hall had kindled an ember deep within him, a burning hunger he was trying hard to ignore since he couldn't seem to put it out no matter how hard he tried.

Jess was mad at her, too, for leading them on, and mad at Rankin for wanting to harm her. But most of all, he was furious with himself for caring about a woman who plainly didn't give a lick about him.

Sometimes, Jess reflected, as he barreled headlong down the path, life could kick a man where it hurt the most.

This wasn't the first time. Jess had been in love once before, or as close to love as a boy of twelve could get to the real article. Her name was Sally Mortinsen and she lived on a farm not far from his family's small ranch. He had known her since they were six; they played together at church socials and the like. In the one-room schoolhouse on Tomahawk Creek they sat next to each other and slipped notes back and forth when crusty old Mr. Danforth wasn't looking. During the midday break they often walked and talked or she would sit on the swing and he would push her. All purely kid stuff, until that magical day about midway through his twelfth year when he began to look at her differently. Something had happened. Something inside him changed. She wasn't just a friend any longer; she was a lot more.

The incredible thing was, she felt the same about him. Had for a while, Sally told him. According to her, girls grew up faster than boys, and she thought he was special long before he thought the same about her.

They took to holding hands when they were alone, and to trading shy pecks on the cheek. From there they graduated to kisses on the lips, and Jess would never, ever, as long as he lived, forget the sweet heady experience of that first moment when her mouth touched his. It made his head spin.

For two years they secretly courted, never letting on to others, never giving their parents an excuse to break them up. They talked of becoming man and wife when they were fifteen. His own parents had married at that age, and her grandmother had been wed when she was only fourteen.

Then a smallpox epidemic struck Texas, and hundreds died. There was no cure. No way to ease the suffering of those afflicted. To his great and lasting horror, Sally's family came down with it, and was quarantined. For a week he was a wreck, unable to sleep, unable to eat, deathly terrified of the inevitable outcome.

Sure enough, one bright sunny morning old Dr. Beaman's buggy came rattling up the road, and he stopped to inform Jess' folks that their good friends, the Mortinsens, were no more. Jess heard the doctor say that Sally had held on the longest, fighting tenaciously, her will to live the strongest the physician had ever seen. But in the end it was not enough and she succumbed.

Jess was crushed. He went about in a daze. He did his chores and went to school and all the rest, but he was numb inside, as dead to the world around him as Sally was in her grave.

Then Jess became mad. The more he thought about the injustice of it all, the madder he became. It was so unfair. Sally had been everything to him, and she was gone. What sort of world was it where a girl so sweet and pure could be so terribly afflicted, and die? What sort of God allowed that to happen?

It did not help that nearly everything Jess did, nearly everywhere he went, reminded him of her. The creek where they lazed away many a pleasant hour. The town where they gazed in store windows and dreamed of the day when they would have the many wondrous things on display. The church where they had played and laughed and been so very happy.

Finally Jess could not stand it anymore. He had to get away. He felt that he had to get out of Texas or he would put a pistol to his head and squeeze the trigger. So when he heard about a new cattle drive to Kansas, when he learned that Rafe Adams was in town hiring, he rode in and convinced Rafe to sign him on.

Jess never told his friends the truth. He had them believe he left home because his parents were holy terrors, but that wasn't true. His parents were as kind and decent as parents came, and they had been deeply saddened when he announced one evening at supper that he was leaving on the morrow for Kansas with a herd of three thousand cattle, and he would be gone for months. His mother tried to talk him out of it, saying he was too young and there were wild Indians along the way, and mentioning the wicked, wicked ways of cowtowns like Dodge. But his father merely smiled a sad sort of smile and bought him the Smith & Wesson he now held in his hand and the gun belt strapped around his waist.

A sharp cry from up ahead ended Jess's reverie. The trail ran straight as a yardstick for a dozen yards, and there, in the center, were Margaret and Ethel—and Warner. Apparently Ethel had tripped and fallen and Margaret was helping her up when Warner had overtaken them. He had Margaret by the arm and she was trying to haul Ethel to her feet, and at the very instant that Jess set eyes on them, Warner slapped Margaret across the month.

Jess should have shot him. He should have gunned the bastard then and there. But instead of squeezing the trigger, he brought the Smith & Wesson crashing down on the back of Warner's skull as the other man turned to confront him. Over and over and over Jess struck him, pistol-whipping Warner with a savagery Jess had never known he was capable of. Ten, fifteen, twenty times he struck, until Warner was prone at his feet and Warner's hat had fallen off and Warner's head was a mass of welts and gashes and oozing blood. Jess might have gone on beating the man indefinitely had Steve Ellsworth not seized his arm.

"Stop it, pard! You're killin' him!"

Jess' blood was roaring in his veins so loudly, Steve's cry almost didn't register. With great reluctance he lowered his arm and his dripping revolver and became aware that Margaret and Ethel had not run off, and Margaret was looking at him with a bewildered, quizzical expression.

"Hellfire!" Steve declared. "You damn near busted his skull. Are you hankerin' for a prison stay?"

"He shouldn't—" Jess said, but he did not finish the statement. He did not say *He shouldn't have put his hands on Margaret.* She was still staring strangely.

Steve offered Ethel his hand and she slowly rose, leaning against him as she did. "I'm glad you weren't hurt," he said thickly.

Ethel poked Warner with her foot. "When he

comes around, we better be long gone or there will be gunplay for sure."

"We'll take you to the boardinghouse," Steve offered. He wouldn't mind if she leaned against him forever but she stepped back and smoothed her dress.

"We don't deserve being treated this nice. Not after how we've treated you."

Margaret saw Jess Donner frown, and she did as she often did when she did not want someone to think poorly of her—she lied. "We were only doin' what Rankin makes us do. I had no desire to ask your friends to meet us." She thought she had been clever, and congratulated herself.

"How can that be?" Jess asked. "I recollect Vince sayin' that meetin' with us after hours was against Rankin's rules."

"Who are you going to believe, him or me?" Margaret demanded, but even to her ears her protest rang false.

Jess did not answer. He couldn't. He was choked with outrage that she had lied to him yet again. A pall fell over him—a pall of simmering anger and resentment and gloom. How could he be so stupid, he asked himself, as to care for a woman who cared so little for him?

Steve turned, took a step, and stopped. "Say. What happened to Heck and Stu? They should have caught up to us by now."

"Let's find out," Jess said. Anything to take his mind off Margaret and Sally Mortinsen and women in general.

The hoot of an owl was the only sound to break the stillness of the night as they hurried back the way they came. Jess brought up the rear. He was more depressed than he had been since Sally's death, and wanted nothing more than to be shed of Margaret. He could forgive her for lying to him once, but not for lying to him twice.

The clearing was empty save for the sprawled form of Rufus. Steve Ellsworth pushed his hat back and said in perplexity, "Where could they have gotten to? It's not like Heck to run off and leave us."

"Stu wouldn't, either," Jess said. He had grown to trust the New Yorker as much as the two Texans, which was saying a lot. He did not extend his trust readily.

Steve took a couple of steps, then stopped and hunkered and pressed his fingers to the grass. "This is blood. A lot of it."

"Pretend you're greased lightnin'," Jess said.

They ran, the women in their long dresses clinging to their legs, until Margaret called out, "Wait!" and picked up something lying beside the trail. "This is where we dropped our bags."

Jess and Steve quickly helped search. Two were in the brush, another lay in high weeds. The women were glad to have reclaimed their few belongings and smiled as they hastened on.

"Are we still leaving town on the morning stage?" Ethel whispered.

"What else can we do?" Margaret answered. "Rankin will be madder than ever. He'll have every weasel on his payroll out huntin' us. Unless we make ourselves scarce, we're liable to end up like Emily Conover."

"Who?" Steve asked. He always had had keen hearing. After the tall Southern belle had explained, he was stunned. "They kill women?" To him women were to be treated special. He had been raised to regard them as ladies, even when they weren't, and the notion of murdering a female was as despicable as despicable could be.

"Six or seven, by my count," Ethel said. "Probably a lot more."

"Of all the dance hall owners in Dodge, Rankin is the worst," Margaret said. "I'd heard stories before I went to work for him but I never figured they could be true. Most of the girls there were just as stupid as me."

Jess, too, had heard sordid accounts of how certain dance halls were run, and he could imagine the ordeal Margaret had been through.

"Signin' a contract to work for Rankin was the worst mistake I ever made," Margaret said. "My only excuse is that I had high hopes of savin' enough money to start a new life for myself. A decent life," she added meaningfully.

Jess caught her looking back at him and grew warm under the collar. He didn't believe her for a second. She had proven to be as sincere and trustworthy as a card sharp. Yet part of him *wanted* to believe, wanted to believe her badly.

The vegetation thinned. Steve spied the lamp in the boardinghouse window. He was so happy to be out of the dark, forbidding woods that he was slow in noticing a figure lying in the grass next to the boardinghouse sign. "Who's that?"

Jess took one look and drew the Smith & Wesson. He dashed past the women to protect them, if need be. Then he drew up in dismay. "No!"

Stu Wilkins was on his back, his arms folded across his chest, his hat on his hands. The white of his face contrasted starkly with the inky black of night.

"Stu?" Steve said and, after running up, dropped to one knee. He touched Stu's face, then pressed his fingers to Stu's neck, feeling for a pulse. "My God. He's dead, Jess! He's dead!"

Jess knelt and confirmed it was true. A cold fury seized him. His mouth went dry and his whole body shook. He had been skeptical of the New Yorker initially, since it had been his experience that Easterners were as worthless as teats on a boar when it came to riding and roping and ranching. But Stu Wilkins had shown him that even an Easterner could have grit.

"Who did this?" Steve wanted to know. He moved one of Stu's arms and tugged at Stu's blood-drenched shirt. "Look at this! He was stabbed."

"Warner," Jess said harshly, and stood.

"What should we do?" Steve realigned the shirt and replaced the arm. "Where's Heck, anyhow? How could he go off and leave his bunkie's body?"

"He went after the coyote responsible," Jess guessed. "It's what I would do if Warner had killed you."

Wiping his fingers on his pants, Steve stood. "Then why didn't we meet up with Heck in the woods?"

"Because Heck is going after the big man himself," Jess said. "He's after Rankin. I figure he'll cut across to Maple Street and take that to Fifth Avenue."

"Do you really think he would take on Rankin's bunch alone?" Steve was doubtful; Heck Myers had never killed a soul in his life. He was a cowpoke, not a shooter.

"Heck is a Texan, ain't he?" Jess said.

Margaret and Ethel were respectfully standing well back, but now Margaret came up and softly asked, "What will you do?"

"What else?" Jess faced west. "Heck is our pard. I just hope we don't get there too late." He beckoned to Steve and took a few steps, then paused and stared at Margaret. "I wish you all the best, wherever you end up." Touching his hat brim, he melted into the night.

"Wait for me!" Steve called. He yearned to talk to Ethel, but all he did was smile and mumble, "Sorry things didn't work out between us." Then he ran to catch up to Jess. He had never seen his friend so fiercely determined before. "Rankin must have a dozen guns at his beck and call. You realize that, don't you?"

"Maybe more," Jess said.

"Wouldn't it be smart to look up the marshal and let the law handle it?" Steve proposed.

"A man who won't fight his own battles is no

man at all," Jess said, summing up his sentiments. "And I don't care how many gun sharks Rankin has. Before this night is done, he'll be as dead as Stu. Or I will."

Chapter Twenty

Heck Myers had never had anyone die in his arms before. For that matter, he had only ever seen two people pass away. One was his grandfather, who died after a long and grueling illness that left him little more than skin and bones; the other was a young neighbor who was showing off at a church social and tried to jump a fence with his new horse, only to break his neck and crush half his ribs when the horse failed to clear the hurdle and both of them tumbled hard in the dust, with the horse on top.

In neither instance had Heck been overcome by shock. It was the natural order of things for people to die. Back east, more often than not, people died in bed. But not west of the Mississippi River. The frontier was as violent as it was vast, and it was said that, in Texas, not four men in ten lived to be fifty. So when his grandfather died and his friend was crushed, although sad a while, Heck was not so deeply troubled as to be in a state of stunned disbelief, as he was now.

Only vaguely aware of his surroundings, Heck walked toward the center of town. He did not know where he was going. He did not know what he was going to do. He only knew he could not bear to be near the body. He could not bear to look down on the pale, lifeless face of one of the best friends he ever had.

Stu Wilkins had been a top-notch pard. As a bunkie, Stu never complained about Heck's personal habits. Stu never minded that Heck was one of the loudest snorers in the outfit, or that Heck often forgot to remove his spurs before he turned in. Stu never once complained about Heck's fondness for tall tales, although nearly everyone else had at one time or another insinuated that Heck was born with a penny dreadful in his mouth. Stu was always willing to lend Heck money if Heck needed some. Stu was always there to listen and offer advice.

"Oh God," Heck breathed, and looked down at his bloodstained hands. He had loved Stu as a brother, and now Stu was gone.

Initially, Heck had his doubts. Stu was a city boy, born and reared in the largest city in America, and only a couple of years earlier had wound up in Texas. Their backgrounds, their worlds, were so different, that Heck was dubious they had anything in common. It didn't help that Heck tended to look down his nose at city boys as lazy and soft, and unable to do a decent day's work if their lives depended on it.

Stu Wilkins had proven him wrong. Never a shirker, Stu always did his share, and more. Stu was always willing to learn how to improve at everything he did, and took criticism for what it was worth. While it was common for city dwellers to put on airs and treat farmers and ranchers as if they were somehow inferior, Stu never did. For Stu, the measure of a person was in who he was, not where he came from.

Heck had grown as close to Stu as he ever had to anyone. They worked together, ate together, and slept together, forging a bond that only men who had lived under like circumstances could understand. And now to have Stu murdered right in front of his eyes, to lose his saddle brother so abruptly, was like having a cold steel blade plunged into his heart.

Heck had a sense that he should do something, and do it quickly, but what that might be eluded him. Grappling with his thoughts, he shuffled toward the lights. He could not stop staring at the blood on his fingers and palms. He could not stop thinking of Stu's final words. His eyes grew damp, and when he blinked, a tear trickled down his right cheek. But he refused to cry. His father always taught him that crying was for females, not grown men. After his grandfather had died, and he started to weep, his father had slapped him, hard, and warned that, if his son bawled, he would be taken out to the woodshed and treated to lashes from the hickory switch his father kept propped in one corner for just such an occasion.

"I will not cry," Heck said aloud, and then, to his great shame, tears streamed down his cheeks and he broke down and sobbed. Squatting, he covered his face with his arms and blubbered like he was six years old. Try as he might, and he did mightily try, he could not stem the flow.

How long Heck wept, he could not say. Eventually the tears stopped, and sniffling, he wiped his face with his sleeves, then straightened and gazed about him, afraid someone had seen. He was lucky. Somehow he had drifted off Fifth Avenue and was on a quiet side street with only a few houses.

"What to do?" Heck asked himself. The vermin responsible for Stu's death had to be punished. But he could not go up against the likes of Lem Rankin alone. He considered trying to find Jess and Steve, then had a better idea.

On a trail drive one man had all the answers. One man always knew exactly what to do in any situation. One man had the solution to every crisis. That one man was the trail boss.

Turning, Heck hurriedly bent his boots toward the Wright House. Rafe Adams might still be up, and if not, then Heck would get him up. Rafe always liked to say that, he could be counted on to stand by his hands through thick and through thin.

Now was the time to put that claim to the test.

Russian Vanes almost blundered into the arms of the law.

First Avenue was ahead. There, Rusty would turn left and in another block be at Rankin's Dance Hall. But he had forgotten about the earlier fracas, and had to dart into the shadows when a procession led by Deputy Trace Morgan filed by. Behind Morgan was a buckboard bearing the bodies of Rankin's three toughs, and behind the buckboard came two more tin stars and a small man in a derby.

"—expect you to find whoever was to blame and see to it they dance a strangulation jig!" the small man was loudly saying to the peace officers. "Mr. Rankin thinks it's an outrage that something like this could happen so close to his place."

"I bet he does, Tilly," said one of the other lawmen. "It's been a coon's age since anyone stood up to your boss."

"What's that supposed to mean?" Tilly snapped. "Mr. Rankin is a highly respected businessman, and is entitled to the same protection under the law as any other citizen of our fair community."

Trace Morgan had slowed to let the buckboard go by. "Your boss should have left Dodge with Luke Short and Earp and the rest of their kind. He's overstayed his welcome."

"A slanderous remark, sir," Tilly said indignantly.

"The truth always stings," Morgan said. "The plain of it is that the days of Dodge being a wide-open town where anything goes are over. It's only a matter of weeks before the mayor and the council pay him a visit and persuade him that Denver or Leadville has a healthier climate."

Tilly found that mildly humorous. "I would like to see anyone tell Lem Rankin he has to do something he doesn't want to."

"Forget him for right now," Morgan said. "I want

to know about Vince Shamblin. What was he up to? Who shot him?"

"Don't you think if I knew I would tell you? Vince had just finished work and was heading home. The same with Lee and Scotty."

"And all three just happened to be wearing firearms in violation of the town ordinance?" Morgan did not try to mask his scorn.

"These streets are unsafe late at night. Any reasonable man would do the same," Tilly said.

"A witness saw some cowboys run off. Your boss wouldn't happen to know who they were, would he?"

"I assure you, he wants to find them as much as you do."

The procession was almost out of earshot. The last Rusty heard was Morgan's statement; "The same witness also saw two women flee the scene. I don't suppose you have any idea who they were, either?"

Rusty did not hear Tilly's reply. He waited a minute to be safe, then glided to the junction. The lawmen were nearing Front Street. Far enough off that even if they glanced back, they would not notice the revolver at his waist. Paralleling the avenue, he stalked toward the dance hall. He paused when he came to where his brother had been shot. Dark stains marked where the rest of the bodies had fallen.

Light glowed in only one window in the dance hall. Rusty jogged toward it, then ducked behind the tree when the door opened and a lot of people filed out. He counted six men and two women. Any one of the men might be Lem Rankin. Palming the Colt, he was all set to rush them and blaze away when caution reared its head. The odds were too lopsided. They might gun him down before he put lead into Rankin—if, indeed, Rankin was with them.

"Quit dawdling, Moose!" someone hollered. "You're slower than molasses in January!"

A seventh man emerged, a towering bull whose massive chest and arms hinted at enormous strength. He closed the door and verified it was locked by giving it a hard shake. "I'm coming, Mr. Brady," he said.

In a group they made for Front Street. Some of the men were talking in hushed tones, the women merrily chattering and giggling.

Rusty strained his ears in the hope one of them would be called Rankin. He thought that a tall, good-looking drink of water in an expensive suit might be his prey, until Moose commented, "Some night tonight, huh, Mr. Brady?"

The tall man swore. "It's the kind of night we can do without. Three men dead, two girls missing."

"I can't get over Mr. Shamblin being killed," Moose said. "I always figured he was good with a gun."

"It doesn't matter how good someone is," Brady said. "There's always someone better."

Behind the tree, Rusty broke out in a smile.

"Do you reckon it was the girls who shot him?"

Moose asked. "Margaret and Ethel were always nice to me."

At that, the two women stopped giggling and a buxom beauty whose hair glinted red in the starlight said crisply, "Margaret Sanger put on more airs than a politician. She thought she was too good to be a dancer, and she was fixing to break her contract with Mr. Rankin. All this trouble is because of her."

"You tell him, Franny," encouraged the other lovely.

"Both of those girls were nothing but trouble," Franny said. "Always griping about how hard the work is. About the long hours and their sore feet and anything else they could carp about. Am I right, Chelsea?"

"More than right," Chelsea confirmed. "They were peculiar. You would think they were twins, the way they clung to one another." She paused. "If you ask me, they were jealous of you because Mr. Rankin favors you, and they were jealous of me because I'm your best friend."

Brady negligently waved a hand. "Enough of this hen talk, ladies. Frankly, I don't care why Margaret and Ethel have flown the coop. The important thing is that Mr. Rankin wants them brought back to face his wrath. That's why he's offering a reward."

"A thousand dollars!" Moose exclaimed. "That's more money than I've ever seen in my whole life. I'd give anything to earn that much."

"You're not the only one," Brady said, "which is

why Mr. Rankin is having the word spread. By morning it will be all over Dodge."

"Why so much?" Franny criticized. "Usually he only offers a hundred."

"Several reasons. First, if Sanger and Heatherton get away, it might give the other girls ideas. Second, Vince, Scotty, and Lee are dead because of them, and Mr. Rankin can't let their deaths go unpunished. It would be taken as a sign of weakness."

"The third reason?" Franny prompted.

"They insulted Mr. Rankin personally. He called them into his office and gave them some friendly advice, and they threw it in his face."

There was more, but Rusty didn't listen. He was thinking about the thousand-dollar reward. Yes, it was a lot of money, but to him it was something more. Grat would be proud of the idea he had, and he grinned as he peered past the tree at the retreating figures.

Rusty was pondering how best to go about finding Sanger and Heatherton when spurs jingled lightly on the breeze and skulking shadows slunk toward the dance hall from the direction of the vegetation bordering the river. When the men discovered the door was locked and no one answered their knock, they came up Fifth toward him.

Rusty indulged in another smile. Things were working out better than he dared to hope. He drew his Colt, and when the men were abreast of the oak, he stepped from concealment. "Hold it right there."

Jess Donner dropped his hand to his Smith &

Wesson but didn't draw. "You!" he exclaimed. "Come back to finish what you started?"

"Where's your brother?" Steve Ellsworth asked. "Fixin' to shoot us in the back?" He twisted and scoured the lot.

"Grat is dead," Rusty informed them. "And if I wanted you two jackasses to join him, I'd have made wolf bait of you before you could blink."

"Then what are you doin' here?" Jess demanded.

"You first, cowpoke," Rusty said.

"We're after Lem Rankin. One of our pards is dead on account of him, and we're out to give Rankin a taste of his own poison." Jess motioned. 'So if you're not after us, out of our way. Time's a-wastin'.'"

Rusty stayed where he was. "We have somethin' in common. Rankin's men killed my brother. I owe the bastard, too. But I can't walk up to him and put a bullet between his eyes. Not alone. He has too many gunnies workin' for him."

"So?" Jess said impatiently.

"So why don't we join up?" Rusty suggested. "I'll help you and you help me. Between us, Rankin is a goner."

"What kind of game are you playin'? Less than an hour ago you were more than willin' to shed our blood."

"That was then, this is now." Rusty holstered his Colt to convince them he was sincere. "My brother was the only kin I had left. I want Rankin dead more than anything, and I'm willin' to forget our misunderstandin's if you are. What do you say?"

"I don't trust you," Jess Donner said.

Steve Ellsworth was rubbing the peach fuzz on his chin. "Neither do I, pard, but we can use him. He's got one talent we lack."

"What's that?" Jess asked.

"He likes to kill folks."

Chapter Twenty-one

"Why are we waiting for?" Ethel Heatherton asked. She did not like standing near the dead cowboy. She did not like being near dead people, period. When she was small—six or seven, she could never quite remember which—a severe influenza epidemic struck Chicago, where she was born and raised. Hundreds perished, including two cousins, an uncle, and her great-grandmother. She had had to attend all their funerals. Her mother made her. To this day she could not think of their sickly white faces and their stiff bodies without shuddering.

"Pardon?" Margaret Sanger was staring in the direction the cowboys had taken.

"We need to find somewhere to lie low until the morning stage to Denver," Ethel reminded her. "Let's go before more of Rankin's men show up."

"Did you see him?" Margaret asked.

"See who?"

"Jess. How he stepped in front of me when the lead was fixin' to fly? Wasn't that sweet?" Margaret asked. "Wasn't that the sweetest thing you ever saw?"

"He might have stepped in front of you by mistake."

"No, he did it on purpose," Margaret said. She had never been so shocked in her life. No one had ever done anything like that for her. "He was willin' to take a bullet for me."

Ethel anxiously regarded the darkness that hemmed them in. "Don't make more out of it than there was. How about if we find a restaurant? I'm hungry."

"How can you eat with all that's been happenin'?" Margaret could not stop thinking about Jess Donner, about the look he had given her right before he hurried off.

"When I get nervous, I get hungry," Ethel said. "Right now I could eat an entire cow, horns and all."

Margaret made no move to go anywhere. "He must really and truly care for me to do somethin' like that. Although, bein' male, he won't admit it, even to himself."

Ethel sighed in irritation. "This is that blacksmith all over again? You remember. The one you were sure you were in love with? The one you pined after for weeks?"

"That was different," Margaret said. "I was fond of him but he wasn't fond of me. Jess is, I tell you, and he proved it the only way a man can."

"Your flights of fancy will be the death of us," Ethel scolded. "Lem Rankin will be out to bury us, and I, for one, do not intend to make it easy for him to fill the graves."

"Go on without me."

Ethel was thunderstruck. Dropping her bags, she gripped Margaret's arms and shook her. "What's gotten into you? You're talking crazy. I thought we were friends. More than friends."

"We are," Margaret conceded. "But someone else can mean something to me, too." She pulled free and took a few halting steps. "I have to give it a try or I'll be wonderin' for the rest of my born days."

"My God," Ethel declared. "You're serious? But he's a cowboy, for crying out loud. He's lucky if he makes fifty dollars a month. Why settle for him when you can snare a man with money?"

"The truth?" Margaret said. "When he and I were in that both and I was feedin' him the usual lies, I felt a twinge."

"Indigestion?" Ethel said hopefully.

"No, silly. A twinge of my heartstrings. There's somethin' about him, somethin' I can't quite explain. I like him, and I want to get to know him better. A lot better." Margaret squared her shoulders, her mind made up. "I don't expect you to put your life in danger by taggin' along. Stick to our original plan and catch the stage."

For a few moments Ethel was speechless. Then she whined like a puppy that had just been kicked and bleated, "You would leave me? Just like that?" She snapped her fingers. "Without so much as a hug or a kiss?"

"It's not that I *want* to do this," Margaret said.

"It's that I *have* to." She headed across the street and into the next yard.

"Wait, damn you!" Ethel could not believe what was happening. Laden with her bags, she had to run to catch up. "Didn't you hear me? We should talk this out."

"I've said all that needs sayin'," Margaret disagreed. "Maybe I'm makin' the biggest mistake of my life, and Lord knows, I've made a lot, but it's my mistake to make, come good or bad."

"Please," Ethel pleaded, "stop and hear me out. Another couple of minutes won't make a difference if it's true love."

Margaret did not stop. "That was uncalled for. I'd never mock you if you lost your heart to someone."

"So long as it was my heart and not my head," Ethel said. "This is too sudden to be real."

"Cupid shoots arrows. He doesn't throw horseshoes. How slow does love have to be to meet your approval?"

"So you think it really is love?" Ethel used words that would turn a minister scarlet. "Will you listen to yourself? You've always had a soft spot for the young ones, but I never thought you would step off a cliff for one."

Margaret refused to respond. She was disappointed. Her girlfriend, of all people, should realize how important this was to her.

"You're only guessing he cares for you," Ethel said, trying another tack. "He could despise you, for all you know, for leading him on like you did."

"I'll ask him when we find them," Margaret said, for her own peace of mind, if for no other reason.

Ethel's annoyance knew no limits. She had never wanted to risk Rankin's anger by running off in the first place. She had let Margaret talk her into it. Now, on the verge of making their escape, Margaret was walking back into the lion's den with no consideration for *her* feelings. "Every step we take puts us in that much greater danger."

"They can't be that far ahead," Margaret said. "Jess will protect us."

"Have you forgotten how many gun sharks work for Rankin?" When Ethel did not receive an answer, she muttered, "Fine. Be this way. But for both our sakes I hope you're right."

The night clerk at the Wright House stifled a yawn as he looked up from the *Police Gazette* he was reading. "Can I help you?" He did not sound eager to be of any assistance.

"I'm lookin' for my trail boss," Heck Myers said. "Rafe Adams. He's supposed to be stayin' the night. Which room is he in?"

The clerk consulted the register. "We have no one by that name staying here. Perhaps you have the wrong hotel."

"Wrong, hell," Heck spat. He had half a mind to march up the stairs and start bellowing Rafe's name. Instead, he pointed at the two chairs Rafe and Tom Cambry had occupied. "They were sittin' there for hours. You must have noticed them."

"Oh. Those two. They haven't taken a room. I

heard them say something about stretching their legs and getting a cup of coffee."

"Did you happen to hear where?" Heck was worried sick that Jess and Steve would end up like Stu Wilkins unless he rustled up help, and quick.

"They went left when they stepped out the door, so I assume they went to Miss Betsy's restaurant just down the street."

Heck was in such a hurry, he nearly collided with a man in a bowler as he barreled down the sidewalk. "Sorry," he apologized.

"Hold it, sonny."

Slowing, Heck said, "I told you I was sorry." Then he saw the badge pinned to the man's vest, and he did as he had been told. "You're a lawdog."

"Marshal Bridges. Are you aware of the city ordinance that prohibits the wearing of firearms within the city limits?"

Heck glanced down at his gun belt. In all the excitement, he had forgotten he was wearing his gun. "Yes, sir, I am."

"Then I will thank you to hand yours over." The marshal held out his left hand. "You can claim it at the jail when you leave."

"I need it," Heck said. With the Vanes brothers running around, he refused to be disarmed.

"You don't have a choice, son," Marshal Bridges said. "The law is the law and it's my job to enforce it." He wagged his arm. "Come on. I don't have all night. I was on my way home to catch some sleep."

"Can't you pretend you didn't see it?" Heck asked. To his way of thinking, it was an ordinary request, and he was unprepared for what the lawman did next, namely, drawing a pistol and pointing it at him.

"All right. Either you're drunk or you're loco. Unstrap your shooting iron and hand it over or you will not like the consequences."

"Let me explain," Heck said, confident that once he had, the lawman would sympathize. "My pard, Stu, was—" But he got no further. Metal flashed in the light spilling from the Wright House and pain exploded in his head. He felt his knees strike the boards and he swayed like a reed in a strong wind but he stayed conscious. "You had no call to do that."

"I have lost my patience with you cowherders," the marshal said. "You think the law doesn't apply to you, that you should have free rein to shoot up the town whenever it strikes your fancy."

"No, no," Heck said thickly. His tongue would not cooperate and the world was spinning. "It's not like that at all."

"Tell it to the judge."

Iran fingers gripped Heck's shirt and he was roughly hauled to his feet. "Stop that," he protested, and swatted at the marshal's arm. He only wanted to explain but his action was misconstrued, and his head exploded in agony a second time. The next thing he knew, he opened his eyes and he was lying on his back on a hard surface and a barred window was above him. "Where am I?" he wondered groggily.

"We've got us a smart one here, Billy," someone said, and cackled.

"Nursing cows for a living must not take much brains, Lester," the one called Billy tittered. "I've yet to meet one of these saddle stiffs who can count to twenty without taking off his boots."

Heck sat up and involuntarily groaned. His head felt as if he had been trampled by a bull The sight of a barred door jolted him into blurting, "I'm in jail!"

"Yes, sir. A real genius," Billy remarked. He was a townsman, not much older than Heck, with pock-marked cheeks and a crooked nose. "Are you in awe, Lester?"

"I'm in awe." Lester was a lump of clay with two chins. His shirt was too small, his jacket too tight.

Their taunts were grating on Heck's nerves. "Did the marshal hire you as comedians or do you work for free?"

"Sassy genius, ain't he?" Billy said. "Makes you want to kick his teeth down his throat."

"I'd like to see you try," Heck snapped. He put his hands flat on the floor and rose unsteadily to his feet. The cell was shared by three others: an old man snoring in his own vomit; a bearded frontiersman in buckskins, who was hunkered under the window with his arms wrapped around his legs; and a farmer in homespun. The cell reeked from a mix of unsavory odors.

"Should we bust him one?" Lester asked Billy.

"Nah. The deputies might hear, and the judge will add to our sentence." Billy grinned at Heck. "Ten days for drunk and disorderly. It doesn't hardly seem fair, given as how all we did was break a few windows."

Heck shambled to the door and gripped the bars. A narrow, murky hall led to a closed wooden door. From the other side came voices. "Marshal!" he hollered. "I'd like a word with you! There's been a mistake!"

"And you're making it," Billy said. "They don't like it when someone raises a fuss."

"Marshal!" Heck tried to shake the bars but they were too firmly imbedded. "I'm not supposed to be in here!" In frustration he kicked the bars, and now his foot hurt almost as much as his head.

The rasp of a bolt being thrown heralded the opening of the door, and down the hall came a familiar figure.

"Deputy Morgan!" Heck said. "You remember me, don't you? You talked to my friends and me about behavin' while we were in Dodge."

"I give that speech to a lot of cowboys," Morgan stated. "And in your case it must have gone in one ear and out the other. You were brought in for wearing a sidearm, I'm told."

"But I had an excuse," Heck sought to justify his mistake. "The marshal wouldn't listen but maybe you will."

Morgan tiredly rubbed his eyes, then said, "No, boy, I won't. I don't much like troublemakers. You've admitted I talked to you, yet you broke the law anyway. Do yourself a favor and take your medicine like a man."

"You've got to hear me out!" Heck cried, and

would have told him about Stu and Rankin's men but Morgan held up a hand.

"Like hell I do. I'm busy, boy. We have three bodies over to the undertaker's, and a fourth was found a few minutes ago. I'm on my way now to fetch it. So you sit back down and behave, you hear?"

"But—"

Morgan's fist flicked between the bars. Taken unawares, Heck was rocked onto his bootheels by the blow. He tasted blood in his mouth and heard the mocking mirth of Billy and Lester. "First the marshal. Now you. That was uncalled for."

"Maybe so," Deputy Morgan conceded, "but I warned you my patience was wearing thin." Wheeling, he added, "Don't let there be a next time."

Heck leaned his forehead against the bars, swallowed a mouthful of blood, and fought down an impulse to scream in rising rage. Now he couldn't get word to Rafe Adams until he was released. Jess and Steve were on their own, and anything could happen to them.

Chances were, come dawn, Stu Wilkins wouldn't be the only one in the outfit being measured for a pine box.

Chapter Twenty-two

Steve Ellsworth did not trust Rusty Vanes any more than he would trust a coiled rattler not to strike, but he had been sincere when he said that Vanes' willingness to throw lead would come in handy should they succeed in tracking down Lem Rankin—especially given the mood his pard was in. He had never seen Jess Donner so grim, so determined to shed blood. "I still think it's a good idea to let the law know about Stu," he commented as they came to Front Street.

Rusty Vanes snorted. "Shows how much you know, cowboy. Rankin has most of the lawmen in town in his pocket."

"There has to be one who isn't."

"I hear tell that Trace Morgan is his own man," Rusty said. "But do you really think they'll take the word of a shiftless no-account like you against that of a leadin' pillar of the community like Rankin?" Rusty shook his head. "Without proof that Rankin was to blame, there's not a thing the law can do."

"He's right," Jess Donner reluctantly admitted. To say he was bewildered by Steve suggesting they temporarily ally themselves with Vanes was an understatement. He wanted nothing to do with the leather slapper, and would as soon deal with Lem Rankin on their own. But he had to admit Vanes was canny as a fox, and he liked the idea the killer had come up with. "Do you see them anywhere?"

"There!" Rusty said, pointing and grinning. "I told you we would catch up to them if we hurried."

A party of seven men and two women were entering a restaurant.

"The walkin' mountain is called Moose," Rusty related. "The tall galoot in the fancy duds is Brady. From what I gather, he's one of Rankin's lieutenants. The women I don't know much about other than their names."

"Franny and Chelsea," Steve Ellsworth said, his emotions tugging at his heartstrings. "We've met them." He was still smitten by Franny, but the fact she worked for the sidewinder they held accountable for Stu's death tempered his fondness.

"I never was one for lettin' moss grow under me," Rusty commented, and started across the street.

Jess immediately trailed after him but Steve dragged his heels. "I'm still not sure this is the best way to go about it," he grumbled.

"They're bound to know where Rankin lives," Jess said. "And remember. They have no idea who we are. To them we're just two more cowpokes. So if we do this right, there shouldn't be a problem."

"If you say so," Steve said. But they were taking an awful gamble, and if things went wrong, word would reach Rankin that they were after him.

The front window was ablaze with yellow light. Despite the late hour, the restaurant was packed; Dodge had more night owls than most any town in the West. Painted on the window was MISS BETSY'S.

Rusty Vanes hooked his thumbs in his gun belt and strolled inside. Jess was in the doorway when two men rose from a corner table and one of them handed money to a middle-aged woman in a checkered apron. Instantly he spun, beckoned to his bunkie, and darted around the corner.

"What's gotten into you?" Steve asked. He assumed Jess had changed his mind about working with Vanes.

"The boss and the *segundo* are in there," Jess informed him. "If they see us, they'll want to know what we're up to."

Steve understood. They would have to lie, and lying to Rafe Adams did not sit well with their trail boss. Rafe had always treated them decent and deserved the same in return. "What do we do? Vanes will think we've ditched him."

"Rafe and Tom are on their way out," Jess whispered. "We'll go in as soon as it's safe."

The door opened and boots thumped the sidewalk. Steve dared to peek out and saw Rafe's broad shoulders and Tom's red bandanna recede into the darkness. He felt an almost overpowering urge to run to them and tell Rafe about Stu, but he didn't. "They're gone."

Rusty Vanes had taken a corner table at the front and was drumming his fingers on it. "Where did you two get to? I thought maybe you had gotten cold feet."

Sliding onto a chair, Jess leaned toward him. "Call me yellow again and you'll be joinin' your brother in hell."

Steve braced for an explosion. Rusty Vanes was not the kind to meekly abide a threat. But strangely enough, all Vanes did was shrug as if Jess's remarks were of no consequence. "Our trail boss just left. We didn't want him to see us."

The group from the dance hall was at a table toward the back. The woman in the checkered apron was taking their orders.

"How do we go about this?" Steve asked. "It's not like we can walk up to them and ask for Rankin's address."

"One of us has to talk to them," Rusty said. "Act real friendly and get them to babble about their boss."

"I'll go," Jess offered.

Steve surprised himself by saying, "No. It has to be me. Franny will remember me from earlier." He would rather walk barefoot across broken glass but he rose and ambled to their table and plastered a smile on his face. "How do you do, ladies?" he said, touching his hat brim and giving a little bow. "Found much use for that parasol yet?"

Franny Brice had been whispering into Chelsea's ear. Looking up, she grinned and declared, "Well, look who it is. Steve Raphael Ellsworth. Enjoying a night on the town, are you, cowboy?"

"Who's this?" the one called Brady suspiciously asked.

"Relax. He's harmless," Franny said. "We met this afternoon and he gave me his parasol."

"*His* parasol?" Brady repeated, and laughed. So did several of the others.

Steve's ears were burning but he coughed to clear his throat and indicated an empty chair next to Franny's. "Mind if I join you for a bit?"

"Yes," Brady said.

Franny patted the chair and crooked a finger. "Pay him no mind, cowboy. He wouldn't know a good mood if he sat on it. Sure, you can join us. How about a coffee on me? It's the least I can do for that nice new parasol."

"Thanks, but a gentleman never lets a lady do the buyin'." Steve's legs were weak, because he was so close to her, and he was more than glad to sit down. He held out his hand to Brady. "A pleasure to meet you too, sir."

Brady scowled but shook. "You've got manners. I'll give you that." He winked, then lewdly asked, "Fancy our buxom redhead, do you, boy?"

"Brady!" Franny scolded, but she giggled merrily.

Steve would just as soon have punched the man in the mouth but he willed himself to relax and go on smiling and said, "She's about the prettiest woman I've ever seen. But I know a cow pusher like me would never have any kind of chance with her."

"You've got that right," one of the other men said.

Franny scolded him, too. "Be nice, Miles. Or have you forgotten what it's like to be his age?" She touched her hand to Steve's chin. "Were I ten years younger, I could do a lot worse."

"Make that fifteen years," Chelsea said. "You started young, remember?"

Both women tittered at their private joke.

Steve noticed Moose glowering at him. Remembering his father's advice that it was always easier to disarm someone with a smile than with a gun, he said, "You must be the biggest gent alive. I wish I had your muscles. I could carry a grown cow on my shoulders."

Clearly flattered, Moose lost some of the scowl. "I picked up a cow once. On a bet. My pa was awful proud of me that day."

"Spare us your farm stories," Brady said.

Steve was desperately trying to think of how to broach the subject of Rankin without seeming to. "I went to the dance hall tonight for that dance you promised," he told Franny, "but I didn't see you anywhere."

"I was there. But finding one person in that crowd is like finding a needle in a haystack. Try again tomorrow night."

"It sure was crowded," Steve agreed. "Whoever owns it must be makin' more money than old King Midas."

"That would be Lem Rankin," Franny said. "And

you're right. He's one of the richest men in all of Kansas."

"I'd like to be rich," Steve said. "Have me a mansion with servants and a carriage to take me everywhere." He held his breath, hoping she would take the bait.

"Lem doesn't live in a mansion but his house is the grandest around. Twenty-two rooms and an indoor convenience. I wouldn't mind living there myself," Franny confessed.

"Twenty-two?" Steve pretended to be awed. "I haven't come across a house in town that size."

"Oh, he lives out a ways," Franny said, but she did not say exactly where.

"On the prairie? Isn't he afraid of losin' his scalp to Injuns?" Steve knew there had not been Indian trouble in that vicinity for years, but he could learn more by playing dumb.

Brady fell for it. "Those were the old days, boy. Besides, Mr. Rankin's place is only a mile east of town. Hostiles never venture in that close."

"I still wouldn't feel safe," Steve said. "Not without a small army to protect me."

"Oh, Mr. Rankin has that, all right," Brady assured him. "He's made a few enemies in his time and he takes precautions. You couldn't get anywhere near his house without his guards or his dog spotting you."

Steve had learned all he needed to learn, and he was eager to pass on the information to Jess and Vanes, but just then the aproned matron returned, bearing a tray. She set a steaming cup of black coffee in front of him and he thanked her.

"You must think you're one tough customer," Brady unexpectedly remarked.

Steve had taken a sip and the coffee was scalding a fiery path down his throat. Coughing, he responded, "What makes you say that?"

"You're walking around with your six-gun in plain sight." Brady patted a bulge under his jacket. "Anyone with a half a brain keeps his hardware concealed."

"I'm plannin' to rejoin my outfit as soon as I'm done here." Steve had not forgotten about the firearms ordinance, and he had his eyes peeled for anyone wearing a badge.

"We're heading out to Rankin's," Franny casually disclosed.

"Three guesses why," Chelsea said, and playfully winked at the redhead.

An image of Franny and Rankin in bed filled Steve's head and he dispelled it with a vigorous shake. "I hope he doesn't resent me givin' you that parasol."

"Not at all," Franny said. "Men bring gifts for me all the time. Most don't know about Rankin and me, and try to win my heart with a cheap ring or necklace or a bottle of lilac water—as if I would ever stoop to marry a clerk or a cowboy." She paused. "No offense meant."

"None taken," Steve said, but any lingering fondness he had felt for her evaporated like dew under the hot sun. She was just another pretty filly who used her body to wrap men around her little finger. In Texas there was a word for that, but not a word a man used in mixed company.

"Most of the stuff I throw out," Franny said as she put her hand on Steve's arm. "But not your parasol. I like it. And it was sweet of you to be so kind."

"That's me. Kind as they come. My ma always said that if you can't be nice to people, you shouldn't bother gettin' out of bed."

Moose was spearing a fork into a piece of apple pie. "My ma used to say pretty much the same thing," he said with his mouth full. "She was always nice to everyone."

"And look at where it got her," Brady said. "She died dirt poor in the dead of winter. Froze to death because she couldn't afford a meal and was too weak to buy firewood or an ax to chop some."

"I wish you wouldn't keep reminding me of that, Mr. Brady." Moose's features clouded with sorrow. "I blame myself for not being there when she needed me."

"Finish your pie," Brady said gruffly. "It's late, and we have a long ride ahead of us."

Steve steeled himself and gulped the rest of his coffee. Setting the cup down, he fished the right amount from his pocket and went to place the coins on the table.

"No, you don't," Franny said. "It's on me. And if you show up at the dance hall tonight, I'll save a dance for you."

Steve had heard that one before. "I'm obliged."

Rising, he touched his hat and jangled to the front of the restaurant.

"Well?" Jess eagerly asked. "Did you find out where the polecat lives?"

"That I did," Steve said.

Rusty Vanes stirred. "Is it a secret or do I have to beat it out of you?"

Reminding himself that polecats could not help being polecats, Steve imparted the information he had learned. "We won't be able to get anywhere near Rankin until he comes back into town."

"That's what you think," Rusty Vanes said.

"What about the guards and the dog?" Steve did not like how Jess's brow was knit, as if he were seriously considering going out there. "I want to make Rankin pay as much as you do, but I'd rather go on breathin' once I'm done."

Franny Brice came sashaying toward the door. Her lustrous red hair, her full red lips, and the sweep of her dress drew the gaze of every male on the premises. Stopping next to Steve's chair, she winked and said, "See you around, cowboy."

Steve breathed deep of her perfume but it had no effect. "See you around," he said. He was one of the few men there who did not watch her go out.

"We'll give them a ten-minute head start," Jess said. "That should be enough." He shifted toward the front window. "I only wish Heck was here. Where in blazes did he get to?"

Steve's wish was that his partner would come to his senses. "We should think this through better."

"I aim to do my thinkin' with my hogleg," was Jess's rejoinder.

The ten minutes passed much too swiftly for Steve's liking. His head bowed in thought, he followed the other two down the street to claim their mounts. The people he passed might as well have been ghosts. Then perfume tingled his nose, different perfume from that which Franny Brice wore, but a perfume he knew just as well, and he glanced up, flabbergasted, as Margaret Sanger and Ethel Heatherton came out of the shadows.

Chapter Twenty-three

Rusty Vanes always did have luck. A lot of it. The first time he could remember was when he was ten. His ma had baked a cherry pie and set it on the windowsill to cool. She told Grat and him not to touch it and went off to hang clothes on the line. Grat had to go help their pa rig a pump for the well, leaving Rusty alone in the house.

He had stared at that pie for the longest while. He stood at the window and sniffed the delicious aroma. He picked it up and felt how warm it was. His mouth watered and his stomach growled, and before he could stop himself, he dipped his fingers into the pie and scooped out a handful of sugary cherries and crust and crammed it into his mouth. Once he started, he couldn't stop. He ate and ate until he had an ache in his guts and there was barely a quarter of the pie left.

The enormity of what he had done sank in, and Rusty dropped the pie pan on the floor and ran out the back door and off into the corn field. His ma would he upset and scold him. His pa would be plain out mad and haul him to the woodshed. Rusty hated that more than anything. His pa kept a hickory stick there and was not averse to using it. Quite the contrary. It wasn't uncommon for his pa to hit him forty or fifty times. He would be so sore and bruised, he wouldn't be able to sit for a week.

So Rusty had crouched among the cornstalks, his heart hammering wildly, and frantically licked his fingers and palms clean while debating whether he should run away. When he heard his ma screech, he almost did. But then he heard his pa bellow in anger, and rising onto the tips of his toes, he beheld his pa dragging their dog out the back door by the scruff of its neck. In his other hand, his pa had the shotgun that always hung over the fireplace.

"Eat our food, will you?" his pa had raged, and as Rusty looked on, his pa pointed the shotgun at their cowering dog and fired both barrels.

Rusty had liked that dog. They called it Daisy even though it was a boy dog because once, when it was a puppy, it was playing in the yard and waddled up to the porch with a clump of daisies in its mouth. Rusty walked out of the corn and stared at the brains and tufts of hair and the pitifully few shreds left of Daisy's head. "You killed him, Pa."

"It had to be done, Russian. He ate your ma's pie, and a dog that will do that once will make a habit of it."

Any sadness Rusty felt at Daisy's death was eclipsed by the sweetly giddy feeling that he had gotten away with eating the pie and not been punished. The dog had come along and licked at the pan on the floor just as his ma happened to walk in, and she naturally assumed Daisy had eaten the rest.

Luck.

Once, at school, during the midday break when everyone was outside, Rusty snuck in through the side window and helped himself to several coins he had seen the teacher put in a drawer. As he slipped out the window, another boy came in the door after an apple he had brought from home to snack on.

Their teacher saw the other boy enter the schoolhouse and come back out; he did not spot Rusty. So when the coins turned up missing, the teacher leaped to the wrong conclusion and blamed the other boy.

Luck.

Similar incidents convinced Rusty he was born naturally lucky. He stole and wasn't caught. He lied and was believed. But the most memorable event of his early life was that day at the rock quarry.

Kids often went there on hot summer days to frolic in the pond at the base of a low cliff. The bravest would leap from the cliff into the water, which was not all that deep. Grat jumped without fear. But Rusty was younger and not much of a swimmer, so he always refused.

That day, several of the older boys were teasing him, taunting him to give it a try. One boy, in particular, would not stop egging him on. A straw-haired bully nicknamed Porker who liked to pick on anyone younger and smaller than he was. That day, Porker called Rusty a coward and a sissy, and said that they should put a dress on him so everyone would know he was a girl and not a boy.

Grat stood up for Rusty, and Porker and Grat nearly came to blows. Then the older boys ran up the trail to the top of the cliff to jump. Rusty was the only other kid there that morning, and he walked around the pond to the shadowy base of the cliff and waded out until the water came as high as his knees. The bottom was littered with rocks, and groping about, he found one about the size of a hen's egg.

The boys jumped in turns. Grat was first, then another, and they came to the surface with their backs to him. Rusty heard Porker whoop for joy and saw Porker in midair with his knees tucked to his chest to make a big splash.

Rusty threw the rock with all his might. He just wanted to hurt Porker. He was not consciously trying to hit Porker in the head, but that was exactly where the rock caught him, and only Rusty saw. Porker went under and did not reappear. The other boys laughed, thinking it was another of Porker's stunts, until the body bobbed to the surface.

The sheriff came, and the doctor examined Porker and decided his death was an accident, that Porker had struck his head on the bottom hard enough to knock him out, and drowned.

Luck yet again.

And now the two women Rusty was most anxious to find came walking out of the night. He smiled at his stroke of fortune, and they froze in surprise.

"What the devil is *he* doin' here?" Margaret Sanger exclaimed.

"He's helpin' us," Jess Donner said. The sight of her had set his blood to racing but he refused to show it.

Ethel was poised to flee. "A while ago he was all set to kill us. How can you trust him?"

"Hear us out," Steve Ellsworth coaxed, and explained about Grat, and how Rusty was out for revenge, the same as they were. "So we've partnered up until Rankin is taken care of."

Rusty could see the women were still skeptical. Since he did not want them to run off, he said, "I don't blame you for bein' scared. But the last thing I would ever do is harm a hair on your pretty heads. Honest." Especially since they would be much more useful to him than the two cowboys.

"You expect us to believe you?" Margaret frowned at Jess. "I credited you with more smarts than this. Here I was, worried sick about you, and now I find out you have a death wish."

"You were worried about me?"

Steve Ellsworth stepped close to Ethel. "What's goin' on? I thought you planned to lie low and take the mornin' stage out."

"I still would," Ethel said, "but where Margaret goes, I go, and she's grown powerful fond of your friend." Her resentment shone through.

Jess Donner stared hard at Margaret. "What's this

all about? I'm just another set of britches as far as you're concerned."

"That was harsh," Margaret said. "I'm sorry for what I did. It was wrong. Terribly wrong. And it won't ever happen again."

"It sure won't," Jess vowed, "because I won't let it. I might be thickheaded but I'm not solid bone between the ears."

Margaret's eyes brimmed with tears. "Please don't talk like that. This isn't easy." She dabbed at an eye. "We're here to help. We want Rankin dead, too."

Ethel, startled, blurted out, "We do? Since when?"

"It's him or us," Margaret said. "Or would you rather be lookin' over your shoulder the rest of your life? There's only one way to be sure."

"I could never kill someone," Ethel said.

Rusty seized the moment to say, "I can. And have. Which is why you need me. None of you has ever shot anyone before. I could blow out the wicks of half the human race and not lose a minute's sleep."

Jess Donner patted his Smith & Wesson. "You're not so special. I can pull the trigger if I have to."

"You hope," Rusty said, careful not to make it sound like an insult. "A lot of hombres think they can, but when they have it to, they can't. It's not that they're yellow or weak. They just can't." He had seen it before.

Steve Ellsworth gazed up and down Front Street. "All this talk is well and dandy, but we shouldn't be standin' out in the open like this. What if a lawman comes along and sees our pistols?" He moved toward a gap between the next two buildings, where the light barely penetrated.

Rusty entered last and leaned against a wall. He would play along a while yet, he decided, and spring his surprise when they were off guard.

Ellsworth faced the women. "This is where we part company. We're on our way to Rankin's house and lead is liable to fly."

"We're going with you," Margaret said.

Ethel swore, and Steve almost did. "Don't be silly. What are you tryin' to prove? You've escaped Rankin's clutches once tonight. Why push your luck?"

Margaret looked down at the ground, her face inscrutable in the shadows. She did not answer right away, and when she did, she looked directly at Jess Donner. "I want to be at your side if you'll have me."

Struck speechless, Jess Donner stepped up close to her and intently studied her face.

"Damn it!" Ethel stamped a foot. "All we've been through, and you throw yourself at the likes of him? I've never been so disappointed in anyone in my life."

"I'm sorry," Margaret said softly, still facing Jess Donner. "What will it be? I'll understand if you say no. You can do better than a dance hall girl."

"Are you sayin' what I think you're sayin'?"

Rusty glanced away to keep from laughing. He had never fallen for a woman and, frankly, didn't get what all the fuss was about. It had been his experience women were next to useless, other than when cooking or in bed. Few could ride all that well, even fewer could shoot, and most were so spoiled, they would rather sleep in a soft bed under a roof than on the hard ground under the stars. The only purpose they served that he could figure was to nag men into early graves. That wasn't for him.

Jess Donner was in a daze. He put a hand to his head and said, "This can't be. This just can't be."

"Yes or no?" Margaret asked. "If I'm makin' a fool of myself, say so, and you will never set eyes on me again."

"Please say no," Ethel urged.

Rusty heard the clomp of boots, and peering out, he tensed. "Hush!" he whispered, pressing flat against the wall. "A deputy is comin'!"

Another few seconds and Trace Morgan walked past. He was yawning and staring at the other side of the street and did not notice them.

Only after the footfalls faded did Rusty risk another look. "That was a close one. I'll fetch my horse and meet you at the east end of town in fifteen minutes."

"But the women—" Steve Ellsworth began.

"What about them?" Rusty wanted to give the impression he did not care one way or the other, so he said, "If they want to tag along, let them. They can watch our mounts while we're tanglin' with Rankin." He left them to mull that while he went for his *grulla*.

Rusty grinned at how clever he was being. But

then, he had always been clever when it came to pulling the wool over the eyes of others. As Grat used to put it, Rusty could trick his way out of hell if he had to.

Before forking leather, Rusty made sure he had six pills in the wheel. Some men only loaded five for safety's sake but he would rather have the extra bullet than be short when he needed one the most.

Gigging the *grulla*, Rusty followed Locust Street to Third Avenue, and from there took Maple Street east. Crossing the railroad tracks, he reined up in a stand of trees. He did not have to wait long. The cowboys had circled around the north end of town and came past the cattle pens. Jess Donner was riding double with Margaret. Steve Ellsworth had Ethel behind him.

Rusty grinned. The jackasses had played right into his hands without realizing it. Riding into the open, he said, "I'm ready if you are."

"One thing," Steve Ellsworth said. "We've been talkin' it over, and we don't want you to go on a killin' spree. It's Rankin we're after and Rankin we'll fill with lead, and no one else unless we absolutely have to."

"Fine by me," Rusty said. He had no intention of doing as they asked. Before he was done, the prairie would run red with blood.

Jess Donner assumed the lead. Rusty was content to bring up the rear, his right hand on his Colt. He preferred to shoot the two cowboys in the back but he might hit the women, and he needed the women alive.

They had gone half a mile when Rusty jabbed his spurs and brought the *grulla* up alongside Jess Donner's bay. "Hold up. We need to talk."

Donner came to a halt. Steve Ellsworth drew rein only a few yards behind them and leaned on his saddle horn. "Why have we stopped?"

"Because this is as far as you go," Rusty said, and drew his Colt. Jess Donner was expecting treachery and went for his Smith & Wesson but Rusty had him covered before he could clear leather. "I wouldn't," he cautioned. "I'll shoot you plumb center, and it might go through you and hit your daffodil."

"What is this?" Steve Ellsworth demanded. "Why are you turnin' on us?"

"I knew something like this would happen," Ethel said.

"First things first " Rusty enjoyed having them at his mercy. "The ladies will stay right where they are. You cowboys climb down, one at a time and nice and slow, and reach for the Big Dipper." He half hoped they would give him an excuse to curl up their toes right then but they did exactly as he told them. "Now shuck the artillery. One at a time, and only use one hand."

Their revolvers raised puffs of dust, and Rusty let himself relax a bit. "There. That wasn't so hard, was it?"

"You still haven't said what you're up to," Margaret said.

"Well, darlin', it's like this." Rusty grinned with vicious glee. "I have use for you and your chubby friend there. You can help me get my revenge on Lem Rankin. But I don't have any more use for these cowboys." He slowly took deliberate aim at Jess Donner. "Any last words, you stupid son of a bitch?"

Chapter Twenty-four

Jess Donner had only himself to blame.

Ever since Margaret Sanger waltzed out of the dark and back into his life, he could not stop thinking about her. He tried—he truly tried—but when she made plain she cared for him, truly and really did care for him, the shock rattled him to his marrow.

Jess had opened up to her at the dance hall, and been kicked in the teeth. He was loath to make the same mistake twice. He kept telling himself that she must be up to something, that she must have a secret motive, but for the life of him he could not think of what that motive might be.

It rattled him. Distracted him, at a time when he could scarcely afford to be distracted. He should be alert for treachery from Rusty Vanes, because not for a second did Jess believe Vanes was sincere about wanting to help them against Rankin. Vanes *was* up to something, but once again, Jess could not figure out what.

Then came the ride out of Dodge. The feel of Margaret behind him in the saddle, the press of her warm body, and the soft contours of her bosom on his shoulder blades were all he could think about. It made his mouth go dry and turned his mind to mush and his body break out in a sweat. He could not form a thought about anything or anyone other than Margaret. He liked having her so close, liked it more than he had ever liked anything, and that alone was troubling enough to create a riot of confusion.

So it was that Jess let Rusty Vanes ride at the rear, when if he had been in his right senses he would have ridden last himself in order to keep an eye on Vanes. And so it was that he did not suspect anything was amiss when Vanes asked him to rein up. And his yearning for Margaret caused him to be more than a shade slow when Vanes pulled his fancy Colt and trained it on them.

Now Jess seethed with suppressed fury. He was furious at himself for being so stupid. Furious at Margaret for the hope he had tried to smother. But most of all, he was furious at Rusty Vanes for his rank betrayal even though Jess had expected it all along. "Yeah, I have some last words," he said in answer to the killer's mocking question.

Rusty's lips quirked. "Oh really? Tell you what. Out of gratitude for you makin' this so easy, I'll let you say them."

"I thought you wanted Lem Rankin dead for the killin' of your brother?"

"That's not last words. That's a question. But yes,

I want him to feed the worms, and thanks to these ladies, it's as good as done."

"I don't savvy," Jess said. He was stalling. Desperately stalling. He was not close enough to the *grulla* to reach Vanes before the Colt went off. He had to think of something else and he had to think of it fast. Steve would be no help; he seemed paralyzed and was as rigid as a board, his gaze glued to the lethal end of the Colt's barrel.

"I don't understand, either," Margaret Sanger said. She was trying to get Rusty Vanes to take his eyes off the cowboys so Jess and Steve could jump him but her ruse didn't work. She glanced at Ethel and nodded at Vanes to hint at what she was up to but Ethel was slack-mouthed with shock.

"It's simple," Rusty said. "The three of us go in with guns blazin', there's no guarantee we'll get to Rankin before we're gunned down."

"You can't do any better alone," Jess said.

"True," Rusty admitted. "If I show up at Rankin's by my lonesome and ask to see him, his gunnies will watch me like hawks the whole time, and probably take my pistols, too. Either way, killin' Rankin and gettin' away is an iffy proposition."

"Takin the ladies won't help any," Jess remarked, and as he did, he slid his left leg to the left. "All you'll do is get them gunned down in the cross fire." He slid his right leg to the left.

"Shows how much you know," Rusty Vanes scoffed. "You see, I know somethin' you don't."

"What would that be?" Jess sidled another half a

foot, careful to do it as slow as molasses in February. Now he was almost directly in front of the *grulla*.

"Rankin wants your lady friends back. Wants them back bad. So bad, he's offerin' a thousand dollars to anyone who turns them over to him." Rusty grinned. "That someone will be me. I'll not only get to blow out his wick—he'll pay me a thousand dollars to do it."

"There's a hitch in your plan," Jess said. He kept glancing at Steve from under his hat brim to catch the other man's attention but Steve didn't notice. "It was Grat and you who shot Shamblin and those others."

Rusty snickered and responded, "It's a wonder you can dress yourself without help. Rankin doesn't know it was me. He'll think I'm there for the money, and that's all. I'll insist on seein' him in person, and he'll be so glad to get his hands on these bitches, I'd bet my bottom dollar he'll welcome me with open arms."

"You have it all worked out." Jess could not think of anything else to say. He had stalled as long as he could.

"Damn right I do," Rusty bragged. "I've always been twice as smart as everyone else. It's why I've never been caught."

"Every outlaw makes a mistake sooner or later," Jess said. "I don't call it smart to end your days dressed in hemp."

"And I don't call it smart to rile a man who is about to have you for breakfast," Rusty retorted, and raised the Colt a fraction.

It was do or die, Jess realized, and streaking his right hand to his hat, he whipped it off and sprang at the *grulla* while shrieking like a berserk Comanche. The *grulla* whinnied and reared just as the Colt spat flame and lead, and the slug meant for Jess's head sizzled through empty air. Instantly, Jess grabbed for Steve and spun to dart into the dark, but the shot had shattered Steve's paralysis and he was lunging for their revolvers on the ground.

Trying to regain control of the *grulla*, Rusty Vanes saw him, and snapped off a shot from the hip.

Steve Ellsworth was spun half-around. He pitched to his knees; then Jess had an arm around him and was bounding into the tall grass that bordered the dirt road. They sprinted a dozen yards, Steve clenching his teeth against the agony. Then Jess dived flat, pulling Steve down with him.

Jess had been expecting a slug in the back but Vanes didn't fire. As he landed on his belly he twisted and discovered why.

Margaret Sanger had slid forward on the saddle, grabbed the bay's reins, and kneed the bay between Vanes and the tall grass.

Swearing savagely, Rusty pointed the Colt at her and roared, "Out of my way, damn you, or I'll take you to Rankin slung over that nag!"

"It's the horse, not me," Margaret lied. She clucked to the bay but it did not move. "It's as skittish as yours."

More swearing, and Rusty reined the *grulla* past her and rose in the stirrups. "Where the hell did they get to?" he snarled, scanning the prairie. "This is what I get for lettin' that cowboy jabber."

Ethel came to life. She, too, slid forward on her saddle, and tried to turn her mount and flee.

"I'd think twice, girl!" Rusty declared, training the Colt on her. "Killin' a woman is nothin' to me."

Ethel froze, except for tears trickling down her cheeks. "Please," she whimpered, "you can't do this. You must let us go."

"I'm surrounded by stupidity," Rusty Vanes spat. He scoured the prairie again, and vented more profanity. "All right. What's done is done. Those two had a little luck of their own but it doesn't change things. Keep headin' east, ladies, and remember, I'll be right behind you."

"I'm not much of a rider," Margaret said. "I'm not sure I can make this horse go."

"You better," Rusty said, "or when you get to Rankin's, you'll be bleedin' like a stuck hog."

Ethel began to sob. "Please, Mr. Vanes, we have some money saved. We'll pay you to let us go."

"How much?" Rusty asked.

"Close to four hundred dollars," Ethel said, blossoming with hope.

"Where is this windfall?"

"I have half." Ethel reached back and patted the bags Steve Ellsworth had tied on behind his bedroll.

"It's a regular epidemic," Rusty Vanes said, and kneed the *grulla* around behind them. He never once took his eyes off the grass. He was sure the cowboys were watching, and might be tempted to rashly try a rescue. "Mr. Rankin awaits, ladies. No tricks, now, you hear?"

"But what about our money for our lives?" Ethel plaintively asked.

"I never agreed." Rusty sensed she was close to breaking, and the last thing he needed was a blubbering female on his hands. He had to keep them moving, keep their minds off what lay head. "Now ride, damn it!"

His tone brooked no delay. Margaret jabbed her heels against the bay. She was so relieved Jess was safe, she was positively happy. Then it struck her that she should be thinking about her own life. She had been to Rankin's house once, and they had half a mile to go. Plenty of opportunity for her to outwit Vanes, if only she could think of a way to do it.

Rusty had a cramp in his neck from twisting his head. He did not face eastward until he was certain the cowboys posed no further threat. Then he hollered, "Ride faster, you slugs!" and brought the *grulla* to a canter.

Ethel was flopping about like a puppet with its strings cut. She was the world's worst rider, in Rusty's estimation, and he could not help laughing. His spirits were brightening. So what if the cowboys were on the loose? They couldn't stop him. Soon he would have fourteen hundred dollars *and* his revenge on Rankin.

That old luck of his couldn't be beat.

Suddenly a strong gust of wind bent the long grass. It brought with it the scent of moisture. Rusty shifted, and frowned. To the west the stars were being blotted out. A storm front was sweeping across the prairie. In the far distance lightning flashed. He doubted the storm would last long. They seldom did at that time of year. But the rain could complicate things.

Ethel Heatherton was weeping in great, racking sobs, and barely able to stay in the saddle.

"Quit your damned blubberin'," Rusty snapped. He had to raise his voice to be heard about the drum of their hooves.

"I can't help it," Ethel choked back her tears to say. "I don't want to die."

"Who does?" Rusty retorted. "Do you think my brother wanted to die tonight or that Rankin is lookin' to have his life snuffed out?" He breathed deep of the rain-laced breeze. "Me, I never give any thought to it. When my times comes, it comes. Losin' sleep over it is a waste of worry."

"Tell me something. How many people have you killed?"

"What's that got to do with anything?" Rusty resented the look she gave him, and fought down an urge to smash her in the face with his Colt.

"You're a despicable person, Rusty Vanes. I wish to God I had a gun. I've never shot anyone but I would gladly shoot you."

Rusty's anger changed to amusement. "Oh. I get it. It's all right for you to kill me but not all right for me to do any killin'? Is that how it goes? You're a hypocrite, girl, like most everyone else."

"And you're not, I suppose?" Ethel archly asked.

"I am what I am," Rusty said, "and I don't pretend to be anything else. You're the one who makes her livin' by hoodwinkin' cowpokes and the like."

"I only do what I have to."

"That makes two of us."

The wind was intensifying. In the distance, thunder rumbled. Rusty hoped the rain would hold off until they reached Rankin's. He didn't own a slicker and he hated getting wet.

Lights appeared to the east. A large house and outbuildings were darkly silhouetted against the sky. The house was on a low, broad ridge that afforded a sweeping view of the countryside. A white fence had been erected, and a broad gate installed.

Rusty and the women were almost to it when a pair of guards came out of nowhere and leveled their rifles.

"This is as far as you go!"

Rusty reined up and smiled his friendliest smile. "I'm Russian Vanes. I've come to see Mr. Rankin." The "Russian" slipped out. He never had liked the fact his father named him after the country their family came from. Since his great-grandfather had seen fit to change the family name from Vanechka to Vanes so it would sound more American, he had a perfect excuse to change his from Russian to Rusty.

"A little late for a social visit, isn't it?" the guard said. "What can you want to see him about at this hour?"

"You have eyes, don't you?" Rusty responded. "Or isn't it true he's offerin' a thousand-dollar bounty for these females?"

Both guards took closer looks at Margaret and

Ethel, and one exclaimed, "I'll be damned! It is them! Run up to the house, Joe, and let the boss know."

"Sure thing, Clancy."

Rusty had figured on being escorted right in. "How about openin' that gate so we can hitch our horses and climb down?"

"No one gets past us without Mr. Rankin's say so," Clancy said. "Be patient. It won't take Joe but a minute or two."

Margaret Sanger had made up her mind to stop Vanes any way she could. She entertained the thought that if she helped save Rankin's life, he might be inclined to spare Ethel and her from whatever horrible fate he had in store for them. So now she straightened and said, "You're makin' a mistake, Clancy. This gun slick isn't here for the money. He's here to kill Mr. Rankin."

"Shut up," Rusty hissed. To the guard he said, "Don't listen to her. She lyin' to try and save her skin."

"I'm tellin' the truth," Margaret said. "This is the one who shot Vince. His brother was killed in the gunfight and now he—"

Rusty leaned to the right and backhanded her across the mouth. "I said to shut up!" It had been a mistake not to gag them, he realized, and now it was too late.

"She's telling you the truth, Clancy," Ethel chimed in. "You know me. We've danced at the dance hall. I wouldn't lie about a thing like this."

"You might," Clancy said, then trained his Winchester on Rusty Vanes. "Still, I'm afraid I'll have to ask you to shuck your hardware, mister."

Rusty smiled and nodded. "Sure, sure, whatever you want. Just don't be hasty, friend. These women wouldn't know the truth if it bit them on the ass." With his left hand he reached for the buckle to his brother's gun belt.

With his right hand, he went for his Colt.

Chapter Twenty-five

Invisible fingers had wrapped around Jess Donner's heart and were slowly crushing the vitality from his limbs. As he lay watching Rusty Vanes ride off with Margaret, he grew strangely weak and queasy. An insane impulse came over him, an urge to rise and race after them and haul Vanes from the saddle and stomp him to a pulp. Only the certain knowledge that Vanes would gun him down before he could lay a hand on him kept him rooted to the ground.

When the sound of hooves faded, Steve Ellsworth raised his head, and groaned. Slowly, painfully, he rose to his knees. He felt sorry for Ethel but there was nothing he could do for her. Not in his condition. The slug had caught him high in the right shoulder and he was bleeding profusely. Waves of torment washed over him, threatening to make him pass out.

"Damn!" Jess sprang to his feet. "We have to follow them! I just hope we don't get there too late."

"Sorry, pard," Steve said, "but you'll have to count me out."

Jess turned to him. "It's that bad?"

Nodding, Steve tried to rise and bit off a whine. "I think my shoulder is busted. I can't move it."

Jess looped an arm around his waist. "Here. Hold on to me." The stain darkening Steve's shirt jolted him. It occurred to him that Steve could die from loss of blood unless they got him to town, and a sawbones. Yet that meant abandoning Margaret to whatever cruelty Vanes had in store.

"I reckon I'm plumb worthless at dodgin' bullets," Steve joked as they shuffled to the road. Moving helped, though; the pain lessened a bit.

"Can you stand on your own?" Jess asked, and when Steve nodded, he quickly moved to where their revolvers lay. "That Vanes ain't so smart or he wouldn't have left these behind." He wiped a sleeve over the Smith & Wesson and slid it into his holster, then replaced Steve's.

"Get goin'," Steve said. "I'll head back to town on my own."

Jess was torn between affection for his friend and his budding affection for Margaret. He had a decision to make, maybe the most important decision of his life. He stared after Vanes and the girls, then took a deep breath and said, "I can't leave you like this."

"You don't have any choice. The women come first." Steve said that even though he was no longer all that fond of Ethel. But he had been raised to always treat women with respect and to put their welfare before his own.

Jess Donner wavered. He was being ripped apart inside. He had never been very religious. Except when his ma made him, he never set foot in a church. And what little he knew about the Bible came from her evening readings, which he had listened to only because she insisted and then he forgot the lessons as soon as she was done. But now he did something he hadn't done since he was old enough to think for himself; he prayed, prayed with all his heart and mind and soul that the Almighty would bend his steps in the right direction. And then, as he waited tense and tingling for some sign or omen that would show him what to do, the creak and clatter of a wagon wafted to his ears from the west, and down the road came a buckboard hitched to a two-horse team.

Jess nearly whooped for joy.

The driver was singing to himself and swaying from side to side. He swore lustily and hauled on the reins when the two young cowboys materialized out of the night in front of him. "What the hell! Are you idiots trying to get run over?"

Dashing to the seat, Jess smelled the reek of alcohol. By the looks of him, the man was a farmer, on his way home after a late night doing the town. "We need help, mister."

"Help, you say? Are you sure you're not road agents? If you are, you're too late. I spent every penny I had." The farmer smirked. "I expect my misses will bean me with her rolling pin, but what's another lump when you have forty or fifty?"

"My pard has been shot," Jess explained. "I need to get him back to town."

"Shot, you say?" the farmer peered at Steve. "Was it road agents?"

"A killer is on the loose," Jess said, "and he's kidnapped two women we were with. Let me borrow one of your horses and go after him. You can manage with the other."

"What's that?" The farmer stopped swaying. "No one steals one of my horses, by God."

"I'm not stealin' it," Jess said. "I'm borrowin' it a while. I'll bring it back as soon as the women are out of danger." He turned to undo the harness but the farmer vaulted from the seat with surprising vigor and reared to his full six-foot-plus height. "Just hold on, boy. My horse isn't going anywhere."

"Didn't you hear me?" Jess remonstrated. "Two women might be murdered."

"So you say. But I don't know you from my uncle Hiram. I'll take you back to town and you can report this to the marshal, but that's all I'll allow."

"There's no time for that," Jess said, and reached for the near horse.

"Look out!" Steve cried.

The farmer waded into Jess with his knobby fists flying. He was drunk but not so drunk he couldn't fight, and his first blow clipped Jess on the jaw, knocking him against the horse. Bringing his arms up, Jess sought to ward off a brutal succession of blows, but the farmer had the shoulders of a bull and the strength of two men. Jess was buffeted and battered like a twig in a tornado, barely able to prevent his teeth from being hammered down his throat.

"I warned you, boy!" the farmer roared. "I warned you!"

Jess could draw and shoot him but that would be murder, and the man was only protecting his property. Setting himself, he ducked a wide swing, then drove his right fist into the farmer's chin. It was akin to hitting an iron skillet. His knuckles nearly broke, and his punch had no more effect than if he had flicked a feather.

"Now you've done it!" the farmer raged. "We hang horse thieves in these parts!"

Under the redoubled onslaught, all Jess could do was back away and block, dodge and weave. He avoided most of the blows but the few that slipped through nearly crumpled him. He realized he could not keep up the fight indefinitely. He had to act before the enraged farmer knocked him out and destroyed any hope Margaret had of living out the night.

Suddenly twisting, Jess connected with two solid rights to the cheek. He followed through with an uppercut, but instead of feeling the sweet crunch of his fist on bone, he cleaved empty air, and the next instant the sky turned to solid stone and crashed down on his head and he was lying in the dirt with the stars spinning and the farmer looming over him like a bear about to rip out his throat.

"I've got you now, boy! You're the damnedest

jackrabbit I ever did see, but this is where you learn to mind your elders."

Jess braced for the punch that would seal Margaret's death. He heard a *thump* but did not feel any pain, which was peculiar, but not nearly so peculiar as the sight of the farmer oozing down beside him.

"I can't unhitch the horse for you," Steve said, hefting his revolver. He had done the only thing he could. He had drawn his revolver with his left hand and, when the farmer bent over Jess, slugged him over the head with all the force he could muster. He had never pistol-whipped anyone, and he was amazed at the ease with which the farmer had collapsed. His shoulder, though, was worse than ever, and it was all he could do to stay on his feet.

"I knew you were good for somethin'." Jess smiled and turned to his task, which took far too long for his liking. But at last he had a single horse hitched to the buckboard and the unconscious farmer in the back. He helped Steve onto the seat and handed him the reins. "I'm sorry I can't go with you, pard. You know I would if I could."

"You'd best light a shuck," Steve advised. "That plow horse will make a turtle seem fast."

Jess's vision was blurry and his throat felt constricted. Nodding, he clambered on the gelding and slapped his legs against the animal's sides and did not look back.

"Holler one more time, boy," Lester growled, "and I'll give you a thumping you will never forget."

Heck Myers ignored him and gripped the cell bars. He had sat idle long enough, with worry gnawing at him like a tick on his skin, worry so potent he had to try one more time. "Do you hear me out there?" He kicked the bars and tried to shake them. "People are goin' to die unless you do somethin'!"

Lester heaved up off the seat. "Some jackasses just won't listen. Come on, Billy. We'll shut him up so we can get some shut-eye."

"Aw, you don't need my help," Billy said sleepily. "He's just a puny cowpoke. You can wallop him without half trying. Just remember what I told you about the judge."

Heck spun. Lester was lumbering toward him, his two chins shaking with every ponderous step. "Don't you dare."

"Save your breath," Lester declared. "I'm sick and tired of you cowboys and your airs. Strutting around town like you own it. Looking down your noses at those of us who don't push cows. Maybe I only work at the feed and grain, but you're no better than I am."

"I never claimed I was," Heck said, hoping to avoid a fight. "I don't want any trouble."

"Then you shouldn't be raising a fuss." Lester raised his pudgy fists, his piggish eyes aglitter. "You wouldn't know it to look at me but I'm a holy terror."

"Sure you are," Heck said, and kicked him in the knee.

Yelping, Lester lurched back a step, then plunged

in again, his beefy shoulders bunched and his fore-
arms raised to protect his face. A wicked grin hinted
at the sadistic savagery of his nature. "For that, I'm
going to break your arms and legs and stove in a
few ribs."

Dearly wishing he had his six-shooter, Heck
skipped aside. He would much rather chuck lead
than trade blows. The other occupants of the cell
were sleepily awaiting the outcome. He knew better
than to count on them for help.

"Come on, cowboy," Lester taunted. "Show some
backbone. Quit dancing around and prove you're a
man."

"Says the hombre who outweighs me by two
hundred pounds," Heck said. "Hell, if you trip and
fall on me, I'm a goner."

Billy laughed and howled, which added fuel to
Lester's anger. "Think you're clever, do you? Let's
see how funny you are when you don't have any
teeth in your mouth."

Heck avoided a series of jabs. His confidence
climbed. The townsman had the reflexes of a snail.
So long as he did not let Lester trap him in a corner,
he would do all right.

"You can't avoid me forever, boy."

"I don't have to," Heck said. He was counting on
the ruckus to bring a deputy. In effect, Lester was
doing him a favor. "And I'm grateful for your help."

Confused, Lester halted. "What the hell are you
talking about? I'm out to stomp you silly."

"You and what other hog?" The insult slipped
out without Heck meaning to say it, and he had to

spring back as Lester came at him in renewed rage, swinging those clublike arms. A fist glanced off Heck's shoulder. Another stung his ear. Ducking under a left, he drove his fist into the pit of Lester's stomach. It was like punching a pillow.

Gurgling and grunting, Lester backpedaled. His face reddened and he sucked in long breaths.

Billy was no longer grinning. "You hurt him," he said, and stood. "Seeing as how he's my brother-in-law, I'll have to take a hand."

Heck was midway between them, his back to the barred window. He retreated as they stalked toward him, glancing from one to the other and trying to gauge which one would rush him first. Billy did the honors, lunging quick and low as if to tackle Heck. Heck leaped back and felt his left heel come down on someone else's foot. "Sorry!" he blurted, and skipped to the side.

The frontiersman who had been on the floor with his long arms wrapped around his legs unfurled in the span of a heartbeat. He had a salt-and-pepper beard but he did not appear all that old. Wide shoulders capped a powerful chest, and both were eclipsed by penetrating blue eyes. He did not say anything. Taking two long strides, he slammed a callused fist against Lester's chin and Lester folded like wet paper. Whirling more swiftly than the eye could follow, he gave Billy the same treatment. One punch to each, and they were out to the world.

Heck's mouth went dry. He was sure the frontiersman would turn on him next, but the buckskin-clad Samson returned to the same spot under the window and, after sinking down, wrapped his arms around his legs.

"Why did you hit them?" Heck marveled. "I was the one who stepped on your foot."

"My mistake," the frontiersman said, and in the shadows his eyes seem to glow bright with secret mirth.

Suddenly the outer door opened and in strode Trace Morgan. "What's all the commotion back here?" He saw the prone forms, and stopped. "I'm not back ten minutes and you start up again, cowboy. I reckon I didn't make myself plain enough the last time." He palmed his Remington and inserted a key into the lock. "Step back and turn around with your hands in the air."

"Please," Heck said, "you have to listen!"

Morgan twisted the key and pulled on the door. Thumbing back the Remington's hammer, he pointed it at Heck's chest. "I won't tell you twice."

"I'm beggin' you," Heck said. "My friends are goin' to get themselves killed! I've already lost one tonight and I don't want to lose any more."

Morgan entered the cell. "This friend wouldn't happen to be a cowboy we found over to Mary Richter's boardinghouse?"

"His name was Stu Wilkins," Heck said. "One of Lem Rankin's men, a polecat named Warner, knifed him."

"Charley Warner? I've made the shiftless bastard's acquaintance." Deputy Morgan thoughtfully stroked his mustache. "You wouldn't happen to know anything about three of Rankin's men who were shot full of holes tonight, would you?"

"I was there when it happened."

Trace Morgan twirled the Remington into its holster, and motioned. "Come out here, cowboy. I want to hear more."

Chapter Twenty-six

Rusty Vanes would be the first to admit he was not the most patient person in the world. Grat always liked to joke that when the Lord passed out patience, Rusty was in the outhouse. But Rusty couldn't help himself. It was his nature. Just as it was his nature to get mad when things didn't go the way he wanted. The madder he became, the worse it was for those who set him off.

At the moment Rusty was seething. His bright notion to use the dance hall girls to get in to see Lem Rankin had gone sour. So much for doing it the easy way, he told himself; drawing his Colt, he shot Clancy in the head.

The guard staggered back, his limbs jerking spasmodically as his brains seeped out the exit cavity in his skull.

Shifting in the saddle, Rusty pointed the Colt at Ethel Heatherton, who was transfixed by horror.

"No!" Ethel said.

"Yes," Rusty replied, and shot her in the chest.

She clutched at her bosom, groaned, and pitched headlong to the earth. Twisting, he shot Margaret Sanger in the back as she was reining the bay around to flee. She cried out, flung her arms wide, and toppled in a heap.

From the buildings arose shouts.

Rusty reined to the gate, swung low, and opened it. A kick sent it swinging inward. He galloped toward the house, aware of shadowy shapes running to stop him. Rusty fired twice and one of the shapes shrieked and fell. He fired again and another man seemed to trip over his own feet.

Fireflies sprinkled the dark, to the cadence of cracking guns. Lead buzzed past Rusty's ear. Suddenly the *grulla* whinnied and tumbled headlong, its momentum carrying it in a forward roll. Almost too late, Rusty sprang clear. He rolled and gained his knees, glad he had not lost his grip on the Colt. Shoving the six-shooter into his holster he scrambled to the wildly thrashing *grulla* and yanked his Winchester from the saddle scabbard.

More fireflies glowed. Rusty answered one, then another, shooting at the muzzle flashes. A scream showed he had scored. To his left, boots drummed. He silenced them with a swift shot.

"What the hell is going on?" hollered someone over by a long, low structure that might be a bunkhouse."

"Is it Injuns?" bawled another voice.

Seven, eight, nine hired guns were converging. Rusty ran toward the house. He had not come this far to be daunted by the odds. Rankin must pay for Grat's life, and that was that.

The guards had lost sight of him and thought he was by the *grulla*. Slugs *thwacked* into its flesh and the horse stopped moving.

Rusty only had twenty yards to go when the front door opened, disgorging another half dozen gun sharks. He was caught in the glare of the rectangle of light that spilled through the doorway, and snapping the Winchester to his shoulder, he cut loose.

The guard called Joe was in the lead. "Kill him, boys! Stop him from reaching Mr. Rankin!"

Rifles and pistols boomed as Rusty threw himself to the grass. He fired, worked the lever, then fired again. Joe and a second short-trigger man died side by side. The rest scattered but not quickly enough. Rusty dispatched one with a slug to the temple, another through the spine.

The open front door beckoned but it might as well have been on the moon. Guns were blasting on all sides now, and unless Rusty got out of the light, he would end up like the *grulla*.

Rusty had to find another way in. To that end, he rose in a crouch and skirted to the right, hugging the dark. Yells confirmed the other men had lost him but that would not last for long. He was nearing the corner when a gruff voice snarled, "Sic him, big fella! Kill! Kill! Kill!" and from nowhere hurtled a bristling, fanged engine of destruction: a dog as black as pitch and as big as a small bear. He snapped off a shot but missed and then the dog was on him, snarling and biting.

Rusty swung the Winchester at the animal's head but the dog was four-legged quicksilver. Before Rusty could plant himself and swing again, the dog leaped. Razor-sharp teeth sought to fasten to Rusty's forearm but closed on the rifle barrel. Instantly, Rusty tugged with all his strength to free the rifle, but the dog clung tenaciously on.

"Let go, damn your hide!" Rusty fumed, and kicked at the dog's throat. He connected but the guard dog did not release the Winchester.

"He's over here!" a man cried.

Thirty seconds more, and Rusty would be up to his armpits in gunnies. He kicked the dog again, harder this time, and when it yipped and relinquished its grip, he shot it smack between the eyes. Guns cracked and boomed as he bolted for the side of the house. Shielded by the corner, he ran as he had never run before. He passed a lit window and glimpsed someone inside, but whether it was Rankin or someone else, he had no way of knowing.

It occurred to Rusty that if he kept on running, he could escape into the night with his life. He dismissed the notion with a toss of his head. Gratton might not have been the best of brothers but he was kin.

No lights were on at the back of the house. Rusty rounded the corner, spurs jangling in his wake. A recessed door caught his eye. Without breaking stride, he threw himself at it. His shoulder struck with a loud *crack* and the jamb splintered under the impact. He tripped and landed on his knees, bruised but unbloodied so far.

A murky hall ran the length of the house. Rusty loped along it, glancing into room after room. Most were dark. One that wasn't contained a rumpled bed. Darting into it, he verified no one was there. Then, with his back to the wall, he propped the Winchester against his leg and reloaded the Colt.

Boots pounded the hallway.

Snatching up the Winchester, Rusty sprang through the doorway and fired as rapidly as he could work the lever. Three of Rankin's underlings were caught flat-footed and expired in a gory dance of death. Rusty emptied the Winchester into them, then cast it down.

Where the hell is Rankin? Rusty wondered as he whipped out his brother's revolver. He hated to think his quarry had escaped.

Then someone out front bellowed, "Surround the house!" and Brady yelled, "You heard Mr. Rankin! Cover the windows and doors, and if the son of a bitch shows himself, blow out his wick!"

Rusty went another ten feet when a door on the left opened, and out stepped the lovely redhead and her raven-haired friend in lacy undergarments. He recognized them as the women from the restaurant, the same pair he had seen leaving the dance hall, Franny and Chelsea. "Move!" he commanded.

The women stayed where they were. Grinning as if Rusty were part of some sort of game, Chelsea said teasingly, "What do we have here?"

"It looks to be a handsome young gentleman,"

Franny said playfully. "Maybe he'd like to enjoy our company a while."

Rusty was astounded, but only for a few moments. "I won't tell you twice, ladies. Out of my way."

"What's your rush, handsome?" Franny asked. Her eyes were oddly dilated and she slurred some of her words. "We only want to please you."

"Then move!" Rusty repeated. He could hear men moving about outside. Soon they would have the house completely ringed.

"Is that any way to talk to a gal who just wants to make your acquaintance?" Franny walked up to him, her hips swaying invitingly, and placed her hands on his shoulders. "Join us." She nodded at the bedroom. "You'll have fun. I promise."

"And what do you think Rankin will be doin' while I'm triflin' with the likes of you?" Rusty asked. "Knittin' me a sweater?"

Chelsea was fiddling with her chemise and somehow or other it came partially undone and her breasts spilled halfway out. Giggling, she said, "Lem won't dare lay a finger on you while you're with us. He wouldn't want us to take lead by accident."

"No, sir," Franny agreed, nodding. "Lem is too fond of us. Calls us his love muffins."

Both women tittered.

Rusty heard a *thump* from the rear of the house and a sound that might have been a window sliding open. "He's right fond of you—is that it?"

"Yes, indeed," Franny verified. "He likes to say

that no one does him like we do. And he should know. Before we came along, he'd been with half the girls in his dance hall."

"Is that a fact?"

Chelsea bobbed her chin. "Do you honestly think we would lie to a handsome devil like yourself?"

"You finally got one thing right," Rusty told them.

"What's that?" Franny asked.

"The devil and me have a lot in common." Rusty shot her in the stomach and she staggered against the wall, her mouth agape.

"Dear God!" Chelsea bleated, and started to back away.

"What's your rush, darkie?" Rusty taunted. "Could it be that you're as fond of Rankin as he is of you? That you two were fixin' to stall me long enough for him to surround the house?"

"No!" Chelsea mewed.

"Liar," Rusty said, and shot her through the throat. Her neck burst in a scarlet geyser and she fell to the floor. Chelsea was gripped by terrible convulsions, and her eyes grew wide and rolled up into her head.

Franny had a hand over the bullet hole and blood was trickling between her fingers. "I could die!" she whimpered.

"There's no might about it," Rusty said, and shot her again, through the mouth this time. Her head left a broad crimson smear on the wall as she slowly sank down until she was sitting on the floor.

"Some folks never outgrow their diapers," was

Rusty's eulogy. Drawing his own Colt, a revolver in each hand, he came to the end of the hall. A dark parlor was on the right, a well-lit room with a piano on his left. He entered the parlor and stalked to a front window. Rankin's hired guns had spread out and were waiting with cocked rifles and revolvers. Over by the stable, torches were being lit. Soon it would be impossible for him to slip out unnoticed.

Rusty spotted Brady talking to a heavyset man in a baggy white cotton nightshirt. It had to be Rankin, Rusty realized, and raised the Colt. But as his finger tightened, a rifle somewhere in the yard boomed. The window shattered and glass shards showered around him like shimmering drops of rain.

More guns chorused the first, and Rusty dropped below the sill. Lead flew as thick as a swarm of bees, reducing what was left of the window to a shambles and making a sieve of the adjoining wall.

Someone shouted, and the firing stopped.

"Can you hear me in there?" Brady bellowed. "Throw out your weapons and come out with your arms where we can see them and Mr. Rankin will let you live!"

"I wasn't born yesterday!" Rusty responded.

Voices murmured, then: "This is Lem Rankin! Who are you and what is this about? Did someone send you or is this personal?"

Rusty crawled toward the hallway. "Personal as hell! My brother is dead on account of you!"

"Does this brother have a name?" Rankin yelled, and when Rusty didn't answer, he said, "Listen to me. I have men on all sides. You can't possibly kill me. Give up and I'll turn you over to the law."

Rusty was about to search for a side room with a window when Rankin gave him pause.

"At least let my lady friends leave! They have no part in this."

Rusty stared down the hall at the bodies.

"They are alive, aren't they? We heard some shooting."

"Sure they're alive!" Rusty grinned as a brain-storm came over him. "Pull your men back and I'll let the ladies walk out."

"I'll pull them back," Rankin said, "but don't try to use the women as shields because it won't work."

"Give me a minute," Rusty replied.

"Take all the time you want." Rankin was confi-dent he had the upper hand. "We're not going any-where. Just don't harm them!"

Chuckling, Rusty hurried to the dead lovelies. Of the two of them, Chelsea had bled more, but most of the blood was in a pool on the wood floor, not on her clothes. Replacing the revolver, he slid his hands under her shoulders and lifted her. She was skinny as a fence post and easy to carry.

Something had to be done about the hole in her neck. Rusty carried her into the room that the women came from and dumped her on a bed cov-ered with a pink quilt. On a nearby dresser lay a dress and other discarded clothes. More were over a chair. None suited his needs. A closet was filled with female finery, including shoes and hats. But it was a shawl that interested him most. Made of silk, it was as red as the blood she had spilled.

"Perfect," Rusty said.

Lem Rankin was growing impatient. "What's keeping you in there? If the women are still alive, prove it!"

"I'm fixin' to send the darkie out!" Rusty hollered. Quickly, he wrapped the shawl around Chelsea's neck to hide the wound and knotted it so it wouldn't slide off. Holding her in front of him, he hurried to the front door but did not open it. "Here comes Chelsea! But how do I know your men don't have itchy trigger fingers?"

Rankin fell for the ruse. "Lower your guns!" he commanded. "Anyone who fires answers to me!"

"Obligin' cuss, ain't he?" Rusty said to the corpse. Bracing her with his left arm, he drew his Colt and held it close to her chemise.

"No more stalling!" Rankin shouted.

Rusty reached for the door. "I hope you're watchin' from hell, Grat. I'm about to send you a heap of company."

Chapter Twenty-seven

Gunfire ahead, thunder behind.

Jess Donner rode with a frenzy born of desperation. He lashed the farmer's horse trying to get it to go faster when it was already galloping as fast as it could. He tried not to think of Margaret, tried not to imagine the worst, but the knot of worry inside him grew and grew.

A gust of wind buffeted Jess's back, the strongest gust yet. He was so intent on reaching Rankin's, he had forgotten about the approaching storm. Nature reminded him with a sudden spattering of large, cold drops. Only a few at first. Then more and more until a steady drizzle was falling. It didn't last long. With a flash of lightning that lit the entire sky and a clap of thunder that shook the ground, the scuttling clouds unleashed a deluge.

Jess could barely see the road. The farm horse didn't like the rain, either. It slowed, and he had to slap his legs against its side to get it to gallop. The *thud* of its heavy hooves became a splashy staccato.

"Hold on, Margaret," Jess breathed aloud. "I'm comin'." His clothes were soon drenched and clammy drops dribbled down his back, causing him to shiver. Pulling his hat brim low to shield his eyes, he probed the prairie before him for some sign of Rankin's house.

Another brilliant, crackling saber cleaved the firmament and struck only a few hundred feet away. The thunder was nigh-deafening.

Every cowboy knew the extreme danger of lightning on the open prairie. A horse and rider were inviting targets, and more than a few had been blasted into eternity by errant bolts. One cowboy of Jess's acquaintance had lost an arm. Another had had a horse charred from under him but miraculously was unscathed himself.

Jess lashed the farm horse anew. Suddenly pinpoints of light appeared. Or was it his imagination? He brushed a hand across his face, and there it was again, lamps or lanterns. He could not tell exactly how far off they were, but he had to be close.

Again lightning seared the plain. Jess saw a riderless horse standing in the middle of the road, and hauled on the reins. But the farm horse slammed into the other animal and they both went down, whinnying and kicking.

Jess pushed clear at the instant of impact. For a few harrowing seconds he feared he would be crushed under hundreds of pounds of horseflesh, but he came to his feet at the edge of the road none the worse for wear.

The horses were rising. Neither appeared hurt,

and Jess ran to the animal he had bowled over and grabbed its reins. Shock struck him with the force of a physical blow. It was the bay! The horse Margaret had been riding! He turned as the prairie lit up again, and spied a fence and a gate. He also saw that which caused his heart to leap to his throat.

A body lay sprawled in the mud. A figure in a dress. Jess ran over, blinking rain from his eyes, and carefully rolled the still form over.

Ethel Heatherton was dead. She had been shot through the heart. Her glazed eyes were frozen in horror.

"Margaret?" Jess said, straightening. Muffled by the downpour, the *pop-pop-pop* of pistol and rifle fire reached his ears. He took a few steps toward the open gate, then froze, the blood in his veins congealing into ice.

From the grass at the edge of the road jutted a pair of shoes and part of a dress. The exact same that Margaret had been wearing.

His legs wooden, Jess ran to her and knelt. Lightning flared, revealing a bullet hole in her back. The world around him spun. He thought he would be sick but he swallowed the bitter bile and bent down. The hole was high on her right side, above the shoulder blade. Gringerly, he touched it and heard her moan.

"Margaret?" Jess gently rolled her onto her side. Pressing his fingers to her neck, he felt for a pulse. It was there, but weak, oh so terribly weak. "Please, no," he said.

Margaret's eyelids fluttered, then opened. "Jess?" she said, and tried to grin. "What kept you?"

Folding her in his arms, Jess pressed her to his chest and uttered a loud sob. "I'll get you to a doctor. Just hang on."

"I'm so cold," Margaret said. Her eyes closed and she shook from head to toe, then was still.

"Don't you die on me!" Jess frantically felt for a pulse again. It was there, but pitifully weak. Scooping her into his arms, he carried her to the bay. To hoist her into the saddle took some doing but he managed, and with her in front of him and one arm around her waist, he reined the bay to the west and applied his spurs.

The bay could move when it had to, and it had to. Jess held Margaret tight, her cheek against his shoulder. The rain was a solid sheet. It felt as if he was being pelted with hail. The wet and the cold would be worse on her. In her weakened condition, it might bring on pneumonia.

Lightning crackled to the north, south, east, and west. Thunder rumbled without cease.

Jess was heading into the fierce center of the storm, and feared worse was to come. Suddenly a vivid bolt rent the air, striking the nearby earth. Jess's skin tingled and his hair felt as if it were standing on end. The blast of thunder nearly burst his eardrums. He had never had lightning strike so close and he never wanted it to strike that close again. But a minute later it did, on the opposite side of the road, and when he glanced up, he could see bright arcs dancing in the clouds above them.

Jess hunkered low over the saddle and rode for their lives. Now and again he looked at Margaret's face, so pale and so near. He hardly knew her, yet here he was risking everything on her behalf. It could be he was a fool. It could be that, if she lived, nothing would come of the hope he harbored. Maybe he was the biggest jackass to ever draw breath. Maybe he was trusting his soul to someone who would crush it. But it was a risk worth taking. As his grandma liked to say, anything worthwhile in life was worth the risk of obtaining it.

Goose bumps broke out all over him. Jess was wet clean through to his skin. Even the socks in his boots were soaked. Margaret's dress was no protection at all; it clung to her like so much wet paper.

Gusts of wind nearly took Jess's breath away. He was amazed his hat was still on. Whenever he raised his head, he was careful not to tilt it too far back.

The dusty road had become a lake of mud. The bay's hooves splashed brown water in all directions. Jess was glad there were no holes in the road. One less worry in a night of nightmare.

The mile seemed like twenty. Eventually the rain tapered off a bit, and so did the lightning. Jess kept hoping to see the lights of Dodge but he saw something else first: a buckboard and a knot of riders. Reining up in a spray of rainwater, he sprang from the saddle. The farmer had revived and was angrily gesturing at someone with a tin star pinned to their vest.

"It's him! The one who stole my horse!"

Jess eased Margaret onto the buckboard's bed and climbed up beside her. Steve Ellsworth was on the seat, a hand pressed to his shoulder. "Get goin'!" Jess hollered. "We have to find a sawbones, pronto!"

"Has she been shot?" Steve was not doing so well. He was pasty white and shivering. "Where's Ethel?"

Jess shook his head.

One of the riders dismounted and climbed onto the seat. "Let me handle the reins," Heck Myers said, taking them from Steve. To Jess he said, "I've brought Deputy Morgan and a posse."

Trace Morgan came over the side of the buckboard and sank onto a knee beside Margaret. He studied the wound, and his mustache curled down.

"Didn't you hear me, Deputy?" the farmer asked, tugging at Morgan's sleeve. "This is the scalawag I was telling you about—the one who stole my horse! I demand you arrest him! And arrest the other one for hitting me with his pistol! I'll be glad to press charges."

A celestial flash lit a face chiseled as hard as flint. "Abner, touch me again and I'll pistol-whip you myself. If you weren't so damn drunk, you would see this woman is in a bad way." Morgan went to swing down but the farmer grabbed his arm.

"What do I care about some trollop? I know my rights! I demand you place these cowboys under arrest!"

"I've got your rights here." Trace Morgan's hand was a blur. The barrel of his Remington slammed against Abner's temple and the farmer slumped over. Springing lithely to the ground, Morgan turned to another man wearing a badge. "Jeeter, see that this girl gets to the doctor. The rest of us will ride on to Rankin's."

"What about Abner?" Jeeter asked.

"Throw him in jail for drunk and disorderly."

"He'll squawk to the judge."

"Remind him I know where he lives." Morgan mounted and looked down at Jess. "Good luck, cowboy."

Then the posse was gone, and Heck was barreling the buckboard down the road with a skill born of long experience on his parents' ranch.

Bouncing in the back, Jess cupped Margaret's chin. Her skin was icy. He felt for a pulse but could not feel one; his breath caught in his throat. Bending, he put an ear to her mouth but could not feel her breathing. "No!" he cried, and probed his fingers deep into her neck.

Steve had twisted around. "Is she . . . ?"

About to nod, Jess detected the faintest trace of life under his fingertips. Slow, erratic beats, the sign of a heart that would soon stop. "She's alive!" he choked out. "But not for long!"

Jeeter had come up alongside the buckboard, leading the bay. "We'll go straight to Doc Samuels on Front Street." He gestured at Margaret. "Who shot her, anyhow?"

"I don't rightly know." Jess suspected it was Rusty Vanes. Once Margaret was tended to, he would go after him. Jess would never be able to live with himself if he didn't.

The buckboard hit a bump, and Margaret groaned. Jess clasped her hand in his and lowered his mouth to her ear. "Don't die on me, darlin'? You hear? I can't get to know you better if you're in a coffin." He whispered more, a lot more, baring his innermost longings, saying things he had never said to anyone his whole life. When the buckboard rattled to a halt, he rose up in angry surprise. "What are we stoppin' for?"

They were in the heart of Dodge. The street was practically deserted. A sign on a building read:

> **DR. HORACE SAMUELS.**
> **REMEDIES FOR MOST KNOWN AILMENTS.**
> **BONES SET. BABIES DELIVERED.**
> **REASONABLE FEES.**

Jess was off the buckboard and at the door before the others. "Dr. Samuels!" he shouted, pounding and kicking. "Open up! It's an emergency!" He went on pounding and shouting until a window on the second floor scraped open and a disheveled man in a bulky robe poked his head out.

"What in God's name is all the commotion about?"

Stepping back, Jess called up, "Someone has been shot! Get down here! We need your help!"

Dr. Samuels yawned and scratched his thatch of gray hair. "Boy, I decide when I will and will not do my doctoring, and right now I'm so tired I can't keep my eyes open."

"I thought doctors took an oath to help folks?" Jess bristled. "Come down or I'll drag you down."

Jeeter kneed his horse to the hitch rail. "It's a woman, Doc."

"A woman?" Samuels blinked at the buckboard and drew back in surprise, hitting his head on the sash. "Why didn't you say so in the first place? I can't see a thing without my spectacles. Give me a minute and I'll let you in."

Jess cradled Margaret's head in his lap until the front door opened. The doctor still had his robe on. With him was his wife, who brought out dry blankets to bundle Margaret in. Jess and Jeeter carried her into the doctor's operating room, as Samuels called it. The doctor then shooed them out and was closing the door when he said, "Say. Have you been shot, too?"

The question was directed at Steve Ellsworth. Steve nodded and replied, "I can wait, though. I've stopped bleedin', and it only hurts when I move."

"There's been an awful lot of lead chuckin' tonight," Heck Myers commented.

"Tell me about it," Samuels said. "I've often thought that, if I saved all the bullets I dig out, I could open a lead mine." The door closed.

"Ain't he a caution?" Heck asked no one in particular.

Jess was not in the mood for levity. He slumped on a bench with his chin in his hands.

"That deputy is takin' the buckboard." Steve was gazing glumly out the window. "When the farmer wakes up, he'll be in the hoosegow." He leaned his forehead against the pane and closed his eyes. "I feel sorry about Ethel. She was sweet, even if she did land us in a heap of trouble."

"It wasn't all their fault," Jess said.

The inner door opened and out bustled the doctor's wife. She made for the kitchen, muttering something about hot water.

"Do you need help, ma'am?" Heck asked, but she didn't answer. "I reckon not," he said, and wrung his hands. "This waitin' around isn't for me. Rafe still needs to be told about Stu, so if neither of you object, I'll go break the bad news."

Steve sat on the bench and wearily leaned back. "I'm about tuckered out. If I fall asleep, kick me."

Without looking up, Jess said, "She could die."

After a goodly while, Steve coughed and winced and quietly asked, "Are you sure about this, pard? It's awful sudden."

"As sure as we can be about anything," Jess answered. "We never know if we don't try. If it's a mistake, it's not my first and won't be my last."

"I love an optimist." Steve grinned, then winced again and clutched his shoulder. "I hope things work out. I can always partner up with Heck if I keep my ears plugged."

Now it was Jess who cracked a grin, which instantly faded. "Who can predict? One day to the next, we never know. It's like buckin' the tiger, only the Almighty is dealin' the cards."

"They call that life," Steve Ellsworth said.

Chapter Twenty-eight

Rusty Vanes was grinning. Surrounded by enemies, outnumbered twenty to one and about to
gamble his life on a ruse that could land him in a
shallow grave, he grinned in sheer joy. He lived for
moments like this. For the thrill. For the excitement.

"Don't try any tricks, darlin', you hear?" Rusty
said to Chelsea, and cackled. He was pulling on the
door when a sudden sound gave him pause, loud
pattering on the roof and the walls and, seconds
later, the peal of thunder. It had started to rain.

From outside came Lem Rankin's bellow. "You
have ten seconds, boy, and then I'm sending my
men in!"

"She's on her way out!" Rusty yelled. The pattering had swelled to a steady pounding and a lightning flash lit up a window. Even nature was on his
side tonight; the rain would extinguish their
torches.

"Then do it and quit your damn stalling! I do not
like to be kept waiting!"

Rusty pecked Chelsea on her blood-spattered cheek. "Right fond of himself, isn't he? How could you sleep with a slug like that?" He molded his body to her back. "On the count of three." He opened the door and was instantly buffeted by the wind and the rain.

The storm had broken in all its elemental fury. True to Rankin's word, his hired guns were thirty feet from the house, barely visible in the heavy downpour, a few with sputtering torches held aloft.

Rankin, though, had come close to the front door, and was waiting with his pudgy hands on his broad hips. "Chelsea! Has he hurt you? Is Franny all right?"

Another gust of wind almost tore the door from Rusty's grasp. He stepped into the open, struggling to hold the body upright. Chelsea's head lolled to the left, hanging at an unnatural angle. Rankin would realize she was dead unless Rusty did something. Opening his mouth, he nuzzled the back of her head, taking as much of her hair between his teeth as he could. Then, clamping his mouth shut, he pulled her head back until it appeared fairly natural.

"Cat got your tongue, girl?" Lem Rankin asked the corpse. "Why the hell don't you answer me?"

Rusty moved forward, taking small steps to give the impression Chelsea was afraid. The pelting rain felt good on his cheeks and neck. But the wind was threatening to rip the shawl off.

"You're safe now, sweetheart," Rankin said. "Make a run for it. My men will cover you."

Careful not to show any part of himself, Rusty closed on his prey. He held the Colt close to his leg, his thumb on the hammer, his finger on the trigger. He wanted to be close to Rankin when he avenged Grat. He wanted to see the fear in Rankin's eyes.

"Didn't you hear me, my dear?" Rankin raised a hand to his eyes to shield them from the downpour. "Run to Brady. He'll protect you until this is over." Gazing past her, he shouted at the open doorway. "All right, whoever you are! Send Franny Brice out!"

Rusty thought of the redhead, lying in a pool of blood with half her mouth blown away, and he nearly laughed. Another few steps and he would be where he wanted to be. He slid his right foot forward, then his left. The corpse's legs were dragging slightly, and suddenly her left foot caught and her leg twisted partway around. Rusty felt it slide between his own. He pushed with his knee to dislodge it but couldn't, and came to a stop to keep from tripping.

"What the hell has gotten into you, Chelsea?" Lem Rankin demanded. "And why are you walking like that?"

The rain had become so heavy, Rusty could barely make Rankin out. But he was close enough now. Spitting out Chelsea's hair, he pushed the body from him and extended the Colt. "This is for my brother, you son of a bitch." He fired at Rankin's face, which was an indistinct blob. But as his revolver went off, so did a rifle, fired by someone lying in the grass somewhere behind Rankin, and he was jolted by an unseen blow to the shoulder that smashed him back several steps.

Rankin had fallen, but only to his knees; he had his hands pressed to his forehead. "He shot me!" he bawled. "Kill him, Brady! Kill the bastard!"

The rifle cracked again as Rusty threw himself to the ground. Brady shouted something, and a ragged volley vied with the thunder.

A nearby tree offered the only sanctuary in sight. Rusty scrambled toward it, heedless of his shoulder. Leaden locusts chewed the soil but Rusty reached the tree without being hit, and crouched. He would not leave until he had finished Rankin off.

The white whale had risen and was lumbering toward his men, roaring, "After him! I want that boy dead!"

"Fine," Rusty said, and shot him in the back. All eyes were on Rankin as he stumbled and fell, a mistake Rusty used to his advantage. Breaking away from the tree, he sprinted toward the stable. A scrawny man with a Spenser materialized before him and Rusty sent a slug into his gut. Slowing just long enough to help himself to the rifle, he ran on.

The night resounded to blasts both natural and man-made. A twinge of pain lanced Rusty's left thigh, another seared his ribs. Flesh wounds, nothing more. Shoving the Colt into his holster, he reached the wide stable doors, which hung half open, and raced inside, expecting to find a horse to escape on. But each and every stall was empty. "What the hell?" he blurted.

Shadows were flitting through the rain toward

the stable. Rusty ran to the back door and flung it open. To his right was a corral, and there, milling nervously about, agitated by the storm, were more than twelve horses.

Grinning, Rusty burst outside, then had to drop down as the darkness erupted in gunfire. A shadowy figure awash in rain acquired form and substance. A gunman was sneaking toward him. Rusty chuckled as he took aim. The Winchester's stock kicked against his shoulder, and the figure flopped about like a chicken with its neck snapped.

Another gun spoke, and yet a third. Rusty retreated into the stable. At least here it was dry. He heard bellowing out front. Lem Rankin was still alive, and that wouldn't do—it wouldn't do at all.

Rusty dashed to a ladder and quickly climbed to the hayloft. The loft door was shut and barred. Warily opening it, he counted seven figures converging from different directions.

Limping and carrying a rifle, Rankin was conspicuous by his bulk and the white nightshirt.

Turning, Rusty walked to the end of the loft and lay flat. He thought of his brother, and the many good times they had had together, and he placed his wet cheek to the Spenser. "This is for you, Grat."

The double doors creaked as they were thrown open wider. Wind whipped the straw on the floor and shook the tack hanging on pegs. A bolt of lightning lit up the center aisle as Rankm and the six others cautiously advanced. They were all sopping wet and primed to shoot.

No one thought to look up in the loft. Their backs

were to Rusty, but he recognized Brady and the big ox by the name of Moose. He centered the Spenser's sights on Lem Rankin's moon head. This time he would do it right.

"We know you're in here, boy!" Rankin shouted. "Give up now and I promise you a quick death!"

Rusty couldn't resist. Pursing his lips, he whistled. Rankin glanced over his shoulder and his toad-like eyes bulged. "Got you," Rusty said, and stroked the Spenser's trigger.

For a moment the others were too stunned to return fire, but only for a moment. Brady was the first to stir to life and spin, and he was the next to die. Rusty shot him in the sternum, fed another round into the Spenser's chamber, and shot the man next to him.

The rest were shooting up at the loft, filling the air with gunsmoke. Rusty shot a small man next to Moose and then shot Moose but the slab of sinew refused to go down, so Rusty shot him again, through the throat. He felt a stinging sensation in his side, and the most god-awful pain.

The last two men were running from the stable. Rusty let them go. He was nauseated, his vision blurring. Rolling onto his side, he looked down at himself. A slug had torn through the loft and caught him between the second and third ribs. Black blood was oozing from the hole.

"Damn," Rusty said. Black usually meant the liver, and the liver meant burying. Bracing the rifle under him, he gained his feet and shuffled to the ladder. His vision had cleared, and he refused to lie there and die like a slaughtered lamb. The buzzards who had bucked him out deserved to die with him.

They were out there, shouting to one another. Ten or more, Rusty estimated. His boots touched the floor and he was overcome by dizziness. It only lasted a few seconds. Dropping the Spenser, Rusty filled his hands with his pearl-handled Colt, and Grat's. They molded to his palms like they were part of him.

Lightning seared the heavens and the stable shook to thunder. Cocking both pistols, Rusty strode out into the rain. There they were, clustered together, probably debating what to do. He shot three of them in as many heartbeats. Then the others were scattering and firing, and he was hit, once, twice, three times, but Rusty laughed and planted his legs and kept on shooting, shooting, shooting.

"She's been asking for you. You can go in to see her," Doc Samuels announced, "but only for a couple of minutes." He was wiping his hands with a bloodstained towel.

Jess Donner went in and over to the table. His eyes misted, and he had to blink to see Margaret clearly. She was covered to her chin by a blanket. The doctor's wife smiled and politely left so they would be alone.

"You saved me, I hear," Margaret said softly.

"The sawbones did most of it." Jess admired how her hair spilled over her shoulders, and how red her lips were. "Anyone ever tell you how pretty you are?"

Margaret started to laugh, then grimaced. "Don't do that. The doc said I could start bleedin' again if I'm not real careful."

Her hand rose from the blanket and Jess cradled her fingers in his. "I'm sorry. The last thing I want is to hurt you."

They were quiet awhile, until Margaret looked him in the eyes and said, "So?"

"So," Jess echoed.

"Where do we go from here?"

"I have some pay comin' to me. It will get us wherever you want."

"That's not what I meant."

"I know," Jess said huskily. "I reckon we take it one day at a time, like everyone else. If it works out, it works out."

"I want it to work out," Margaret said. "I want it very much."

Jess fidgeted, yearning to say much more but feeling unable to do his emotions justice. He was spared from trying by Dr. Samuels.

"I'm sorry, son. I won't have my patient dying on me. Help us carry her to the spare bedroom so I can operate on your friend."

Heck Myers had returned an hour earlier with Rafe Adams and Tom Cambry. They each took hold of a corner of the stretcher the physician brought in and carefully conveyed Margaret down the hall to a small but comfortably furnished bedroom. Mrs. Samuels was by her side every step of the way.

Dr. Samuels had Steve Ellsworth on the operating

table when they returned. He bid them take a seat in the waiting room.

Despite all that had happened, despite Stu's death and Ethel dying and the ordeal he had been through with Margaret, Jess was happier than he could recollect being since he was knee-high to a calf. Margaret wanted him, and the future was ripe with promise.

The outer door opened and in walked Deputy Trace Morgan. His clothes were damp, his pants and boots spattered thick with mud, and he had the weary look of someone who had been up all night. Nodding at the others, he came over to Jess. "The girl?"

"She'll live," Jess said.

Morgan smiled a genuinely friendly smile. "So some good came out of this. And your other friend? The one with the freckles?"

"The doc says he'll be fit as new in a couple of weeks."

"I thought you should know. We found the other girl out at Rankin's. She's over to the undertaker's."

Heck Myers could not help overhearing. "That's a shame. Ethel was as sweet as sugar when she wanted to be."

"How about Rankin?" Jess asked.

"Dead, along with his top man, Brady, and eight others," Morgan related. "Six more were wounded bad enough to need doctoring and are being brought into town in wagons. It's the worst one-man massacre since Newton."

"Vanes did all that?" Heck Myers marveled.

"We also found Franny Brice and Chelsea Winthrop shot to pieces. Oh, and Rankin's dog."

"Sweet Jesus!"

"Rusty Vanes was still alive when we got there," Morgan said. "He had been shot eleven times but he lived long enough to brag about what he had done, and to say he'd do it all over again to avenge his brother."

"Damn, he was a hellion," Heck said.

Morgan's voice held a note of respect when he said, "If that boy had lived, he'd have a bigger reputation than Hickok and Hardin combined."

"It's over, then," Jess said, relieved.

"Except for the burying," Trace Morgan said. "Folks will come in from miles around."

"Rankin was that well liked?" Rafe Adams asked.

"Hell, no. The mayor plans to make it a holiday. Invite families to have picnics and then give a speech." Morgan tapped his badge. "There are days when I'd like to take this off just so I can shoot someone." He regarded them somberly, and left.

Jess looked at his hands and was startled to see dry blood on them. He rubbed his palms but the blood would not come off.

Heck stretched and yawned and sauntered to the window. "Hey, the sun is risin'!" He turned to Jess, his face creased in a lopsided grin. "That sure was some night, huh?"

"A writer in the tradition of Louis L'Amour and Zane Grey!" —*Huntsville Times*

National Bestselling Author

RALPH COMPTON

Available wherever books are sold or at
www.penguin.com

SIGNET

Charles G. West
EVIL BREED
0-451-21004-2

The U.S. Army doesn't take kindly to civilians
killing their officers—even in self-defense. But
Jim Culver has two things in his favor: the new .73
Winchester he's carrying—and the ability to use it.

"RARELY HAS AN AUTHOR PAINTED THE
GREAT AMERICAN WEST IN STROKES SO
BOLD, VIVID AND TRUE."
—RALPH COMTON

Available wherever books are sold or at
www.penguin.com

S805

No other series has this much historical action!

THE TRAILSMAN

Available wherever books are sold or at
www.penguin.com